SANCTUARY

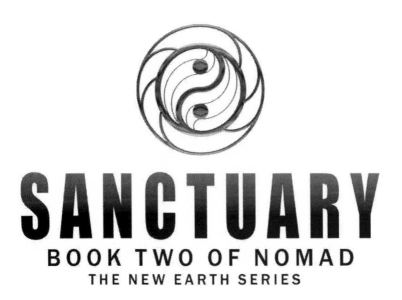

SANCTUARY

BOOK TWO OF NOMAD
THE NEW EARTH SERIES

MATTHEW MATHER

SANCTUARY

Matthew Mather ULC
www.matthewmather.com

ISBN: 978-1-987942-06-4
Cover image by Momir

This is a work of fiction, apart from the parts
that aren't.

NOTE FROM THE AUTHOR

FOR THEIR GENEROUS HELP
developing the science and story behind Nomad,
I would like to thank the generosity of

Dr. Ramin Skibba
Center for Space Sciences at UC San Diego

Dr. Kevin Rauch
University of Maryland Astrophysics

Dr. Seth Shostak
Director of SETI

Dr. James Gillies
Research Fellow at CERN

For free Advance Reading Copies of my next
book and more, join my community at
MatthewMather.com

Find me on Facebook and YouTube
search for
Author Matthew Mather

OTHER BOOKS

Standalone Titles
Darknet
CyberStorm
Polar Vortex

The Atopia Series
Atopia Chronicles
Dystopia Chronicles
Utopia Chronicles

The New Earth Series
Nomad
Sanctuary
Resistance
Destiny

The Delta Devlin Series
The Dreaming Tree
Meet Your Maker
Out of Time

SANCTUARY

NOVEMBER 1st

Eight Days A.N.
(After Nomad)

1

A BULLET RICOCHETED off the open truck door.

"Get out!" Jessica Rollins screamed at Lucca and Raffael.

The faces of the teenaged brothers shone white in the dim light, their eyes wide. A second bullet punched a frosted hole through the windshield and lodged itself in the metal screen behind the seats. Jess crouched lower and stole a glance around the door. "*Andare!*" she yelled.

That did the trick. Keeping low, Raffa slithered over the driver seat, opened the opposite door of the Humvee and disappeared. Lucca climbed over Jess and gracelessly tumbled into the dirt and snow at her feet. Jess pointed at her own eyes, then at a pile of twisted metal and bricks ten feet away. *One, two,* she mouthed silently, and on *three* she swung around the truck's door and squeezed the trigger on her AK-47. *Pop. Pop.* Two controlled rounds. She felt Lucca move behind her and fired again, then rolled through the gray snow to scramble next to him. Raffa slithered on his stomach to join them.

A bullet whined overhead.

She had sensed something was wrong the moment they drove up to the bottleneck in the road. A jumble of car parts blocking the street seemed a little too neatly placed. She'd stopped short of the road's choke point, but there had been no easy way to back out.

"Giovanni," Jess whispered into her walkie-talkie, in as low a voice as she could manage. She sucked air in between her teeth and exhaled heavily, trying to ease the flood of adrenaline. Her hands shook. "Do you have Hector?"

The walkie-talkie crackled softly. "In the brick schoolhouse half a block behind you."

Jess turned the volume down. She peered behind her through the murk and saw an arm waving, a hundred feet back on the opposite side of the street, behind the Range Rover. *Schoolhouse.* Indistinguishable from other piles of snowdrift-covered rubble. "And Leone?"

"He's with me. What can you see?"

What can I see? Jess almost laughed. In the dying light, dirty snowflakes fell through an indistinct soup. Daytime was an oozing sludge-brown twilight that clawed its way from the suffocating black of nights. The feeble rays of flashlights and headlamps drowned in the murky aerosolized soup they breathed. It stank of rotten eggs, the sulfurous-brimstone stench burrowing its way into the brain and filling their lungs with black phlegm, smothering everything in a pasty layer that scratched the eyeballs and coated tongues.

Removing her goggles, Jess rubbed her eyes and strained to see through the semidarkness. The temperature had dropped ten degrees in the past two hours. Another frigid night. The Humvee's headlights barely pierced the muck.

There. A head peered around the corner of what looked like the entrance to an open garage. No more than a hundred yards away. A second shape appeared behind the first, the body and head twitching, more like a cornered animal than predator. Jess pushed the *talk* button. "I see two, probably men. Do you see anything?"

"Nothing."

Jess brushed snow from her face and pulled her gloves back on. Three-story buildings lined the street, some with windows still strangely intact. It reminded her of bombed-out villages she'd seen on her tour of duty in Afghanistan; almost everything destroyed, buildings reduced to twisted piles of brick and steel. Yet every now and then a reminder of civilization endured, like the marble statue that stood untouched and defiant at this town's entrance as they drove in.

The two figures ran, doubled-over, behind the jumble of car parts blocking the middle. Had they seen Giovanni exit the rear car and run into the school? She had to act fast. This had been planned as an ambush, but the playing field was level now. Whoever had lain in wait for them had lost their advantage.

"Leave Leone with the shotgun to protect Hector," she instructed Giovanni over the walkie-talkie. "Then take Lucca and Raffa down the side street, south. Sending them to you now." She looked at Lucca, his rifle gripped in white-knuckled fists, and flicked her chin in Giovanni's direction. The teenager crouched and took off at a half-run with his brother trailing. "I'm going up to the

4

roof. When we get into position, toss two grenades into the open garage door of the red building. That'll force them out. Open fire from one side; I'll pick them off from the other." Flank-and-flush.

Static hissed over the walkie-talkie. "Maybe we just turn the trucks?"

Two heads bobbed out from behind the burnt-out car in front of her, and one of the men jumped into the open to duck behind a pile of rubble twenty feet closer to Jess. Her hands tightened on the AK-47. "We need to scare them off."

Hissing silence. "Okay. I have the boys."

"Tell me when you get there."

"You're *sure* you want to do this?"

She closed her eyes and tried to take a deep lungful of air, but a wet cough erupted mid-breath. She pushed the *talk* button. "We have to."

A pause. "We're on our way."

Jess tried to steady her shaking hands by clenching them into fists. Her army consisted of two teenagers, the elderly groundskeeper Leone and the Baron Giovanni Ruspoli, who'd probably never shot at anything more threatening than a clay pigeon before. It was on her to keep them safe.

A third head appeared carelessly out from the doorway ahead. She hoped a few grenades and some well-placed sniper fire would be enough to scare them off, but people were desperate. Beyond desperate.

Jess slung her assault rifle over her back and tightened the strap snug. She shuffled behind the Humvee on her knees and kept going until she reached the cover of a fallen wall on the other side of the street. She stopped. Listened. Peered into the gloom. Sensing nothing, she got to her feet and jogged to the drainpipe going up the side of the three-story building. She removed her gloves, stuffing them into the pockets of her parka, then blew on her hands and gripped the frozen pipe to begin climbing. She pulled herself up onto the railing of the first floor balcony and slid over into a pile of snow, but landed awkwardly and her prosthetic leg wrenched loose.

She cursed and pulled it back into place, feeling it rub into the raw stump just below her left knee. Getting to her feet, she balanced against the wall and propped herself against the railing. She shimmied her way onto the second floor balcony and stopped there, straddling the railing so she could pull her gloves back on to warm her already frozen hands. Leaning out, she saw one of the scavengers emerge from the pile of car wreckage to take a potshot at their Humvee.

"In position," Giovanni's voice whispered over the walkie-talkie.

Jumping up to grab another drainpipe, Jess pulled herself up to the edge of the roof. She held herself there as she scanned the debris for signs of movement. Nothing. She hauled herself up and twisted through more ash-ridden snow onto her back.

She thumbed the *talk* button and whispered: "One second."

Rolling onto her knees, she pulled her rifle off her back and popped the cover of its telescopic sight. She hunkered low and moved to the edge of the rooftop, then dropped flat onto her stomach. The lead scavenger had almost reached the Humvee. "Okay, in position. Drop those grenades in."

She slowed her breathing, steadying herself as she zeroed the crosshairs in on her target. The man turned, almost to face her, and her breath caught. He was no more than a teenager. Just a boy.

From the corner of her eye, she saw the shadows of Giovanni and Raffa dart out from behind the building across the street. With the crosshairs on the boy's chest, Jess's felt the pressure of the trigger beneath her finger, but released. How many had she killed already? She shifted the sight down, leveling the crosshairs on the fleshy part of the boy's leg, and pulled the trigger as a blinding flash burst in the street below. The first grenade's heaving concussion was followed by another a second later.

Windows blinked and shattered.

Screams filled the air.

A man ran out of the building beneath her, both hands to his belly. Another sprinted out, a gun clutched in shaking hands that he pointed at Giovanni. Jess swung her rifle left, this time aiming mid-torso, and fired. A red mist puffed from the man's chest and he fell. She glanced to her right. The boy held his leg, hopping back toward the wall.

More screaming.

An engine roared, and a second later a vehicle skidded out of the garage entrance.

Jess squinted hard, trying to understand what she was seeing. The body of an old Volkswagen Beetle, but with the wheel wells torn away. Large, circular rollers with jagged spikes had been welded onto the back axle, replacing the tires. Rudimentary skis had been placed where the front wheels should have been.

Slipping to a stop, the boy staggered to get in the passenger door, while two more of the scavengers perched in the open front-trunk. They fired random shots in Giovanni's direction. Jess lifted her rifle, locked a round into the chamber, aimed and fired. Her bullet punched through the roof. The two men ducked and the strange vehicle accelerated, kicking up a spray of dirty snow. It veered up the street and disappeared into the gloom.

It had been enough, but it could so easily have been worse. The man she had shot lay motionless. A seeping pool of black spread around him in the light of the Humvee's headlamps.

"Help."

Was that the man in the snow? She held her breath. Listened.

"Help me."

Was Giovanni hurt? In the sudden silence, she strained to hear.

"Please, help me."

No. It was coming from *inside* the building. Below her. Not Italian either; a distinctly American accent.

Giovanni, accompanied by Raffa and Lucca, appeared from the darkness on the other side of the street. Jess heaved a shaky sigh of relief and gave them a quick wave. Stepping through the foot of snow and ash covering the roof, she found the stairway down. The door was locked. She chambered a round and fired into the lock. The door kicked open. Clicking on her headlamp, she inched her way down to the first landing, scanning the frozen gloom, leading with the rifle.

"Please, help me," came the muffled call again.

Her finger dropped onto the trigger.

She swept each room with the AK-47, barrel just under her line of vision. Stomach tight, constantly searching behind and up. Clearing doorframes first, then into each room. Eyes wide, sucking in every detail. Sweat gathering despite the cold. Something kicked in her gut. Even scavengers should have been more prepared, put up more of a fight. Had it been too easy?

She shoved the thought aside and focused. Clearing the last set of stairs, she entered the lobby and opened the door to the garage. In the light of their headlamps, Giovanni, Raffa and Lucca stood encircling three people, all of them tied by hands and feet to a radiator. Rough sack bags covered their heads.

"Please, whoever you are, please let me go," one of them moaned. A man whose voice she recognized.

She marched to the pleading man, pulled the bag off his head, and stared in open-mouthed disbelief. "Roger?"

"Jessica?" The man's eyes bulged. "Thank God."

Her knife already out, she knelt and brought the blade to his face. Her hand trembled.

"Jess…" Giovanni took a step forward.

In one quick motion, Jess grabbed Roger's arms and wrenched them to the side. She cut the cords binding him, then the ropes around his feet.

Roger pulled his arms free and rubbed his wrists. He winced and extended a hand to be helped up. Instead she seized him by the throat, pulled him to his feet and pushed him back against the wall, the knife still in her hand. "What the hell happened?"

"Jesus Christ, what are you—"

"My father?"

"I don't know," Roger gurgled. "Where is he?"

"He's dead. They're both dead."

Giovanni put an arm on her shoulder and tried to ease her back with gentle pressure. She released her grip on the man's neck.

Roger wheezed and doubled over.

"How did you get here?"

"I was knocked unconscious when I went out with your father."

Wind whistled outside.

"Jessica?" A woman's voice echoed from the darkness.

Giovanni and Lucca raised their rifles. Dropping her hands, Jess turned. Someone limped across the dirt-streaked marble floor, but even in the dim light she recognized the shining blue eyes.

"Massarra?"

2

JESS EXHALED A long plume of vapor, which quickly dissipated in the dry air despite the cold. The air was the first thing she noticed every morning. She could smell it before she opened her eyes. A cloying thickness devoid of life that suffused itself into the last moments of her dreams, the belching stench of the inner Earth, its underworld of brimstone and sulfur, but without heat. Dante, an Italian Jess had spent time thinking about, understood cold. He'd placed circles of ice beneath the circles of fire in his vision of Hell's inner sanctum.

She panned her flashlight around the room. Two wrought-iron chandeliers hung from a wooden ceiling twenty feet overhead, a border of family crests and shields painted around the top edge. Wood paneling lined the walls to half-height, the hallway about sixty feet long with a huge wooden door flanked by cathedral windows in the front, next to a set of extra-wide double doors leading to a concrete-floored garage. "What is this place?"

"*Comune*, ah, how do you say…" Giovanni's face was lit by the glow of his headlamp, the shadows exaggerating the creases of his frown. "Town hall. I think this is a town hall."

Jess swept her light across the front wall. In block letters over the door, she found the name of the town. "*Bandita.*" She snorted. "Fitting. Let's set camp here for the night."

How many days now? Eight days since the destruction, since Nomad had repaved the surface of the Earth, churned its oceans to submerge the continents and tore the crust apart to belch a miles-thick layer of dust and vapor to blanket the globe. America was gone, the Midwest torn apart and covered in a chest-deep blanket of ash from the eruption of Yellowstone, the coasts blasted by thousand-foot tidal waves and rocked by apocalyptic earthquakes. Sea levels surged upward as glacial icecaps tipped into the oceans, drowning everything left behind. The Baikal rift had detonated, wrecking Asia's interior, along with dozens of secondary yet massive eruptions around the Pacific Rim and mid-oceanic ridge. In just days, the entire planet had been plunged into a shadowy new world, the dawn of a dark new ice age.

Nomad, two black holes—massive in the experience of the Earth, but tiny on any cosmic scale—had ripped the solar system apart, and either thrown the planets into radical new orbits, or slung them away into interstellar space. Because of the lucky geometry of the encounter, Earth's own orbit had only shifted into a slightly more elliptic one around the Sun. One still within the habitable range.

Lucky.

This stinking hell was *lucky*. A mass extinction event as the Earth hadn't witnessed in two hundred and fifty million years. Little had survived. The plants, the animals, almost everything was dead or dying.

But not quite *everything*.

Like warm-blooded cockroaches, humans couldn't be stamped out so easily. Everywhere from the gloom, bloodied and battered survivors appeared. While electric grids and most electronics had been fried in the intense barrage of solar irradiation during the event, older, solid-state electronics, like shortwave radios, had survived. Giovanni had contacted dozens of survivor groups, and along the roads small encampments of people appeared, marked by the luminous mushrooms of glowing artificial light and buzzing generators.

"You think they won't come back?" Giovanni asked.

Jess surveyed the room again. "I'm not sure."

How could she be sure about anything? The whole day today she'd been on edge, the distance growing between their small convoy and the relative safety of the *Castello Ruspoli*. The point of no return was fast approaching. Maybe it had already been crossed. Their plan had seemed the only way forward when she was sitting in the safety of the castle's catacombs, but out here?

"They sure as hell looked like they were going somewhere when they left." She clicked off her flashlight. "Then again, we killed one. Might have been someone's brother."

"So we go?"

"Being out at night could be deadly, for us and them. Let's get the trucks in the garage. We leave at first light."

Giovanni spoke to Raffa and Lucca in Italian, and they nodded in unison and strode to the front door, opening it cautiously and looking around, their headlamps flashing in the darkness, before heading out.

Jess clicked her flashlight on again and shone it on Roger. He sat on the wood-beam floor, rubbing the red, flayed skin where his wrists had been bound. Giovanni had started on helping free the women.

"Who the hell were they?" Jess took a step toward Roger. "And how are you even *alive*?"

Roger squinted into the glare of her high-beam light. "You don't know how happy I am to see you." His voice trembled. His face was caked with blood. He held up a shaking hand to shield his eyes.

He raised his right arm, even though she knew he was left-handed. His left shoulder was still wrapped in the same dirty bandage that covered the wound from where Jess had accidentally shot him with a crossbow. At *Castello Ruspoli*, when they had confronted Nico in his deranged, final attempt to bring closure to a centuries-old vendetta. A bloody feud between his family and the Ruspolis, into which she and her mother had been mistakenly dragged. The whole incident seemed like a long-ago dream. A surreal juxtaposition to the violence and terror of Nomad's passing.

But it hadn't been a dream.

Her mother and father were dead.

They weren't killed by Nico, not directly, but only because Jess had managed to save them, and save the young boy Hector from the lunatic in the final moments as Nomad tore the Earth apart. Her mother and father had died trying to recover her father's data, the information he'd collected as Harvard's preeminent astronomer.

Her father had been convinced that his data was the only surviving evidence of Nomad from more than thirty years earlier. He risked his life to recover the backpack containing the data—a collection of old tape spools and CDs, along with his laptop—and had died in the process. Why he'd risked his life, the reason he thought the information was still so valuable, Jess could only guess.

Did it pinpoint some future cosmic collision? Perhaps with Saturn in eighteen months, as Jess had been able to recreate on the simulations on his laptop? Or was it something else, some other event? Or something she couldn't even guess at?

The only person who might be able to answer this question now sat before her—Roger Hargate, who was her father's student, and who she had her own relationship with back in New York before any of this began. She knew a lot about Roger Hargate, more than she wanted. How long until he asked if they had any pain medication? Then again, she had impaled a wooden crossbow bolt through his shoulder only a week ago.

Jess clicked her full-beam flashlight off, throwing the hallway into a near darkness illuminated only by their red, low-power headlamps. A gale howled outside, and in her mind's eye Jess saw her father's crushed body, frozen on that mountaintop, his face mottled blue. This man had gone out with them. He *must* have been the last person to see her parents alive. She knelt and looked him in the eye. "What happened, Roger?"

He winced and stared at the floor. "We went out to get his backpack. Just as we got outside, something impacted the castle walls like a bomb. I was knocked out, Jess, and when I came to, everything was black. I was screaming for help. For hours. Somebody found me. They dragged me into a shelter."

"Who are *they*? What shelter?"

"At first, I thought they were rescuing people, but it wasn't like that."

Jess waited. "What do you mean?"

"They were collecting people, rounding them up."

"For what?"

"We were loaded onto trucks. I don't know what they were going to do with us." He covered his eyes in the crook of his elbow. His body shuddered.

"What are you saying, Roger?" It seemed impossible that scavengers had organized themselves to traffic in human beings, not in a little more than a week, but then, she'd already seen some of the horrible things people could do to each other. Her skin crawled. "How many of them were there?"

"A small group. Five or six men."

"And they've already modified their cars like that? For snow?"

Giovanni sniffed. "Italians and cars, no big surprise."

12

"They saw you on the road," Roger added. "They had me tied up in the back."

"So they followed us?" Jess said. "They were *hunting* us?"

The front door swung open and Jess spun on her heel, bringing her rifle up. Leone's bald head shone ghostly gray, with wisps of white hair floating above it. At waist level, a small white face. Hector. She lowered her rifle, kneeling as he ran toward her, scooping him up into her arms. His little hands dug into her neck, squeezing her tight.

"It's okay," she whispered.

Leone followed, loaded with backpacks and carrying a crate in his arms. The old man must have started unpacking before Jess had even decided to stay. She felt some relief with the decision being shared, and she smiled at Leone.

"*Chi è?*" he grunted, squinting at Roger and the two women still tied to the radiator.

"Ah, this is Roger, *un amico del professor* Rollins," Giovanni said. "The women, we don't know."

Leone stopped mid-stride. "*Amico de professore* Rollins? Who came with him from *Germania?*" He spoke only broken English. His eyes narrowed.

"He was kidnapped by those men," Jess added, swiveling her body around so Hector could see Roger.

"Okay." Leone dropped the crate and backpacks to the floor. The edges of his mouth stretched down. *Strange,* his face said. "And her?" He pointed to the front door, at Massarra, the slender, brown-skinned, blue-eyed woman. She stood by the front door, seeming halfway in and out at the same time, jumpy perhaps but somehow not frightened.

"She was the woman you followed, the one who drove me to the castle, you remember?"

"I never saw the face."

"That's her."

Leone shrugged, and seeing he had nothing else to add, exited to the garage.

Jess had first met Massarra in Rome, when the woman had helped her after she was locked out of her apartment. It was just before the Vatican was bombed, just when all the madness had

13

started, and Massarra had perhaps saved her and her mothers' lives by driving them from Rome to *Castello Ruspoli*. Without Massarra, Jess might not have been here, might not even have survived. She'd already had a brief word with Massarra, who said she'd tried to return to the castle when she became trapped in Italy.

"Who are they?" Jess gestured to the women with Roger. They huddled together silently, their eyes skittish, darting from her to Roger and back again.

"I have no idea." Roger struggled to his feet. "They don't speak any English."

Giovanni knelt beside one of them, whispering in Italian. She sobbed and wrapped her arms around his neck as he freed her.

The walls shook as the Humvee rumbled into the garage next door, followed by the softer growls of the Range Rover and Jeep. Car doors opened and slammed shut. The double doors to the hallway swung open, spilling reflected headlight into the room. Jess cast a long shadow over Roger and Giovanni and the women. Lucca and Raffa started unloading the cars to pile equipment in the hallway.

Jess put Hector down. "Get some blankets," she said softly, nodding at the women, now untied. Hector followed her eyes, then ran off to the boxes Raffa and Lucca were stacking.

"Did you come to rescue me?" Roger pulled two chairs from a stack near the wall and motioned for the women to sit.

Shaking her head, Jess shouldered her rifle. "I had no idea you were alive."

Helping the women onto the chairs, Giovanni exchanged a few words. He looked at Jess. "They're okay. I'll set up the radio."

"Get the boys to see if they can find anything of use in the Euromobile next door." The gas station. Not everything from the old world had been scavenged. Not yet.

Lucca unfurled the sleeping mats, while Raffa set up the cooking table. Leone worked on venting the wood stove he'd dragged from the back of the Humvee. Three days on the road, and everyone knew their jobs.

"So what are you doing here?" Roger asked, getting two more chairs.

Hector came over with blankets and bottles of water for the

two women, which they accepted, mumbling, *grazie, grazie.* Tears streamed down their faces.

"We're…" Jess paused.

"They don't speak English, trust me." Roger dropped a chair beside her, and sat heavily on one himself.

She shifted from one foot to the other, still keeping her eyes on the women. "We're going south. Giovanni has family in Tunisia, in the Atlas mountains. Beyond that, into Libya. It's still warm there. There's rain in the Sahara."

"How do you know?"

Jess nodded in Giovanni's direction. "Shortwave. Most electronics were fried, but shortwave works for long distances. We're in touch with dozens of survivor stations. A lot of people left alive out there. At least for now."

Roger brought one hand to his mouth to chew on his thumbnail. "Did Ben get his data?"

Jess took a long look at him. "I got it." She felt the weight of her father's tape spools and laptop in her backpack. She never took it off, even when she slept.

He rubbed the back of his neck. "At least you have what he wanted. Can't imagine it's of any use to anyone now."

"What was so important?" Her voice cracked, despite her best efforts to remain calm. Roger had worked with her father for years. Maybe he knew something more than she did.

"Ben tried to publish that paper thirty years ago, the one hypothesizing about Nomad. A lucky guess." He grimaced. "Maybe not so lucky. Nobody paid attention at the time."

"But they have now." Giovanni finished setting up a folding table and unspooled the radio's antenna, draping it over pictures along the wall. "It's been all over the radios. The famous Dr. Ben Rollins on TV, saying to stay calm, but somebody dug up that old research paper."

"They're saying it proves he knew about it." Jess spat the words out. "But it's not true."

Roger held her gaze. "It wasn't true. He didn't know. But the information in that old paper wasn't accurate. He made mistakes calculating Nomad's position thirty years ago. That's why he thought what was in the bags was so important. Those are the originals."

Maybe it was important, maybe it wasn't. Maybe it was just her father's guilt. For Jess it was an act of faith. Her father had died for this bag. She swung the backpack around and cradled it in her lap. "It's all tape spools and CDs, stuff from twenty or thirty years ago. Can you decode it?"

"Maybe. But we should go back to the castle and wait for help. It's too dangerous out here." He pulled the blanket tight around him, his body shaking.

"Help?" Jess understood what Roger hoped for, understood the terror, but this new world wasn't forgiving, and she was fighting for more than just her own life.

"There's no help coming," Giovanni said, sitting in front of his radio. He switched it on, pulling out a sheaf of papers. "We're getting broadcasts from many survivor camps, but nothing from governments."

"But traveling through that"—Roger held one shaking hand toward the front door—"is madness. How do we even go south?" He turned to Giovanni. "Do you have a ship?"

Giovanni was busy tuning the shortwave, but managed a shrug. "We drive. We walk."

Roger's eyes grew wide. "Across water?"

"Across ice." Jess shouldered her backpack. "It's going to get colder, maybe for years, maybe decades. Maybe forever. If we don't go now, we die."

NOVEMBER 2nd

Nine Days A.N.

3

FOUR BODIES HUDDLED together in terror, a mother cradling two children, a man with his arms around them, all their faces turned in toward each other. Their bodies glittered in the cold light of Jess's LED flashlight, their features softened by a frosted coating of ice crystals and ash. Frozen in time forever. Even before Nomad, Jess had seen bodies crouched together like this when she had visited Pompeii, Romans that had been trapped by the rushing mud and gasses of the explosion of that ancient volcano. Jess took a moment to say a small prayer, to let herself feel sadness at this lost family, but at least their struggle was over. Death's unbroken winning streak now littered the entire world with frozen corpses.

"What should we do with them?" Giovanni wasn't referring to the four dead souls. He stroked his chin, purposely not turning to look at Elsa and Rita, the two women they'd saved the night before. They were asleep, curled up under a pile of blankets near the wood stove, next to the double doors leading into the garage.

It was five a.m., still pitch black outside.

Flames flickered in the hearth of the stove, radiating warmth, the comforting scent of burning wood struggling to overcome the pervasive stench of sulfur. The women slept under the improvised ductwork vent Leone had built from the back of it into the garage outside. A dim brown light seeped in through the high arched windows in the front of the hall. Massarra stood by the front door, peering out the window. Jess hadn't seen her sleep, although Jess hadn't really slept herself. Roger sat on a crate near the wood stove. He fiddled with the controls of the shortwave.

"*Non abbiamo scelta.* We leave them," grunted Leone. The old man had stood watch over their new arrivals all night.

"*Si,*" agreed Giovanni. "We leave them some food, some water."

"We need Roger," Jess said, her gaze still fixed on the frozen corpses. She squeezed the remainder of a ration pack of chili into her mouth. Some breakfast. At least it was warm. "And I won't leave Massarra." The woman had probably saved her and her mother's life in Rome, so bringing her was the least she could do to repay some of this debt. Giovanni had said what she'd done didn't matter, that it was ancient history and they had to look forward to survive.

"You need Roger?"

"I said *we*." Jess clicked off her flashlight and turned to Giovanni. "He has a degree in astrophysics."

"Say again, Jolly Roger. Do you read me?" From across the hallway, Roger's voice echoed as he tried to make himself heard over the shortwave.

Giovanni had told him about the survivor groups he'd contacted on the radio and the logs he kept, shown him the shortwave and explained the trouble he had keeping in touch with them. Roger had explained to Giovanni how shortwaves bounced off the ionosphere, and theorized about how Nomad might have altered the upper atmosphere, explaining the static as ionization, the day and night cycles.

"We have food for five adults for four months," Giovanni said as he watched Roger play with the radio's controls. "Maybe six if we ration. For nine people we last three months at most."

They had five hundred more miles of overland travel to the south of Sicily, and then a walk of a hundred or more across sea ice, and who knew what beyond that? The drive here, fifty miles, took three days—often negotiating twisted knots of frozen magma that they had to winch the trucks over.

"And in cold weather we are consuming even more energy," Giovanni added. "Maybe four thousand—"

"Our mission is to figure out what's in this bag." Jess cocked her thumb at her backpack. "Anything that helps me do that, is what we need to do."

"No."

"What do you mean, no?"

"Our mission, if you must put it like this, is to stay alive. Only if we are alive do we figure out what's in that bag. To stay alive, we need to get south. Doubling the number of people in our party risks our lives."

Jess clicked on her flashlight again to illuminate the corpses. "I'm not saying we take all of them."

"So we leave the women, just take Roger and Massarra?" Giovanni said. "You believe their stories?"

"Something is not right," Leone grunted, gesturing to the women, but not saying any more. Instead, the old man shrugged and shuffled away toward the stove where they slept.

"A lot of things aren't right." Jess clicked off her light again. She turned to face Giovanni. "Massarra came back looking for help, *our* help, and without her I wouldn't even be here."

"This is no time for—"

"For what? Abandoning someone who risked her life for me? And I need Roger. Maybe this is finally some good luck."

"It is a risk. That is all I am saying."

"If we come across any big encampment, any kind of survivors' commune or trace of organized activity, we'll drop them off. At least Massarra. The two women, we leave here with some food and some gear to help them get by."

Giovanni's face remained blank. Eventually, he nodded and walked away to join Leone and begin packing.

The night before had turned heated during a discussion of the plan to head south. The layer of snow and ash covering the ground grew steadily deeper each day as temperatures plummeted. It was ten below freezing at midnight, and barely a few degrees above that inside the room, even with the wood stove going. Roger had been adamant that they should go back to the castle and dig in, wait for the outside world to get organized. Giovanni was equally as convinced that such a course would be disaster.

Either way, the odds were against them surviving for long.

For Jess, back at the castle, part of the deciding factor in going south was to find someone to decode her father's data. He'd sacrificed his life to retrieve it. It might be the only surviving record of the Nomad's trajectory from thirty years ago. Was it valuable? Her father had been desperate to retrieve it, and she trusted that it therefore had to be more important than they could know. Jess needed to go south, to the growing city in the Sahara desert, at an oil refinery in Al-Jawf, Libya, the only place they'd contacted that still had some technical capacity. They were in nearly constant contact with Al-Jawf. It was raining there every day. Life might be possible in the south.

But now they had Roger.

He might be able to scavenge what was needed, might be able to program the laptops they possessed to decode the contents of her bag. With his help, getting south might not need to be their top priority.

Jess glanced at Roger, who was twiddling the dials of the old shortwave. She was glad he was alive, but she was also conflicted, and not only about going south. In the days since her parents' deaths, the week of time since Nomad had ripped past the Earth, her relationship with Giovanni had deepened. He'd held her, comforted her, and she'd taken to sleeping huddled together with him and Hector, nestled under blankets. She hadn't healed enough and was too exhausted and drained to give it much thought, but something was changing within her and between them.

She wondered how much of it was the situation they were in, latching onto whatever solace they could find. Something normal amidst the chaos. Part of her wanted to talk to Giovanni about it, but mostly she retreated. But why? Was it because she could trust nothing, take nothing for granted in this madness? Or was it because she was worried she might be forced to do something cruel—to make a decision that may tear them apart?

After the argument about going south, Jess had retreated with Giovanni and Hector to get some sleep, but had felt Roger watching her. She had almost lived with him in New York, but that was more than a year ago now and in a very different world. In the old world. She'd run away without explanation, and her father had felt Roger had come to Italy to find her. He was in love with her, her father had said. Almost the last words he had said to her.

Last night she felt Roger's eyes following her, and when she went to bed, she'd inched away from Giovanni.

"Jessica, we need to get going, yes?" Giovanni said, returning to Jess ten minutes later. "Those bandits? Morning will be here soon."

Jess blinked, still transfixed, gazing at the corpses. She flicked her chin at the sleeping women, the two who were still alive. "We can't leave them here."

Giovanni frowned. "I thought—"

"We're involved now. If those bandits come back for us, no

telling what they might do to them. We'll get them to scavenge when we stop at night, help with the camp. Everyone pulls their weight. We can't leave them. It's a death sentence."

From across the room, Leone heard this and scowled, glanced at Giovanni, but then shrugged, seeing there was no arguing.

"I repeat, this is Station Saline. We are now in the town of Bandita in Italy, with Jessica Rollins and Giovanni Ruspoli," Roger almost shouted into the radio. "This is Roger Hargate with Jessica R—"

"Hey!" Jess tossed the empty ration package in her hand at him. "What are you doing?"

Roger ducked, the projectile missing his head by inches. "What?"

Elsa and Rita startled awake, and Raffa and Lucca came running in from the garage. Jess took three quick strides and raised her hand, but instead of smacking Roger, she switched off the shortwave. "What the hell was that?"

"Station identification, just like you said to do."

Jess balled her fists. "You told him no names?" she said to Giovanni.

The Italian pulled one hand through his hair. "I did."

"You didn't." Roger held his palms out. "I thought the whole point was to communicate—"

"We are identified as Station Saline. That's all. You understand? Anyone could be listening." She exhaled loud and hard. "Pack up the radio. Pack everything up." She turned to the women. "Elsa, Rita, *andiamo*. Let's go." When nobody moved, she clapped her hands together. "Let's go, goddamn it!"

A woman raised a child in her arms, held the swaddled infant high. Jess tried not to look at her as they swept past. The Humvee's engine growled, the improvised snowplow they had welded onto the front scraped the asphalt of the highway. The woman disappeared behind them in a swirl of snow and ash.

She wanted them to take the baby.

How long would they survive? Another day. Maybe two? Jess

had slowed the Humvee when she saw the woman appear through the fog, but Giovanni tapped her arm and shook his head. She put her foot back on the gas. Of course he was right—they couldn't stop for every person they swept past. She told herself every one of them represented a danger. Any one of them might have friends, hiding out of sight, ready to ambush the convoy and steal what they could get away with in their own desperate struggle to survive.

She couldn't get the woman out of her mind. Why had she brought these two women, Elsa and Rita, with them? Risked their lives, their rations, for people she didn't know? Maybe the feeling that her father was watching, or maybe she just wasn't hard enough yet, hadn't seen enough death to devalue another human life—to reduce it to an equation related solely to rations or risk. Why not exchange them for this woman and her baby? No, rational decisions still had to be made in an irrational world.

Jess had packed up in silence, shifting some of the gear from the Range Rover to make new space for Hector in the back of the Humvee. Leone had put the two women, along with Massarra, into the Range Rover with him. In their convoy, Leone took the rear, with Lucca and Raffa in the middle in the Jeep, while the Humvee took the rest, with its snow-chained tires and plow, to open a path through the two-foot-deep slurry of snow and ash.

When they had left the castle, progress through the secondary roads winding through the Tuscan hills was painfully slow, but in the few hours since leaving Bandita, they'd made as many miles as the past two days. The Autostrada A1 highway was the main trunk that ran the length of Italy, and remained in good shape. They were only slowed by the litter of abandoned cars.

"Do you believe Roger's story?" Giovanni asked.

Jess reached down to scratch her stump. Did she believe what? That Roger was separated from her father in an explosion at the castle? Or that he was captured by scavengers? "I don't know." She kept her eyes on the road. She had taken the first driving shift, and these were the first words they'd exchanged in three hours since they'd left. "You were the one who let him use the shortwave."

Giovanni leaned forward to look out the windshield, up into the gray-brown sludge of a sky.

Jess downshifted to get around the snow-hump of a car ahead.

The truck lurched, and she stomped on the accelerator. The distance between her and Giovanni edged inches wider.

"Please, be careful." He looked over his shoulder, into the backseat, at Hector. Not a peep from him all morning.

Jess eased off the gas but said nothing.

The wind picked up, and a thin layer of ice crystals whipped sideways over the highway, sheeting across the half-buried cars dotting the road. Her emotions were coiled tight, and deciding the right thing to say or do was a constant struggle. Something caught her eye. A smudge moved through the dark sky. Something moving fast.

When she was a kid, her father used to take her canoe camping in Upstate New York. The end of each day began a cycle of making camp, preparing dinner, sleeping, then in the morning tearing down camp and getting out on the water. Her father taught her the importance of watching the sky, reading the clouds, noting the wind. Getting out of the way of bad weather was important, especially when that meant getting off the water and under shelter. Her time in the Marines had re-iterated those lessons.

Jess peered through the grimy windscreen. Something had changed up there. The aerosolized sludge still stung her eyes and clogged her lungs. This morning she had coughed up the same gray phlegm she had every morning since Nomad. But the sky was somehow different. Usually dark during the day, like the thickest thunderhead she'd ever seen—gray tinged with shifting yellows, but now, as she watched, the sky gained form, mushrooms of brown sprouting downward. Any sudden change in air could signal some kind of pressure front. A wave of rain pelted the windshield. No, not rain. Sleet. Ice and snow. The wind picked up and howled. Pellets of ice rattled off the hood.

"We better get off the road." Jess shifted into a higher gear and accelerated, snow exploding in waves off the plow. There it was again. A vague shape that might have been, what? A helicopter? Not possible, not in this wind. Her eyes must be playing tricks, her mind seeing patterns in the swirling sky.

Giovanni craned his neck forward. "I think there's an exit—"

Before he could finish, the sky lit up, a flashbulb-bright burst illuminating the black clouds towering overhead. It momentarily

25

blinded Jess, the image of the clouds still dancing in fading green in her vision when the thunder hit. A splintering crack followed by a rolling, echoing boom that shook the Humvee. The skies lit up again, and this time Jess watched a halo of lightning flicker through the clouds as a dense squall of sleet hit. The thunder reverberated, echoed off the hills around them.

Jess eased on her brakes, the Humvee's headlights illuminating a swirling globe of snow. She switched to fog lights, but that was no better. A total whiteout. The snow, blowing sideways, reduced visibility to "zero-zero"—zero feet upward and zero feet sideways. She screamed into her walkie-talkie: "Stop! Stop!"

The sky flashed again and again. Blinded in the furious storm, she slammed on the brakes as another splintering crackle rattled the windows, punctuated by hollow thuds and rolling booms.

NOVEMBER 3rd

Ten Days A.N.

4

A YOUNG MAN stared at Jess, his eyes silent but damning. I'm sorry, Jess tried say, but she couldn't speak. Couldn't reach out. She was frozen, stuck in place. With a start, Jess shivered awake. The image of the young man faded, replaced by a thin yellow light. Dreams were the place where wishes and fears came to life, she understood now, and when wishes and fears were the same, the dreams became nightmares.

Blinking, her mind reassembled, one nightmare replaced by another.

She leaned into Giovanni, breathing in his now-familiar scent. "Hey," she whispered, nudging his shoulder. Hector was cradled between them, their sleeping bags piled together in a nest in the back seat of the Humvee.

Jess pulled her arms free, felt the cold outside of her burrow and wished she could stay wrapped up all day. The windows of the Humvee seemed coated, but not in snow. Something translucent. A dirty yellow light filtered through, just enough to see. They had turned off the Humvee's engine in the night, turned off the heating, after they got their sleeping bags out. Giovanni jumped up, his eyes wide.

"It's okay," Jess whispered, holding one finger to her mouth, looking down at Hector. "Everything's fine. I think it's morning. I'm going to look outside."

He nodded and pulled his arms around the boy, who mewled and curled into him. Jess extricated herself from the bundle of sleeping bags and blankets, shivering. The cold of the leather seat seeped into her back. She pulled on a fleece and slid into her boots, then wriggled into the front seat and pulled on her parka, hat and mitts. Taking a deep breath, bracing herself for the cold, she steadied herself and unlocked the passenger side door.

She pushed, but it didn't budge.

A hard edge crept into her chest. With a twinge of desperation she threw her shoulder into it. Not an inch. Her heart rate kicked up. Had they been buried? She remembered grinding to a halt in the white out, the thundersnow, bursts of lightning crackling around them deep into the night. Violent surges of wind had buffeted the Humvee, strong enough to rock the heavy vehicle. It seemed to come from all points on the compass. Between the blasts of wind were stretches of eerie calm, just long enough to think it might be over, until the relentless assault began again. Eventually, they had wrapped themselves up and fallen asleep.

This time she threw all her weight into the door, and with a tearing crack it opened a couple of inches. Shards of ice fell into the seat. She leaned back and threw her shoulder into the door again, and this time it opened a little further, a mini-avalanche of snow tumbling onto her through the opening. Giovanni was rousing himself behind her, asking her to hang on, but she didn't stop. Squeezing through the gap, Jess pulled herself upright and stood.

The Humvee was coated in a smooth layer of ice, the air a mud fog. She took hold of the door in her right hand and put her left onto the roof, then levered herself upward and swung her feet onto the sloping ice. She slid down the embankment, coming to a stop about ten feet away. Slipping and sliding, she got to her feet. Before packing it in for the night she'd registered the outside temperature at minus ten Celsius, but now the air was strangely warm. Definitely above freezing. A layer of wandering mist had settled onto the ice, coating it in a slick ochre film. She kicked one foot down and broke through the inch-thick ice into crystalline gray snow beneath.

Giovanni's head stuck up through the doorway.

"I'm okay," Jess said before he could ask.

Behind them, the Jeep and Range Rover were similarly buried under a glimmering yellow veil. The highway divider, a gray metal barrier, was coated as well. The skeletons of trees lining the road looked encased in inches of dirty glass. Ahead, the roadway buckled, knots of frozen magma thirty feet high spilling from a ravine rising up into hills on her left. In the distance to her right, a low building was just visible off the highway, at the intersection of a road leading away to the west.

"Good thing we stopped." Giovanni pulled himself from the truck and slid down to join her. He pointed at the magma flows blocking the road.

She kicked at the ice again. "We can't drive on this." She

couldn't fight the elements. This wasn't an enemy she could beat.

"We'll drive as far as we can."

"Drive?" She gestured around her. "On this? *Through* this? This is insane."

"If we have to, we walk," Giovanni said matter-of-factly.

"We're still fifty miles from Rome, so that's five hundred to Tunisia."

"So you'd rather give up? And go back to what? Or should we just sit here and wait for the cold to take us?"

Jess let her eyes slide along the frozen carpet that disappeared into the sulfurous mist. "This is crazy."

"I once walked two hundred miles across Greenland. It's slow and painful, but it can be done. One step at a time." He pointed at the building just off the highway. "Let's see what's inside there. Maybe a little present for us, no?"

Jess squinted. She hadn't noticed before, but half-buried machinery dotted the outside of the building, and she needed a mission, something to distract her mind from the yawning abyss. "All right. Wake up the others."

With two hard tugs, Giovanni heaved open the metal door. He clicked on his headlamp and peered inside.

Before leaving to explore the building, they gave Raffa, Lucca and Leone instructions to dig out the trucks with the shovels and picks, and then use the winches to pull them free of the ice. Roger was put back on radio duty while looking after Hector, trying to get updates on conditions from other survivor camps. Jess asked Massarra to watch over Elsa and Rita, as they got together some breakfast.

Scouting ahead, the highway was rough. Crevasses fractured the ground for as far as they could see through the smog, but Giovanni thought they could still thread their way through. The building was on an off-ramp that led to SS675, a freeway leading west. It looked in much better shape. They could follow that to the Rome ring road, but driving south along the coast was a patchwork of much smaller roads and rougher terrain.

"Looks like a garage," Giovanni said. He stepped through the door.

"Anything we can use?" Jess said.

"We look around, yes?" he called from inside.

She clicked on her headlamp and stepped through after him. The lamplight cut a speckled beam through floating dust particles. There were tractors outside the building, what they'd seen from the road, but it was wreckage, not even salvageable. She hoped for a nice surprise inside—maybe a shiny earthmover on treads—but it was empty. She picked up a plastic gas canister by the door and shook it. Also empty. She tossed it and opened the carryall bag she had brought along, scanning a workbench next to the wall. Wrenches, hammers, but nothing they didn't already have. She followed Giovanni into a small office off the main room.

And swore softly.

A man sat at the desk in the office, cradling a little girl in his arms. They looked asleep, except that they were covered in a glistening blue gel. The window to the office was smashed. With temperatures above freezing today, the coating had partially melted, leaving behind a slick film.

"Must have been gases from the rupture across the highway," Giovanni said. Careful not to disturb them, he knelt and began searching through the drawers of the desk. Jess stared at the man and his daughter. They looked so peaceful. No more terror. Cold storage. For eternity.

"Let's go." Giovanni took her hand and led her away.

On the counter sat a laptop, coated in the same slick blue film. It wouldn't turn on. Dead, like most of the electronics they found. She pulled a box from the top shelf and was rewarded with a shower of wet ash. Jackpot. A CD player appeared amid the mess of cables, and an ancient disk drive was wedged under an equally ancient laptop. Jess stuffed them into her carryall. She could add them to her growing collection of scavenged electronics.

Click. Click. Hiss. A blue light leapt from the darkness. "We take it?" Giovanni held up an acetylene torch, its tip flaming and sparkling.

Jess nodded, her attention on a coil of rusting metal tracks resting against a pile of tractor rims. The tracks were like tank treads, probably for one of the wrecked tractors outside. In her mind she saw the bandits' car, its rear wheel replaced with spiked rims, skis replacing the front wheels.

"You know how to use that?" Jess asked.

Giovanni turned the torch's gas off, dousing the garage back into darkness. "More or less, but Raffael is our *meccanico*."

"Maybe wrap those treads around the rear Humvee wheels?" They already had spiked wheels on them, but the metal links of the tractor treads were at least three times the width and would sink less on snow. "Maybe make skis on the front of the Humvee? From metal or something?"

"Not metal." Giovanni clued in to what she was thinking. "Too sticky on snow. But we could use the sleds."

"They're tough enough?" She knew he meant the arctic expedition sleds strapped to the roof of the Range Rover.

"Half-inch polycarbonate. Very slippery on snow and ice, and we could reinforce them with metal plates, maybe weld on the tractor rims onto the outside of the Humvee's rims, then fit treads onto that."

They could transform the Humvee into their own snowmobile. Their own snow *tank*.

Halfway back up the icy embankment to the truck, in the middle of discussing how to cut away the Humvee's wheel wells to accommodate the tractor rims, Jess noticed Roger standing on top of the Range Rover, waving his arms.

"Jess!" he yelled.

Giovanni scanned the road, looking for signs of danger.

Jess dropped the sack she had on her shoulder and took off at a run. Had the scavengers returned? Only three hundred yards, but the wind picked up and drowned out Roger's cries. What was it? Something about Hector? She scrambled up the embankment, adrenaline spiking into her bloodstream.

"What happened?" she screamed over the wind, digging her crampons into the ice to pull herself up on a tree next to the road. She unslung her assault rifle.

Roger held out his hands. "Everything is fine."

She hauled herself over the icy guardrail and grabbed onto the metal cable thrown around it to the Humvee's winch.

Raffa and Lucca waved. They'd already pulled the truck out of the ice, and were busy digging around the Range Rover.

"I made contact with a new survivor camp in Civitavecchia," Roger said, his hands still out.

"You yelled at us for that?" Jess doubled over, her breath coming in labored gasps. *Civitavecchia.* She'd heard of it. Rome's main port, where cruise ships came in. They hadn't contacted there before, but still… "Jesus, Roger, you scared the cr—"

"They're evacuating people."

She straightened. "What?"

Snow had begun to fall again, at first tiny crystals from the charcoal sky, but now thick flakes fell soundlessly around them.

"In boats. To Tunis, Algiers, Tripoli across the Mediterranean. They're evacuating people south." He held up the shortwave radio mike. "You can talk to them yourself."

Giovanni swung one leg over the guardrail behind Jess. "Sixty miles from here. We can go that way." He pointed down the road leading away from the highway, to the west. He smiled. "See? One thing at a time."

5

"ARE YOU CRAZY?" Roger jerked his hands up so hard he threw half his cup of chickpea soup over the interior of the Humvee.

"We stick to the plan." Jess calmly spooned some of her own soup into her mouth. She looked at Roger. His face was slick with sweat, his eyes glassy. "And clean that up."

Roger grimaced, holding his ration pack in the air as if he couldn't figure out what do to with it. "We can hitch a ride on a ship fifty miles from here, but you want to drag our asses down five hundred miles of wrecked highway, then walk over ice that hasn't even formed yet?"

"That's right."

Jess took her meal towel and wiped away some of Roger's mess from the Humvee's scratched metal console. The interior was stripped down, khaki-green, Italian-army issue, complete with a thick, square windshield and scratched riveted metal, the steering wheel a donut of hard black plastic that hovered over glass-faced analog dials and over-sized switches. The least comfortable seating of any vehicle in their convoy trio, and it retained the same musty, gunmetal-oil smell Jess remembered from her tour. She found her hand drifting to her leg, resting it just above where it joined the prosthetic. Not even a Humvee provided much protection against an improvised roadside explosive.

"*Andiamo in barca*," Leone said from the back seat behind Jess. He had Hector on his lap and gripped him in his big arms. "*È più sicuro.*"

"That's not true, we don't know if the boats will be safer," Jess said, her voice rising.

Leone didn't say anything in a way that let Jess know he didn't agree.

"We stay away from populated areas, we move south as quick as we can, wasn't that the plan?"

"Hector, do you like boats, *barche*?" Giovanni smiled and leaned from the driver seat to ruffle Hector's hair. The boy smiled weakly in return. They spoke mostly in English, so he didn't understand much, but his face reflected the rising tension.

"Don't do that." Jess jabbed her spoon at Giovanni.

"Don't do what?"

"You know what. Don't be an asshole."

"I think I might not be the one being an asshole, as you say."

"Meaning?"

He put his ration tin down carefully. "It doesn't mean anything."

"Say what's on your mind, Giovanni."

"All our lives are at risk. We had a plan. We can have a new plan."

"We need to protect this." Jess patted the backpack, now resting in her lap. "Right now, we have a plan that doesn't depend on anyone else. We have vehicles, we have supplies."

"I'm getting sick of that goddamn backpack." Roger wound down his window and threw out the remainder of his dinner. "Your father almost killed me over—"

"My father *died* for this," Jess interrupted.

Roger paused to take a deep breath. "That box of electronics you found, was it in a metal crate?"

"Metal shelves. Why?"

"Must have acted as a Galvanic box, took away the brunt of EM radiation. There's a modem in there; I think it works."

"We can read the disks?" Jess shifted in her seat toward him, her voice losing its edge. "Does the CD player work?"

"If the modem works, I can transmit data over the shortwave."

"But it's not digital."

"We go old school. Audio frequency modulation. Slow, but it works."

"And how does this change anything?" Giovanni leaned forward to insert himself between Roger and Jess.

"Because I might be able to transmit the data to your engineer friends in Al-Jawf. Down in the Sahara where we're heading."

Jess pressed her lips together.

"If we're not the only ones hanging onto this data"—Roger pointed at the backpack—"then we're no longer humanity's custodians. So we head for the boats."

"First, show me that it works," Jess conceded, but she was a

36

long way from sending her heritage off into someone else's hands. "And that you can read the data."

"If the data's even still there."

Jess gripped the backpack tight.

"I need time," Roger added when she didn't respond.

"You've got time. All the time we have on the road."

"I mean time not spent bouncing off the inside of this truck. We need to sit still for a few days."

"That we can't do." Jess shook her head. "South. We keep to the plan."

"I agree." Massarra leaned in through the Humvee's window. "Anyone want more?" She held up the steaming pot of chickpea soup.

Roger spat out the remains of a chickpea husk, the edges of his mouth working into a sour frown. "Who invited you to this talk?"

"You know"—Giovanni jabbed a finger at Roger—"I was thinking the same thing about *you*."

The astrophysicist's face turned beet red. "This is my *life* we're talking about. We should head for the boats. It's only fifty miles. We could almost walk."

"So then walk." A smile edged across Giovanni's face. He turned his finger from pointing at Roger to pointing out the window. "Get out. And take some chickpea stew with you."

"Hey." Jess held her hands up, palms out to the two men.

The color drained from Roger's cheeks. "I've had enough of chickpeas. I'm going hunting." He opened his door.

"Take someone with you," Jess said, her hands still up.

"I hunt better alone." He stepped out.

Jess watched Massarra give Roger a long, hard look as he pushed his way past her. He picked up a rifle from next to the cooking stove. The blade of a knife glinted in Massarra's hand.

"If you don't come back, we're not looking for you," Giovanni offered as Roger stalked away.

Jess jabbed his shoulder. "Stop that."

The Italian shrugged and settled back into his seat to resume eating.

Roger made his way along the tracks leading down to the buildings. Reaching the edge of the structure, he glanced over his shoulder and stepped from the broken ice of the trail onto the slick yellow crust. Each step broke through the inch-thick layer above into the knee-deep slurry below, earning a multitude of curses as snow wedged into his low leather boots. He tightened the strap of the rifle over his shoulder and squinted into the gray-orange sky. A flattened yellow sun-blob hovered near the horizon. He still had an hour or more of murky light.

Glancing over his shoulder again, he found the trucks now barely visible. Massarra was keeping Elsa busy with the cooking and cleaning, and Rita had her head in the Humvee, talking with Raffa. Satisfied, he entered the edge of the forest and made his way around the back of the building, and then, slipping over the ice, he double-backed across the road into the forest on the other side.

Roger had seen the flashes on the road during the day, back the way they'd already traveled.

Sweat poured from his brow, soaking his woolen cap. He'd hunted as a kid, in Pennsylvania backcountry with his father. He learned from him and was good with a rifle. He figured it was one of the reasons the Organization had been interested in him. That and his astrophysics degree. Today, though, he wasn't hunting. At least not for anything he could eat.

"*Abbastanza lontano.*" A man appeared from the trees behind him, holding a rifle up.

Roger didn't raise his arms. "Make this quick."

The man motioned with his gun. At the edge of the trees was a well-worn path leading along the edge of the highway. They quick-marched along it a half-mile back. A car came into view, though not exactly a car anymore. The Volkswagen Beetle had large circular rollers, with jagged spikes, welded onto the back axle. Behind it was a gray Mercedes SUV with snow chains over the wheels. The doors to the Mercedes opened, and two men stepped out.

"So, Mr. Roger, where's my *bag*?" said one of the men, stepping forward.

Strands of white hair clung to his liver-spotted scalp, jowls of loose skin hung from his angular face dominated by the angry red

38

slash of a cleft lip. His eyes, beady and black, penetrated from below bushy gray eyebrows.

"I'm slowing them down as much as I can."

"You can do better than that."

"She doesn't let go of it. Sleeps with it tied to her."

The old man stepped in close to Roger. "Maybe I'll have my girl cut their throats?" He leaned forward, his nose just inches from Roger's. "And maybe cut *your* throat, too."

"Salman, I want that bag as much as you do." Roger didn't flinch or retreat. The old man's breath stank of garlic. "If you want it undamaged, we do it my way. I can't just cut the straps off the bag and run with it. We need to do this right."

"Maybe I just kill all of you and call your friends myself." Salman produced a slab of black plastic from his pocket. It had a white yin-yang symbol emblazoned on it.

"Activate that without me, and nobody's coming."

"Maybe, maybe not."

The two men with Salman stepped behind him. One of them wasn't a man, though, more of a boy, a teenager, his ruddy cheeks flushed with the cold. He limped, his right leg bandaged where he'd been shot.

"Maybe it's more of your lies," Salman added.

"You need me."

"For now." He put the black emergency beacon back in his pocket. "But I am not a violent man. When my nephew called me, with wild stories, I came to find out for myself. But I only want what you want."

Roger doubted that was true. He wanted Salman dead.

"Somewhere safe, somewhere we might survive," continued Salman. "That's all I want. But any funny business, as you *Americanos* say, and I cut you up into tomorrow's dinner. *Capire?* You understand? And I kill your girlfriend Jessica first, so you can watch."

"Don't touch her."

Salman smiled an oily grin.

"We need her," Roger added. "You want my friends to come get us, we need her, and we need that bag."

"I think *you* need her." Salman's smile widened. "I wonder what

Miss Jessica would think if we told her you were spying on her father, for your…how do you call it?"

"The Organization."

"Mysterious, yes?" The smile slid from Salman's face. "I grow tired of this, Roger. Maybe I should have just let you die on that mountain. My nephew Nico was foolish."

"I'll get the bag. And they won't get far south. I've sabotaged the trucks."

"So you're not heading to the coast?"

"She's stubborn."

"Two days. You have two days." Salman turned to the boy, raising one hand. The boy pulled his rucksack off and produced a buckshot-riddled rabbit. Salman took it and tossed it at Roger.

"What about my other bag?"

Salman rolled his eyes but nodded at the boy, who produced a small brown paper sack. "Your weaknesses will be your undoing. And that's the last of it."

"We had a deal."

"Who's the other woman?"

"Massarra. Jessica seems to know her."

"How is that possible? She finds somebody she knows in this chaos? What is the relationship?"

"I don't know yet. When you left me—"

"When my man, Adriano, was killed by your girlfriend."

"You knew the risks." Roger took plastic bags from one pocket of his parka and wrapped the bloody rabbit. "Like I told you before, she claimed she was kidnapped by the bandits. That's all I know. Massarra won't talk to me."

"But *we*"—Salman held his arms wide—"were the bandits, and *we* didn't kidnap her."

"I know."

"Then kill her. Kill this Massarra woman, I don't care how. But before you do, find out who the hell she is."

6

"SO, WHO ARE you?" Jess asked Massarra.

They stood shoulder to shoulder, inspecting the spur of fractured earth rising up in front of them, an almost vertical wall of rock and ice that cut right across the highway. Jess had asked Massarra to help her scout north, but there was no way around this. At least, not for the rest of them. Jess had to resist the urge to climb, to scramble up it and look on the other side—but this wasn't a time to take chances.

"You saved my life, back in Rome," Jess added. "My mother's too. I don't even know your full name or where you're from."

Massarra smiled to show she wasn't offended. "Mizrahi is my family name."

"Middle Eastern…?" Jess said hesitantly. "Arab?"

"Israeli, but my given name is Arabic."

"An Israeli Arab?"

Massarra snorted and smiled. "Jews and Arabs have been brothers and sisters for a thousand years."

"I didn't mean—"

"It's okay."

"But your family lived in Turkey."

"My uncles, yes. Too many troubles in Israel. Well, perhaps not anymore." Her smile softened from one of amusement into one of sadness.

"What happened to your uncle, the one that was in the car with us when you took us to Giovanni's castle?"

"He is with God now."

"I'm so sorry."

"He is in Allah's hands. He lived a good life."

An unnatural silence descended. No wind. No hum of machines. No clatter of life.

"So you and Roger, you were…" Massarra searched for the words.

"I don't know what we were, to be honest," Jess said for her. "We were together for a while, back in New York, before I came

41

here."

"And you and Giovanni…"

"Awkward would be the word." Jess took one more look at the wall of rock. "Let's head back." She turned on her skis and tried to scramble up a short, icy incline they'd just slid down.

"How did you survive?" Jess asked as she reached the top of the hill, huffing and puffing. Her stump throbbed. She had never been much of a cross-country skier, but she'd volunteered for this short reconnaissance. If she wanted to cross a hundred miles of sea ice, she better get some practice in. Massarra seemed very comfortable on skis. She seemed comfortable with almost everything they did.

"When we were turned back at the border, I made it most of the way to *Castello* Ruspoli before Nomad, but I couldn't save my uncle. He asked me to leave him."

Jess left a respectful silence.

"I was in the Israeli army. We were taught ways to survive. I agreed to Special Forces training, but it was more for the hiking and outdoors than a love of weapons."

"I was in the Marine Corps."

"Your mother told me."

Jess shoved forward hard on her ski poles. One of them broke through the icy hard pack, almost pulling her off her feet.

"She was a beautiful woman, your mother, very warm."

Jess pulled ahead again. She fought the tears, the wound still fresh.

"They are with God now."

"That's not what my Dad would have said."

"He was not a man of God?"

Jess skidded to a halt and surveyed the flattened countryside around them. The trees were knocked flat as if by some giant's hand, everything covered in a coating of frost. Nothing moved.

"I fear that only the evil, stupid and cowardly remain in this world," Massarra said. "The world is ruled by a million evil men, did you know?"

"That wouldn't surprise me."

"And ten million stupid ones, and a hundred million cowards. The evil men are the power—the politicians, the rich, the fanatics of religion. The cowards are the bureaucrats and paper pushers who are just doing their jobs. The billions of others that existed here were just cattle herded, but I fear the cattle are gone."

"So much for the meek inheriting the Earth."

"When we spoke of Nomad, around the fire, do you remember?" Massarra asked. "You said your father knew of Nomad, years ago."

Just weeks ago, but in a different world. "I was mad at him," Jess admitted after a pause. "He didn't know about Nomad."

Massarra laid a hand on Jess's arm. "But you said—"

"He was supposed to meet us, but he got dragged to Germany. It was stupid, what I said. I said he lied, but I wasn't speaking about Nomad." Jess shrugged away from the woman. "What does it matter? I shouldn't have said it."

Massarra watched Jess ski off ahead of her. She waited a long time before following.

The Humvee roared, wreaths of smoke rising from its engine. The new rear-wheel tank treads clattered against ice clinging to the ruptured spur of earth they were trying to cross. A haze rolled in from the west on a breeze, the sun a weary smudge in the orange pall over their heads.

Jess watched the action from a distance. Hector nestled beside her as he finished off the last of the stew they'd made with the rabbit Roger caught on his hunting trip the day before. It had redeemed him a little in the eyes of Giovanni, and Elsa had fawned over him when he returned.

"Start the winch!"

Lucca leaned out of the driver side window of the Humvee and gave a thumbs-up. The winch's high-geared electric motor whined, and Lucca gunned the engine again. The wheel-tracks tore into the ice, and the truck clawed its way up a foot, slid back two feet, then juddered up three. Jess looked left and right, at the rocky spine rising from the ground, a deep fracturing of the earth that stretched north and south as far as she could see into the murky distance.

They'd spent a day camped at the intersection after making the decision to convert the Humvee. That whole day it snowed—or something resembling snow—a flesh-colored ice-dust that covered everything in a putrid blanket. Giovanni thought it would only take a few hours to make the modifications, but it had taken most of one day just to use the sleds to pull the tractor rims and tracks from the garage.

Jess got her first taste of what it would be like to haul equipment and supplies across ice and snow, pulling the gear across the less-than-half-mile open field. Giovanni had an easier time of it, more accustomed to sleds and skis, but it was torture for Jess. The constant pulling-pressure of her stump against the ill-fitting prosthetic made it excruciating.

Sitting in the warmth of the castle caves a week ago, the prospect of sledding a hundred miles on foot seemed like a challenge, but reality had set in. Maybe by themselves, Jess and Giovanni might be able to manage some distance, might be able to cheat death in the snow and ice—but with Hector, and with their one-and-a-half tons of supplies? She couldn't even imagine how it would be possible, but it didn't stop her resolve from pushing forward.

After finishing and testing the modifications the night before, they left at first light. The new tank treads worked beautifully for the first few miles, but the snow deepened. In low gear, the Humvee ground its way forward and managed walking speed, but at least it worked. The sled-skis raised the truck off the snow enough, and the new tank-tread rear wheels crunched into the ice beneath, driving the truck forward, compacting the ice-slurry enough for the Range Rover to follow with its chained wheels. The Jeep followed in their tracks.

When they encountered a crevasse, they went around. When they really got stuck, they winched. This was their third winch-stop of the day. Night was falling. Jess stood on the tailgate of the open rear of the Range Rover, digging through the boxes and packsacks while she waited for the Humvee to crest the ridge. She'd just finished emptying supplies from the Humvee so it could climb easier, and had totally cleared out the Jeep. It kept getting stuck in the snow, its clearance not quite high enough.

"Are there any more tents?" she asked Roger. Hector got up from beside her and fished a handful of snow to clean his plate. A trick Giovanni had shown him. He presented her his handiwork, dropped the plate in the kitchen box, and scuttled off to join his uncle.

"Just the three on top," Roger replied from the front seat, headphones on, cycling frequencies on the shortwave.

She added them to her inventory. At each stop they'd scavenged anything and everything they could, so she wanted a clearer idea of what they had, but more importantly, she was certain things seemed to be missing. A whole box of truck parts was gone.

She scanned her growing list: six tents, eight sleeping bags, four sleeping mats, twelve blankets, nine fleece tops and sweaters and three complete sets of outdoor wet gear. Keeping things dry, never mind clean, was almost impossible, and the wetter and dirtier it got, the less it kept out the cold. And it was getting colder by the day. Minus twelve Celsius the night before.

Four ice axes, their two semi-automatic AKs, a Remington .308 caliber rifle with scope and four handguns as defensive weapons. A few boxes of cartridges and shells, plus four grenades, squat gray tubes swaddled in foam packing. Add to that a two-hundred-year-old crossbow with a dozen bolts, a sword and three daggers that they'd salvaged from the castle armory museum. Weapons that had already saved them once.

"So if Civitavecchia has ships working, what about jets, helicopters?" Jess asked. On the shortwave, she'd talked to the people running the sea rescue operations, a stitched-together patchwork of emergency workers.

"The ash in the air would melt the turbines of jets," Roger replied. "Same with turboprops, but older-model propeller planes work, and maybe non-turbine helicopters. A few of the survivor camps have them."

"Any near here?"

"Not for a thousand miles."

Jess stacked two backpacks of clothing to one side, and counted one, two, three parachutes. She was a skydiver and BASE jumper— but she couldn't imagine they would be doing much of either. The silk fabric could be used for bedding or shelter, and was well packed. The parasailing kit was another matter. Giovanni had thought they might be able to pull him along behind one of the trucks, to get an aerial view if needed.

Wishful thinking, given the limited visibility, but Jess wasn't ready to throw it away yet. Instinct made her want to keep it around, just in case—in case of what, she didn't know, but then they were facing the unknown. A set of scuba tanks rested beneath it, with three regulators and masks but no flippers. Not for the water, but in case of noxious fumes. A compressor was lashed to the sidewall.

"Why are you asking?" Roger pulled his headphones off.

Jess wasn't ready to talk about the smudge in the sky she thought she saw. She looked up from her inventory sheet. "Just curious."

Roger switched off the radio.

She sat next to him on the Range Rover's tailgate and watched the Humvee scrape its way up the ridge. At the base of the ridge, beside the Jeep, they'd stacked the fuel canisters and food. She looked at her inventory. They kept a reserve of a hundred liters of distilled water, and tried to use the water filters as much as possible. Melting snow was a long process, but Giovanni insisted they all stay properly hydrated as much as they could. Ninety liters of distilled water remained after five days on the road.

At least they'd never be in the dark: a hundred packs of twelve AAA batteries meant they could run their ten headlamps at full power for half a year uninterrupted. They had a full toolkit of spanners and wrenches, vise grips and anything else they'd need to fix the vehicles, along with a thousand feet of yellow nylon cordage, and eight hundred-and-fifty-foot climbing ropes and six harnesses. Add to that the high-tensile steel cable on the two winches on the fronts of the truck, three hundred feet on the Humvee and two hundred on the Range Rover. They packed all of Giovanni's expedition gear onto the roof of the Range Rover. Four sleds, two of which were now on the front of the Humvee itself.

They carried with them two thousand pounds of fuel, half of it for the trucks and the other half for humans.

After Jess had warned of Nomad, Giovanni had converted the caves under Ruspoli Castle into a survival bunker. They couldn't take everything he'd stored there, but for their expedition they packed five hundred pounds of rice in fifty ten-pound sacks, two hundred and forty cans of spam, ten fifty-pounds bags of chickpeas, a hundred pounds of beef jerky and a hundred liters of olive oil. Add to that two hundred and forty pounds of emergency food bars, nearly three thousand of them with three hundred calories each.

This half-ton load of food added up to over two million calories, enough for five people to eat for six months. Jess wanted to pack lighter to move faster, but Giovanni had insisted they plan for the worst. While a human needed about two thousand calories a day, arctic explorers sometimes used up three times that, he'd explained, in exertion and fighting off the cold.

Then came the diesel and gasoline.

They filled the trucks up before they left, of course; twenty-three gallons into the Range Rover, twenty-five into the Humvee and twenty into the Jeep. Their fuel consumption varied; just seven miles-per-gallon for the Humvee, even modified for high mileage, with up to eighteen miles-per-gallon for the Jeep and the Range Rover in between.

The drive was five hundred miles to the tip of Sicily, so Giovanni had made a rough guess and packed about enough to refuel each vehicle twice; using twenty-liter German-style military canisters, they filled eight with gasoline, eight with diesel and nine with kerosene. The kerosene could be used for heating and light as well as fueling the diesel trucks, although it would burn hotter and might damage the engines over a long time, but they didn't need more than a week or two.

Twenty-five canisters, at forty pounds each, made a thousand pounds of explosive petrochemicals strapped to their roof racks. So far they had so much fuel they hadn't even bothered to check cars they passed.

More or less, it should have given them a range of a thousand miles, but the deep snow and constant back and forth driving had used far more per linear-mile traveled. Even so, by ditching trucks and lightening their load as they went, they could consolidate everything and everyone into the Humvee and still make the distance. With the new tank-treads, Jess thought they might even be able to cross sea-ice with the Humvee, but Giovanni insisted it

47

would be impossible.

"I don't see why? We can try," she'd protested.

"You'll see. Walking is the only way," he'd replied.

Screeching metal tore against rock, the Humvee's engine growling a staccato roar, like hammers hitting sheet metal.

"*Brutto figlio di puttana bastardo!*" Giovanni unleashed a torrent of expletive Italian from the top of the ridge, and Lucca answered back something.

The engine noise stopped.

"Everything okay?" Jess called out. The truck, two hundred feet away, was almost lost in the blue haze.

The engine turned over, wheezed once, twice, and roared back to life, but now a weeping squeak whined from somewhere inside it.

Giovanni didn't answer. The tank-treads clattered against the ice and the Humvee disappeared into the gloom, climbing to the top of the ridge.

Jess noticed Leone doubled over next to the stacked gas canisters, his face contorted. "What is it, Leone?" She took a closer look at him. He looked ill.

Leone noticed her watching him, and he straightened up and smiled at her, lowering his head and shaking it. He was fine, his expression said.

Suddenly, Giovanni yelled at her from the top of the ridge. "Jess! Jess! Come up here. You need to see this!"

The high-pitched whine of the winch's engine pierced the fog with a hollow clinking sound that echoed. He was lowering the winch harness, with three hollow aluminum tubes lashed to the hook with yellow cord. It slid down the slope toward her. Jess tossed her inventory papers onto the sacks in the rear of the Range Rover.

"Roger, come with me." He'd just turned the shortwave back on.

He looked up, his headlamp blinding her. "Why?"

"Just come."

He clicked the radio off after a second of hesitation and shrugged.

They trudged through two feet of blue snow, picked up the

aluminum-rope harness and stepped into it, first Jess, then Roger. "Okay?" she asked.

Roger nodded. "Good to go."

"Pull us up!" Jess yelled.

The winch's engine whined to life, the steel cable going taut, almost pulling Jess and Roger from their feet. They regained their balance and stepped up the slope with the winch hauling them.

"I can use the shortwave to transmit data," Roger said. "Pretty sure I can code up something to use the laptop's microphone as an audible modem."

Jess quick-stepped forward, watching for patches of ice.

"I talked to one of the engineers at Al-Jawf," Roger continued. "He has old software, x86 code, for decoding the LZW compression format on your dad's CDs. I think I could unpack the 1980s data."

"So let's do it."

"You need to give me some time to work."

The ground flattened out as they crested the ridge, the Humvee coming into view through the fog. Only a dim glow was visible on the horizon now—the sun hiding behind the cloudbanks. The winch stopped, Lucca waving from the driver seat, while Giovanni stood behind him, staring into the darkness, his back to Jess.

She stepped out of the harness and approached him. "So what's so important?"

"That." He pointed at the glow on the horizon.

"The sun?" Jess squinted and took a better look. On the other side of the ridge, the soupy atmosphere cleared.

In the distance, the fog glowed bright, but it didn't come from the sky—dots of light spread across the plateau, electric lights, fires burning. In rows and lines.

A city.

NOVEMBER 4th

Eleven Days A.N.

7

"I'M NOT SURE this is a good idea."

Jess studied the dark circles under Giovanni's eyes, the speckled stubble on his cheeks. "We need to." She looked away, toward the chimneys of fire-smoke rising into the fog-orange sky. Taking a step forward, the ground crackled and shattered. Her foot sank two inches through fine shards of ice crystal.

"Pipkrakes," Giovanni said.

Jess took another unsteady crunching stride away from him and glanced down.

"That's what it's called, what you're stepping on." He pointed at her feet. "Gives the crunch to frozen ground in early winter. Some call it needle ice or mush frost, *kammeis* to the Germans, *shimobashira* to the Japanese. Ice that grows within the soil, from the bottom up, when the temperature drops below freezing. The freezing water sucks more water up from beneath and vertical crystals grow."

Jess didn't know it had a name. The slopes of the hills just visible in the distance looked almost skiable. It was late afternoon. Shadows dusted the mountainsides, and a breeze carried the cold air downward onto them. Up above, the sun was almost visible, a patch of waxy brightness behind a semi-translucent crimson shade. Every day they were transported into a different world. At night the thundersnow had crackled again, with tendrils of cold lightning that snaked through the blackness above.

"I'm trying to say I know a lot more than you about cold weather survival. I should go."

"And that's exactly why you should stay here," Jess replied. "It's better if I go with Raffa. We go as man and wife. Less threatening than two men. Raffa knows what we need. You stay with Hector."

"Then I should go with Elsa, or Rita."

They reached the open back of the Humvee. "We don't know them, or how they might react in a fight—and you don't know cars like Raffa."

Giovanni reached into the truck and picked up a wooden crate of food, grunting at its weight. He set it down and sat on it. "Then let's not go in at all."

"I want to drop Massarra and the women here. Maybe even Raffa and Lucca and Leone too, if it looks good. We don't all need to go south."

"You know they wouldn't want that."

They spent the night on top of the ridge, waited until the brick-red dawn came so they could watch the city they'd found. What was it? A camp this size, they should have heard about it on the radio. They tried cycling through all the VHF and emergency frequencies to see if someone was broadcasting. But nothing. Jess argued that maybe they didn't have any communications gear, but it looked like thousands of people were camped there. To Giovanni it seemed too strange, and strange meant dangerous.

At first, they'd decided to give this strange city a wide berth. They lowered the Humvee back down on the side of the ridge away from the lights before crossing it again a mile further down. By midday, as they finished winching the Jeep over the ridge, the Humvee's engine had gone from a smooth roar to rough and jittery, sometimes surging, sometimes coughing.

Raffa said it could be the spark plugs getting gummed up. They tore through all the supplies the night before, but couldn't find the spares. Worse, when Jess confided in Giovanni that Leone looked like he was in pain, he replied that the old man couldn't find his heart medication. Leone had made him promise not to tell Jess.

They'd covered less than a hundred miles in the week since they left the castle, and they'd ground to a halt. Still more than four hundred miles to go on land in Italy, and that was before the walking began.

"Raffa said the Humvee's engine might overheat. And the Rover's, too."

"Jessica, please—"

"We've never seen a camp as big as this. They might have meds, or car parts we can trade for." Jess dropped the last of the crates from the back of the Jeep and motioned for Raffa to come over. She bent down and kissed Giovanni on his stubbled cheek. "I can take care of myself." She took off her precious backpack and stared at it for a second before giving it to Giovanni. "Don't ever take it off."

Red snow drifted through a pink fog that settled in the hummocks between the hills, the air aglow as the sun set over the cloudbanks. Raffa turned on the Jeep's windshield wipers. The engine's heat melted the ash-snow into blood-red rivulets that streamed off the hood. In the distance, a beacon shone above the scattered dots of flickering firelight from a villa on a hilltop in the center of the encampment. Bolts of light streamed away from it and stabbed the darkening sky.

Jess held one hand over the passenger-side heating vent, more as a distraction than to push away the cold. Something to take the edge off the tension. There had been no way to gain any insight into what they might find down here. Her whole body was tensed. She tightened her grip on the AK, drawing only small comfort from its presence. If something happened here, if things went bad, getting out would be tricky.

Entering the outskirts of the village, the truck filled with the smell of charred wood and the noisome stink of open latrines. Ragged people, wearing misshapen mountains of frayed clothing, huddled and hunched around feeble fires. Some turned to watch Jess, the firelight reflecting hunger in their eyes. On the outskirts, the huts were pitiful structures made from scraps of wood and plastic, even cardboard, erected over trampled earth.

What made them want to come here? There were plenty of destroyed villages they could be rebuilding.

Raffa followed tire tracks through the crowd as it opened before them. Empty, the Jeep's cabin felt strange, the engine's howl echoing up and down in pitch as Raffa gunned it and turned the wheels back and forth to control sliding through the frozen muck. They'd emptied the Jeep out, then piled in some diesel and food they felt they could afford to trade.

A figure appeared through the haze and raised one arm. A rifle dangled from his shoulder. He was wrapped from head to foot in black. Raffa eased on the brakes and the truck slid to a halt. More men with rifles manned a barricade of upturned barrels and cinder blocks.

"*Facciamo affari*," Raffa yelled as he rolled down his window.

The guard approached. "*Cos'hai?*"

"*Diesel.*" The teenager pointed over his shoulder at the four twenty-liter canisters in the back seat.

"*Nient'altro?*" The guard clicked on a flashlight and peered through the back window, craning his neck up. He stepped beside them, shone the light in their faces.

"*Sì, abbiamo del cibo.*" Raffa squinted but tried to smile. He had to be even more nervous than she was, but he held it together well.

The guard shone the light into Jess's eyes, then down at the AK she gripped. He stepped back and yelled, shouldering his rifle. Raffa held up his hands, palms out, to the guard in surrender. The other men ran over, their weapons raised. Raffa and the guard exchanged a stream of Italian Jess couldn't keep up with.

Raffa turned to Jess. "Put the gun down," he said, his voice low.

"What do they want?" She'd raised her weapon on purpose, to show them they were armed. Men encircled the Jeep, their own guns pointed at Jess.

"They want our weapons."

"No way. Tell them no way. We'll leave."

Raffa exchanged more quick words with the guard, back and forth, gesticulating and waving his arms. The man shook his head and turned away. He spoke to another beside him. Jess licked her lips, dropping her finger onto the trigger. The guard turned back to the truck and spoke again.

Raffa leaned toward Jess, his hands still up. "They're not happy about it, but they agree. Two men will come with us, and we can only enter the outside."

Jess nodded first to Raffa and then to the man holding the flashlight, lowering her AK at the same time. Raffa clicked the unlock button. Two of the men opened the back doors and slid in behind them, bringing with them the stench of tobacco and sweat.

Raffa put the truck back into gear. "I said we were from a camp to the north, that we want spare truck parts and medicine, but we won't give up our weapons. I told him we have the Jeep and a hundred liters of gasoline if they help us."

If they could drop Elsa and Rita—maybe even Leone and the

boys here, if they wanted, if Leone could get the medicine he needed—they wouldn't need three trucks. She was keenly aware that Raffa and Lucca had their own families just south of Rome, if they could find them. She knew she would. In her mind, Jess saw the voyage south as one of attrition, shedding supplies and weight as they went, getting lighter and faster the further south they went.

The guard walked forward and swung open a gate, motioning for Raffa to follow him in the Jeep. Red snowflakes drifted through snaking tendrils of cooking-fire smoke. Inside the compound, the road was plowed-clear asphalt, and the structures went from thrown-together shacks of scrap to pre-fab shelters and tents, with electric lights shining from windows. A black and red flag draped from a wooden pole just past the entrance. Jess didn't recognize it.

They trailed the guard into a low corrugated metal building, past a depot piled with green camouflage cases. Chickens squawked in slatted wooden crates stacked at the entrance, and inside were parked four trucks, one of them a Humvee. Raffa pulled beside it and turned off the engine. The men in the backseat opened their doors and immediately started to unload the diesel.

Jess jumped out of her door. "Tell them they only get it when we agree to a trade."

She hit the concrete floor, slipped on a patch of grease and had to steady herself, her prosthetic leg clanging against a metal post supporting the roof. Maybe she was more tired than she realized. Raffa made to help her, but she waved him away.

The guard walked over, and she thought he intended to offer her a hand, but instead he tapped her leg with the muzzle of his rifle and pulled back the fabric.

"Hey!" Jess swatted him away. Beside her, Raffa tensed, said something curt to the man in Italian. She laid a hand on his arm and gave him a don't-say-anything-stupid smile.

The guard ignored Raffa and turned to his men. Said something in a language Jess didn't understand, then looked at her. "You come with us," he said in halting English. Gently but firmly, he took hold of the muzzle of her AK. She tried to pull away, but the two other guards raised their weapons.

"Raffa, what's going on?" Jess held her rifle firm.

The teenager fired off a series of quick back-and-forth

questions with the one holding Jess's gun. "He says we need to come with him, to talk with someone."

"I'm not giving my weapon up."

More men streamed in from the open door to the garage. At least six, Jess estimated, seeing them from the corner of her eye as she held her gaze on the guard in front of her.

"I don't think there's a choice." Raffa held his arms up.

At least a half a dozen rifle muzzles now pointed at Jess. Exhaling, she let go of her weapon. What just happened? The atmosphere in the room changed the moment the guard saw Jess slip.

"That way," the guard said to Jess, motioning with his rifle muzzle for Raffa to come as well.

Maybe they wanted more information about their camp. Jess had a story ready, using the *Bandita* town as her fictional camp-base. Shuffled forward by the pack of men, she and Raffa were walked outside and into a cinder block building next door. They pushed them through the front door, down a flight of steps and into a corridor.

Jess's stomach lurched.

It was a jail cell, crowded with people. The guard shoved them forward into an empty holding cell, ten foot square. Green paint peeled from the rusted metal bars. The other prisoners watched them silently.

The door swung shut behind them. The lock clinked. She'd given up without even a fight, but as gentle as they had been, they must want *something*. Raffa sat on a wooden cot against the wall, and she slumped next to him.

Swearing softly, she pressed her face into her hands and closed her eyes. "Sorry, this is my fault."

"This is an unexpected pleasure, Miss Rollins. Welcome to our home."

Jess opened her eyes. She must have fallen asleep. What time was it? She pushed herself up on the wooden bench, startling Raffa who was curled up on the bench beside her. A man stood smiling at her from behind the rusting metal bars of the cage. The other cells had been emptied.

"Excuse me?" Jess managed to groan, squinting at the man.

He had perfectly-parted blond hair, translucent pale skin, his nose thin and almost effeminate—a surgical beauty—but his eyes were hard and blue. His accent was well-spoken, educated British.

"Bring her," he said to two guards flanking him. He walked away without looking back.

The prison door squeaked open. One of the guards motioned at Jess.

"We go together," she said, pressing her back against the wall and reaching for Raffa, who'd bolted awake to stand in front of her.

The guard shook his head. "Only you," he said in Italian-accented English.

"Together, or we go nowhere."

The blond-haired man stopped at the stairs leading up. The guard holding the door open turned to look at him. Blond-hair paused to consider, then nodded.

Sandwiched between the two guards, they followed up the stairs and back out of the cinder-block jailhouse. The air outside was biting cold and sucked the wind from Jess's lungs; the sky an impenetrable black. She gasped, using one arm to hold her parka tight around her, and keeping the other arm behind her to clutch Raffa's hand.

The Englishman led them up the hill a hundred yards, toward the central villa with its shining beacon, but just when Jess thought that was where they were headed, he took a sharp left into an entranceway carved into the ground.

Uniformed soldiers guarding the door snapped to attention. One of them opened the door. Inside, the tunnel was brightly lit, with a curving, sweeping marble floor that angled downward. Glowing picture frames lined the walls, scenes of glistening old growth forests and quiet ocean bays dotted with seaweed covered rocks. A soft hiss, and a door-panel opened in the wall ahead of them. The blond-haired man strode through the opening as lights blinked on inside.

"Please, sit." He indicated a white plastic chair to one side of a brushed metal table in the middle of the room. He sat at a matching chair on the other side.

The room was spotlessly white, smelled antiseptically clean.

Jess became aware of how filthy she was, of her own fetid stink. She hadn't had a shower, or even properly cleaned herself, in more than a week. She had on the same clothes she'd worn for almost that time. In front of her, smiling, the man looked freshly shaved, his blond hair coiffed, blue eyes clear, his polished leather shoes gleaming in the overhead LED lighting. And was that…cologne she smelled?

A large mirror dominated one wall of the twenty-by-twenty foot room. Jess guessed they were being watched. She sat. Behind her, the guards pulled Raffa back and stood him by the wall.

The man's smile widened, revealing a perfect row of white teeth. "Miss Rollins, it is a pleasure."

Jess frowned, looked at the glass mirror-wall, then back at the Englishman. *How do they know my name?* "And you are…?"

"Who I am is not important."

"And how do you know me?"

"You're famous, Jessica." He glanced at the mirror-wall. "Or perhaps I should say, infamous. A lot of people are looking for you."

"Me?"

"Your father, where is he?"

"I don't know."

"We'll find him, you know. We have scouts out looking. Right now."

"We got separated." Jess turned to check on Raffa. "We just came to see if you had some medication. His uncle is sick." She cocked one thumb over her shoulder. "And some car parts. We have our Jeep, some fuel we could trade."

The man tapped a stack of file folders on the desk. In way of reply, he opened one of the file folders and spread a set of glossy eight-by-ten inch photographs on the table in front of Jess. She leaned in to look. They were pictures of her and her mother, in Rome. Grainy and in black-and-white, as if captured from a security camera. One of them was a partial image of her sitting under awnings, to get out of the rain, talking to Massarra's uncles.

She fought a surreal sense of vertigo. *What the hell was going on?*

60

"So you have vacation pictures of me and my mother. What do you want me to say?"

"Do you know, before this, I made a living from being able to tell if people are lying?"

"You're a cop?"

The man laughed, baring his teeth in a flash of white. "Nothing so pedestrian. More of a…businessman, and you are going to help me with some business."

Jess sat back in her chair and crossed her arms. She held his gaze, the calm expression on her face betraying nothing of the whirlwind in her mind. What did he want? They didn't have much of value in their possession. Maybe the gold bars? But how would that relate to her father? The only thing that made sense was the backpack. Her father's data. But how could this guy know about it? She glanced around the room, then at the file on the desk. Was this some sort of government bunker? Why would they have dug up surveillance pictures of her? In all the survivor groups they'd contacted, everyone was struggling to get basic power, to survive, but here…

"What is this place?" she asked.

The man nodded, keeping the high-wattage smile at full-beam. "I could say that I'm the one asking the questions, but that would be tiresome." He held his hands out. "You could describe this as a luxury disaster retreat."

"You built this to survive Nomad?"

"It could have been a pandemic, an asteroid, a nuclear war. Nomad was a surprise to all of us." He eyed her merrily. "Almost all. This is Vivas Twelve. Kind of a billionaires' preppers club, in your American vernacular."

His words flashed through her mind. "So who's looking for me? Is it Ufuk Erdogmus?" She said this before she thought it through. It was one of the last things her father said to her before he died: find the billionaire Ufuk Erdogmus.

The man straightened. "Interesting."

"So he *is* looking for me."

The Englishman's face remained smilingly blank, but said everything by saying nothing.

"Is he here?"

61

The man shrugged. "First, you help me. Then we'll see about me helping you. Where is your father?"

"I told you, we got separated."

For the first time, the smile slid from his face. "Jessica. You must understand the landscape ahead of you. There is the world out there—the sick, the hungry, the dying, the *diseased*." He paused to linger on this last word. "And then," he continued brightly, "there is the world in here; safe and warm. Each Vivas shelter is a tiny self-contained underground city, hundreds of us at each location. Bury us, and we have equipment to dig ourselves out. Attack us, and we can seal our doors for two years without needing to breathe the air above or drink a drop of contaminated water. Would you like to see a garden again? Plants? Perhaps"—he crinkled his nose—"take a hot shower? We have movie theaters, swimming pools…"

"I don't know where he is."

Closing his eyes, the man sighed. He flicked one hand at the guards. "Take them back to the cell block."

NOVEMBER 5th

Twelve Days A.N.

8

"SEE ANYTHING?"

"Nothing coming our way," Roger replied.

Giovanni cupped his hands and blew on them. "Give me the binoculars."

"All yours." Roger handed them over. "Should we haul the Range Rover?"

Giovanni shook his head and tightened the straps on his backpack—Jess's backpack. "I'm going to get them."

He looked through the binoculars, the two circles of vision merging into one. The twinkling glow of the encampment separated into dots of light. He focused on one fire near the edge, then looked further in. The shacks seemed to merge into a more regular pattern of buildings toward the center, all surrounding a central villa, illuminated by what looked like searchlights blazing into the sky. Jess was supposed to be back last night, but she wasn't. At first light, he climbed a ridge above their tents to watch. All day he'd been up here, waiting for any sign of the Jeep.

Roger stuffed his hands back into his mittens. "If we take the Humvee, and we get stuck…"

Giovanni focused on what looked like a barricade at the interface between the outer and inner circle of structures. "I don't need lessons from you."

He lowered the binoculars. Night was falling again, the weak glow in the sky fading back to darkness. Today the mists were pink-orange, but clear enough to see the encampment, about two miles away across a snowed-in valley. "I'm going to get her. On foot."

The cold numbed Giovanni's fingertips. The first stages of frostbite were painless, but he knew the warming up afterward was excruciating.

"Leave the backpack with me. I can work on the data while you're gone," Roger offered.

"I don't think so."

Roger exhaled, a plume of white vapor shooting into the pink ice crystals shimmering in the air. He looked at the encampment glowing in the distance, then back at Giovanni. "If I don't have anything to do, I'd better go with you."

"And we'll take Lucca. He'll want to find his brother." Giovanni stuffed the binoculars into the pocket of his parka, cupped his hands and blew on them again. "We leave at first light tomorrow morning." He glanced around. "Where's Massarra?"

"Jessica!"

The young man's face stared accusingly at Jess. I'm dead, his eyes said to her. He wasn't more than a teenager, his face smooth, pink, fresh. You killed me.

"Jessica, wake up!"

The young man's face faded, replaced with cinder block walls. Jess shivered and clutched the thin blanket they had given her and Raffa to huddle under on the metal cot.

"Jessica," the voice hissed again, lower this time, but still urgent.

She turned her stiff neck. Was it someone in the cell next to her? No. All the other cells were empty.

"Look up," urged the familiar voice.

Massarra's piercing blue eyes hovered behind the metal grates of the tiny window of their cell. "We must hurry."

Jess glanced left and right. No guards. "What are you—"

"You need to get out of here, right now."

"I know that."

"No, I mean *right* now. You need to get outside of the Vivas encampment. You are in grave danger."

Jess nudged Raffa awake but held one hand over his mouth. She pointed up at the metal grate.

"How can we get out?" Jess asked.

Massarra shook her head in violent shivers. "You must find a way. Quickly. Yourself." Her thin hand extended through the grate, her exposed wrist fragile and pale. From her fingers something fell into the dirt. "Outside the camp I can help." Her arm and face disappeared.

Jess rocked forward to her feet and knelt in the dirt. A switchblade. She clicked it open and tested the blade. Razor sharp.

They'd strip searched both her and Raffa after returning them to the cell, put them into stained prisoners' clothes, but they'd given them back their boots. Jess slipped the blade into hers.

She needed to get out of here. But how? Get the guard over, stab him? Take the keys? Maybe. Maybe she could be fast enough by herself. She glanced at Raffa.

"Guard!" she shouted as loud as she could.

Raffa looked at the cellblock door, then back at Jess and down at her boot. He clutched the soiled blanket, but then straightened and stood. His hands shook but he balled his fists and nodded at Jess.

"I need to speak to the English man!" Jess shouted again.

A small metal opening over the main cellblock door slid open. *"Cosa c'è?"*

"I need to speak to your boss! I know where my father is, but he's very sick. We need to hurry."

The truck crested a ridge and Jess rolled sideways onto Raffa. She struggled to right herself, but her wrists were bound. She'd stood her ground in the jail, said that she'd only bring them to her father if Raffa was brought along. She insisted they had to go right away. The blond-haired man was suspicious, but he'd relented. He seemed in a hurry as well.

A team was hastily assembled, and Jess and Raffa were tied together and pushed at gunpoint into the backseat of a truck.

The vehicle's engine growled. Jess marveled at how it had been modified for snow. Its four wheels sat atop triangular tank treads, but not a hack job like Raffa and Giovanni had performed on their Humvee—this transformation took expertise and resources and looked like a pre-fabricated kit.

The Englishman drove the truck himself, sitting directly in front of Jess. A dark-eyed man with his face covered sat beside him. He held an automatic rifle, pointed up, and glanced into the back seat every few minutes. The truck's headlights lit up conical swaths of fresh pink-white snow. Crystals of ice twinkled. Three snowmobiles—*where the hell did they get snowmobiles?*—whined in front of the truck, following hollows in the snow that hinted at the road. Outside of the lights of the truck and snowmobiles, she saw nothing but dead black.

Hitting another bump, Jess tossed onto Raffa. "*Andiamo*," she whispered. "Just follow me." Raffa nodded. Fear in his eyes, but he steadied himself. Brave kid. She rocked back into her seat.

The man holding the rifle looked over his shoulder at them.

Jess waited until he turned back to lean down and take the switchblade from her boot. The whites of Raffa's eyes gleamed in the light of the truck's instrumentation. She began working the blade into the rough nylon cord binding her wrists.

"We're almost there," Jess said in a loud voice, keeping her eyes on the man with the AK in the front.

The roar of the truck's engine lowered in pitch as the blond-haired man shifted down. An almost vertical wall of dirt, rock and ice appeared from the black gloom. The same ridge of earth across the highway that had stopped them the day before, the one they had to haul the Humvee and Jeep across by winch, the one she was counting on.

Giovanni and Roger were about a mile to the north, she knew. They had to be watching. At the same time, the Englishman was wary of a trap, as was the guard beside him. Two more sat in the trunk, plus the three snowmobiles each with two men. They all appeared to be former military—very likely mercenaries. Ten heavily armed men versus her and Raffa, and maybe Giovanni and Roger and Leone. Even if they saw them coming, they wouldn't be able to get here that fast. The wildcard was Massarra, but even given her apparent toughness and experience, what could a hundred-pound woman add to this unbalanced equation?

There weren't many options, but she had to do something, and fast. Jess cut through her ropes and handed the knife to Raffa, urging him with her eyes to do the same. Reaching forward, she unzipped the truck's emergency kit, felt around inside. She found a flare and stuffed it into her boot. Everyone was distracted looking at the growing wall of rock, searching the darkness for any signs of movement.

The blond-haired man downshifted again. The snowmobiles stopped where the spine of Earth became vertical. It hadn't taken as long as Jess thought it would, but this truck with its modified treads, and the snowmobiles were much faster over the snow, and it was a straight drive down the highway from the Vivas encampment. She hadn't had a lot of time to think. They pulled to a stop, one snowmobile up ahead and one to each side.

The blond-haired man turned to Jess. "So you pulled your truck across here?" He turned back to examine the wall of dirt and ice. "I don't see any marks."

"We brought our Humvee to the top and saw your city, Vivas. We thought it looked dangerous, so we winched up the Jeep and dropped it down here."

"And yet we don't see any tracks from this side."

"The snow, the wind from the north, must have covered them. I came down here and did a reconnaissance. Look!" Jess pointed to their left. Just visible at the edges of the pools of light thrown by the Jeep's headlights were a pair of ski tracks leading south where she and Massarra had come over when they were deciding where to head next. They'd explored a little to the south before deciding to head north.

The blond-haired man leaned out his window. "Follow those tracks and see where they go. And keep in contact." The man on the snowmobile in front nodded and gunned his engine, the other raising his weapon. They disappeared into the darkness. The blond-haired man turned back to Jess. "So where's your father?"

"On the other side. He is very sick. The only way he's going to live is if you help us. I have no choice. If you climb to the top, you'll see them. They're camped at the bottom on the other side."

The man watched her carefully. "We will see."

He opened his door and yelled at the men on the snowmobiles on their right, then at the two men on the one beside him. Both left their engines on, headlights shining. The truck's engine was still running, its lights still flooding the road ahead.

He said something in Italian to the man holding the rifle in the front seat, then stepped out of the truck and walked in front, his backside illuminated by the truck's lights. The man in the front seat glanced at Jess, then at Raffa, and opened his door and stepped out. The two men in the back disembarked and stood guard, one to each side of the truck.

Doing her best to keep her upper body still and in place, Jess took the knife back from Raffa. He nodded. He was free. Keeping his hands low, Raffa shifted his arms toward her. Two of the men scrambled up the rocky embankment, toward the top. The blond-haired man and three of his mercenaries stood in front of the truck, their backs to it, but two men still stood guard to either side of the truck.

Down to six. An improvement, but not enough.

"*Si, si!*" one of the men yelled from the darkness at the top of the embankment.

The blond-haired man turned to Jess. "Perhaps some truth?" He turned back. "You two, get up there and help them."

"Should I get out?" Jess asked. "It might be easier if my father hears my voice."

"Yes, come." The man kept his back to her. Two more of his men scrambled up the rocky embankment.

Down to four on two.

Jess glanced at the snowmobile beside them, still running. She pulled on the door handle, and with a soft *ka-chunk* the door opened an inch. The interior light glowed on. Jess opened her door and slid out of her seat. She motioned for Raffa to follow her. The two men climbing disappeared into the darkness above.

Any second, they'd realize that there was no camp on the other side.

Biting cold assaulted her senses. She smiled at the man beside them, then feigned a slip in the snow. Reflexively, he reached out to help her, his rifle cradled in one arm. She took the arm, pretending her own hands were still bound together. Still giving him the same smile, she accepted his help. He had week-old stubble, his face as worn and weathered as Giovanni's. As he hauled her up, she spun and brought her switchblade up in a quick motion, driving it into the carotid artery in his neck.

He never saw it coming. His eyes went wide as the blade ripped through cartilage and soft tissue. Hot blood spurted across her arms and face. The man, eyes fixed on her, dropped to his knees, his body convulsing, a soft gurgling the only sound from his throat.

She eased him into the snow in a spreading dark pool. Still gripping the man, she turned him, and slid his rifle into her own

70

hands. The hum of the truck's engine was loud enough that the Englishman and his men still stared up the rock face, their backs to her.

Slinging the rifle over her shoulder, she took two quick steps onto the snowmobile and Raffa followed, stumbling at first getting out of the truck, then sprinting. Snowmobiles had no gears. She'd been on many, joyriding as a kid. Her heart pounding, feeling Raffa's hand clutch her ribs, she wrenched back on the throttle.

"Hey!"

She glanced left. The guard on the other side had his rifle up, pointed straight at Jess. Twenty feet away. In slow motion, she felt the snowmobile's engine roar, its track skidding and biting into the snow. In her mind's eye she saw the guard's finger on the trigger. She ducked, expecting a bullet.

But it was his head that exploded in a spray of pink mist.

The snowmobile rocketed forward and she hauled the steering to the left, into the darkness where the other snowmobile had gone. Looking over her right shoulder, she watched another of the mercenaries crumple to the ground.

Jess accelerated down the hill, away from the road. Ice exploded from trunks of trees in front of her as bullets impacted them. Staccato bursts of gunfire. In the black distance, the smudge of the other snowmobile's headlights appeared. The smear of light lengthened as the machine turned around, then formed back into a single bright blob as it headed back directly toward her.

Over the immediate rumble of her own snowmobile's engine, she heard the thin whine of the one at the truck. Reaching the copse of trees, she stole a quick glance back. A headlight bore toward them, following fast behind. The light of the other snowmobile danced in the air over their heads.

She had maybe a two-hundred-yard lead.

Jess pulled the throttle to its maximum and shot across an icy field. Her eyes teared up. The advancing light of the snowmobile in front of them grew brighter. They were sandwiched. She angled away from it at forty-five degrees.

"When I stop," Jess yelled over the engine's noise, "get off and pick up the snowmobile, move it to the right."

Raffa gripped onto her back. "What you say?"

Now wasn't the time for an English lesson.

"Get off when I stop and help me move the snowmobile," Jess yelled again. She jabbed toward the right with her hand.

She slowed to zigzag again through another copse of trees, then gunned the engine. The snowmobile skimmed over the top of the ice-encrusted snow. She kept her eyes searching through the blackness. And there it was. She jammed on the brakes. Raffa's weight slammed forward into her, shoving the handlebars into her stomach. The snowmobile skidded sideways to a halt.

"Grab it!" She disentangled herself and jumped off into the knee-deep snow, turning off the snowmobile's headlight. Blackness. The snowmobile behind them was making its way through the trees, about a hundred yards behind, the headlight of the other one merging beside it.

Around them it was pitch black.

"Quick, quick," Jess urged, pointing to her left. She strained to pick up the front of the snowmobile and pulled it three feet sideways across the ice.

Raffa saw what she meant and he hauled the back of the snowmobile, but he moved it six feet. Jess pulled her end, sloughed it sideways again.

"Again, again, come on."

They pulled it another dozen feet into the cover of some trees and behind a snowdrift.

Jess grabbed the flare she'd stolen from the Jeep's emergency kit, pulled it and it flamed to life. She ran forward ten feet and stuck the flare into the snow, right near the edge of the cliff. The headlight of the other snowmobile, less than thirty yards away, lit her briefly and she rolled sideways and held her breath. At full throttle, the snowmobile roared past her and shot off the edge of the cliff. The driver yelped. The sound of the engine went up an octave as the vehicle roared in midair.

Seconds later a clattering crash as man and machine hit the rocks below. An orange fireball exploded below.

Scrambling back to the trees, Jess helped Raffa drag their snowmobile further away. A wind whipped across the plateau, fresh snow coming with it. Jess and Massarra had explored this area, and discovered this cliff. It was impassible, hundreds of feet high, stretching for several miles north to south. It was why they had decided to go west. The other snowmobile appeared and slowed near the edge of the cliff. Two of the men disembarked and looked tentatively over the edge, at the guttering flames of the wreckage below.

Doing their best to cover their snowmobile with snow and twigs, Jess and Raffa edged away in the darkness as the growl of the big truck's engine became louder. The snow thickened. Jess caught a glimpse of Englishman's face. She had a rifle across her back, but they still outnumbered her. Not the time for a firefight.

"Let's go," she urged Raffa.

9

JESS DUG HER nails into the frozen earth. Something cracked. It might have been a finger. She couldn't feel them. She couldn't feel anything, not her feet, not her face. Somehow, she kept moving. Kept urging her body forward. Every ten feet she'd grope around to feel Raffa, but he wasn't behind her anymore. She felt his arms around her, urging her forward.

The blackness swallowed everything.

She couldn't see her hands in front of her face. The ground, the frozen rock wall on her left, the idea of a world outside this blackness receded from her mind. She just wanted to lie down, be engulfed by sleep and dreams.

For a while she had been shivering, the cold biting into her, the pain throbbing in her fingers and toes. The agony receded, blossomed into warmth. The shivering stopped, the pain went away. Was she still moving? She sensed her arms and legs swinging back and forth, felt herself teetering, and falling over. Strong arms kept returning her back upon her feet, and she heard the constant whispers in her ear.

And then.

Something loomed in the darkness.

Light. Movement.

"Jessica, my God."

A face glowed in the light. Familiar. Her mind struggled.

"*Prendila.*" Raffa's voice croaked from his blistered lips. He lifted Jess one last time, which required all his fading strength, and pushed her forward.

"Giovanni," Jess whispered as he pulled her into his arms. That's right, her frozen mind said to itself, we were trying to find Giovanni. And Hector. Now, stop. We can stop.

She slumped. Her feet fell out from under her.

"Start the Humvee," Giovanni yelled at Roger. His headlamp pierced a thin ray of light through the swirl of falling snow. "Get the heat up to maximum. Keep the lights off." He looked at Jess. "Jesus Christ, is this your blood?"

"*No, non è suo*," Raffa said. He slumped into the snow. "Not hers."

Roger disappeared into the darkness. Lucca emerged from the same darkness and yelped. He ran to his brother Raffa, fell beside him, and pulled his head and shoulders onto his lap.

"What happened?" Giovanni cradled her in his arms. "We were about to leave, to go into—"

A bright orange ball flashed in the distance, obscured by the deepening churning snow that fell from the sky. A half-dozen smaller orange balls flared beside the larger one. Jess stared at the flames, her eyes still unfocused. The orange ball grew into a fiery globule. No sound, but the ground juddered after a few seconds.

Staggering together, they made it to the Humvee as the first shock wave hit them, a concussive, ear-splitting roar that rolled over and over, echoing off the rock wall behind them. The fireballs merged and climbed into the sky, a crazed maelstrom of snow and fire that illuminated the plain before them.

Not fifty feet away, a solitary figure appeared, illuminated by the growing conflagration. Giovanni lifted Jess into the passenger seat of the Humvee and swung his rifle around. The figure jogged toward them. Giovanni raised his gun.

"You must leave now." A woman's voice, stern and unyielding. Her face was invisible against the fireball.

His rifle still up, Giovanni squinted. "Massarra?"

She crossed the final twenty feet and held up one hand to push aside the muzzle of Giovanni's AK. Another explosion lit up the dark clouds above. The Vivas encampment, less than two miles away, blazed. Screams echoed.

"Now," repeated Massarra, pointing at the spine of earth behind them. "Go to the other side and take the Range Rover. Back east, to the coast."

Thick snowflakes fell onto her face and shoulders. "I will take the Humvee, drive south and lead them away. You take the road east. I will meet you in Civiteveccia."

She swung a sack into the passenger seat of the Humvee. A pile of greasy spark plugs spilled out.

"How did you—"

"No time to explain." Massarra shook the snow off and pulled back her hood. "Whoever is doing that"—she pointed at the fire rising into the snow-driven sky—"will soon find us if we don't hurry."

She turned to Roger, sitting in the driver's seat of the Humvee. Her smile widened, revealing her teeth. But it wasn't a smile. "And if any harm comes to her, Mr. Roger," she said, pointing at Jess. "I will personally skin you alive, do you understand?"

You killed me, said the boy, Aberto. Not more than nineteen. So young. Another man's face appeared, this one grizzled, a week's worth of stubble on his cheek, his eyes wide with surprise, a switchblade stuck deep into his throat. We know who you are, said the man.

"They had pictures of me," Jess whispered.

Giovanni's face hovered and came into focus. At the same moment came the pain.

She screamed, "Jesus Christ," her voice whining into high-pitched agony.

"Give it to me," Giovanni yelled at Roger.

The man fumbled and handed something over.

Jess felt a pinprick in her arm, submerged somewhere below the flames burning her fingers and toes, and a moment later a cool wave washed through her body. Giovanni's face retreated from in front of her, disappeared up a tunnel. Her fingers and toes still burned, but it was a fire in another building now.

"Stay with me," Giovanni said, his voice low and soft. "The pain is from frostbite. Your foot, your fingers…it's going to hurt a lot worse before it gets better. I just gave you morphine."

Jess fought back, her mind swimming back to the top of the tunnel. Giovanni's face came back into focus. "Where are we?"

"We're in the Range Rover. You passed out. We had to leave, go back the way we came."

Gritting her teeth, Jess forced her mind out of the fog. She blinked and looked around. She was in the third row of the Range Rover, her body stretched across Raffa and Giovanni. Elsa, Rita, and Roger sat in front of them, in the second row. Leone was driving, with Lucca in the front passenger seat holding Hector. Seeing Jess awake, Hector waved, his face frightened. *"Buongiorno, Jessica."*

"Buongiorno," Jess replied as loud as she could manage, but it came out barely more than a whisper.

She smiled at Hector, trying to convey that everything was all right. He knew it wasn't. He wasn't stupid. But he was brave. Jess could hardly imagine what this world must look like to a six-year-old.

Children adjusted, learned ways to survive and thrive even in hostile environments. As much as she'd imagined children to be fragile, it was actually the other way around. Children were robust, hardy, and easily adaptable. Adults had the more difficult time shifting to new realities, of letting go, of dealing with pain.

Outside the truck's windows, white-orange snow fell in a semi-bright murk. Daytime. Jess took another look around the truck.

"Where's Massarra? Did she come back?"

It was coming back to her now. Someone had taken down several of the mercenaries. Someone very good with a rifle. An expert. A sniper.

"She took the Humvee and went south," Giovanni explained. "To lead them away from us. Said she could circle around Rome, then make it on foot to intercept us again. She insisted."

"Doubt we'll be seeing her again," Roger muttered.

"We stuck an LED searchlight on the top of the Humvee to make sure they won't miss her," Giovanni added, frowning at Roger.

"She saved us." Jess tried to sit upright, but the fire flared again in her toes and fingers as she moved. "It must have been her."

She looked at her hands for the first time. They were wrapped in thick bandages. Dread surged through her. What was underneath those bandages? A black, twisted, gangrenous mess? She lost a leg, but could she stand to lose her toes, her fingers? She'd be worse than crippled. She couldn't hide that. In this new and ravaged world, disabled like that, she'd be dead soon enough.

"Don't worry," Giovanni said, watching her eyes and face. "I don't think you'll lose any of them. I've seen worse." He paused. "Raffa told us what he could. Said you escaped on a snowmobile, then left it and walked in the dark. Two hours, he says, no jacket or gloves…"

That's right, Jess remembered, the memories seeping back. They had walked along the spine of earth in the dark. No way to get lost. They just had to walk along the ridge, keeping it to their left in the pitch black, and stumble forward. They knew that the Humvee was somewhere along there, a few miles.

"Raffa said they took you prisoner almost as soon as you entered the camp. That someone recognized you? You were mumbling about photos when you were asleep."

"They had pictures of me," Jess said. "In Rome, with my mother. An Englishman looking for my father."

"English?"

"He took me into some kind of underground bunker. For billionaires, he said."

"Vivas," Giovanni muttered under his breath.

Jess squirmed upright, ignoring her pain. "You knew it? Why didn't you tell us that was—"

"I didn't know *that* was Vivas. A few years ago, an American salesman came calling, asking us if we'd be willing to pay a hundred millions dollars for a two bedroom unit in a massive bunker. Said it came with underground swimming pools—"

"—movie theaters too, I heard." Jess interrupted. "They wanted my father, but I don't know why. Before he died, my Dad told me to find Ufuk Erdogmus. You remember?"

Giovanni frowned but nodded.

"I mentioned Erdogmus to this Englishman. He knew him."

"So why didn't you wait to speak to Ergodmus? Was he there?"

"Because Massarra appeared and told me to get out of there as fast as I could."

"Good thing," Giovanni said. "Because Vivas was destroyed."

"What?" Jess's mouth fell open. "That place was designed to withstand anything."

"The ground shuddered, explosions a thousand feet into the

78

air. Looked very bad."

"And Massarra rescued you?" Roger snorted and shrugged theatrically. "Who is she? Do you know?" He paused. "Really?"

"I know that she saved all *our* lives today, perhaps." Giovanni pulled Jess closer. "And is risking *hers* now."

Roger was about to object, then reconsidered. Instead, he said: "Jess, while you were away, I talked to Al-Jawf again. Your friends in Libya."

"And?"

"They had a clear night two days ago. I got a new reading on the position of Venus. Look at this." He produced a laptop. "Look at these new simulations."

NOVEMBER 6th

Thirteen Days A.N.

10

"LET'S STOP THERE."

Jess pointed at a collapsed set of buildings just off the road.

Giovanni craned his neck forward to get a better look. "Leone, *andiamo là.*"

"*Sì.*" The old man pulled the steering wheel and the Range Rover skidded through the slush and churned its way up a winding road.

The light was falling. Time to make camp for the night.

In the distance, a sheer rock wall loomed. Lights twinkled at its top.

"Pitigliano," Giovanni said, watching Jess's eyes. "An ancient medieval town. Beautiful to visit, but maybe another time."

"Another time," Jess agreed.

When Jess awoke to the pain, the ash fall brought in on the southerly wind was thick enough to make it very slow going. They missed the off-ramp to the coast road on the first pass. They followed their own tracks back, but found other tire tracks in the snow and muck as well.

If they were being followed, they didn't see anyone.

In silence, they wound their way through the rubble of small towns and past stripped-husk olive groves of half-buried trees. A thick yellow haze replaced the ash fall, stripes from a painter's brush that oozed across the landscape. The sulfurous stench returned, but Giovanni said that they were near the town of Saturnia, where sulfurous hot springs had existed before; tourists came to bathe in them. Jess couldn't imagine anything worse.

As the ash fall stopped, Jess's pain began to ease.

Her fingers and toes still ached, but reduced to a dull throb below another dose of morphine. She'd unwrapped her hands, trembling, expecting the worst. They were raw-red and mottled purple, but not black. Her fingertips tingled. A good thing, Giovanni had laughed, winking, saying that amputating his girlfriend's fingers was always the beginning of the end in his relationships.

The Range Rover skidded to a halt beside a mound of wind-blown ice and brick. One of the farm buildings, two stories of gray brick with terracotta tiles, looked almost intact. Only the windows were shattered.

"Leone, Lucca, Raffa, *guardate dentro*," Giovanni said, motioning at the building. "And take your weapons."

They only had one AK semi-automatic rifle left, which Giovanni kept with him, but Leone kept the other rifle and the two teenagers the pistols. Jess had stolen an AK from her victim, but on the long trek through the cold she had used it as a crutch and eventually let it fall by the wayside.

Roger, Elsa and Rita opened the back doors of the Range Rover and slid out, while Raffa exited the front passenger side with Hector. Eight adults and one child crammed into a Range Rover for ten hours made it feel as though they were in a cattle car. Jess had gotten used to her own body odor, but mixed with the others, the smell was almost overpowering. Giovanni stepped out from the third row of seating to hold Jess as she came out. Pain flashed through her foot as it hit the ground.

"First time I've been glad I only have one foot," Jess tried to laugh, grimacing, Giovanni's arms still around her. She gamely pushed him away and hobbled a few steps. "Hey, Roger, could you run the new simulations again?"

It'd been almost impossible to use the laptop all day, bouncing around over the rough terrain, and anyway, Jess's mind was half gone under the drugs.

"Jessica," Giovanni protested, holding up one hand, "is now really—"

"And set up the shortwave," she added, gritting her teeth, forcing away the pain.

"Sure." Roger stepped back to the truck to retrieve his bag. "Do you want me to look at the data too?" He pointed at Jess's backpack that she clutched in her arms.

"Just get the sims and the shortwave going."

Giovanni didn't say anything more and began tossing equipment from the back of the Range Rover with more energy than the task required. He winced picking up each bag. His own wounds, from the fight at the castle two weeks ago, still hadn't fully healed.

"It's important," Jess said, joining him. "The simulations are important."

"As you wish."

From the farmhouse, Raffa waved the *all-clear* signal from the second floor. Giovanni waved back.

Jess pulled a food crate from the back of the Range Rover. "Is this all we have?" She counted four of the brown plastic containers they used to store the ration packs.

"It's all we had time for."

"That's *it*? Is there more in the roof rack?"

Giovanni dropped his head low and sat heavily on the truck's tailgate. "How do you say...*all hell* was breaking loose when you returned. When you were in Vivas, we pulled across to the other side the most important supplies first—mostly the food. When we had to leave fast, I had to leave it on the other side. We had to drag you unconscious on one of the sleds. Vivas burned before our eyes."

"So what's in the roof rack?"

"Mostly stuff I thought was least important. Most of the stuff I was going to leave."

"Like?"

"The scuba gear, the parasailing kit..."

"Jesus Christ."

"We're halfway to the coast. We'll make it tomorrow." Giovanni sucked air between his teeth. "I talked with the coastal people yesterday, with Roger while you were gone. A ship leaves the day after tomorrow."

"And can we get on it?"

"Yes." He hesitated. "I took the gold bars from the Humvee when we fled." He'd insisted on taking the gold when they left the castle. Said it would still have some value for trading.

"You took gold instead of food?"

He stood quickly and shook his head. "What would you have me do? Leave you there, frozen, half-dead?"

"I want you to make smart decisions. You've been wanting to head for these ships ever since Roger contacted them."

"*Madonne Merde.*" He raised one hand and stared at her for a moment, body tense, then shook his head. "I am going to set up camp, yes?" He turned and walked around the far side of the Range Rover, away from her.

She sighed and cursed softly, "Shit." She could have cut him some slack—the situation back there hadn't been an easy one. He'd saved her life and she should be grateful, but dammit, they needed that food.

Time to do inventory.

"Look at this." Roger pointed at his laptop screen.

An oak dining table had collapsed from ceiling debris, but Roger had propped up the broken legs on stacks of ash-smeared frozen books. He'd then swept a corner of the table clean to set up his computer. Beside him, the shortwave crackled and hissed. He hadn't managed to reach anyone tonight.

Worrying, but not unusual.

At nightfall, the yellow haze had thickened into an electric pea soup as dusk turned to dark. Coils of snow-lightening crackled across distant hillsides.

Jess finished hammering a final nail into a tarp covering the kitchen window, while Lucca and Raffa sealed a tarp over the stairs. The gas generator hummed outside, and a single LED lamp shone in the middle of the room, connected to the generator by a snaking yellow cord. A fire of broken furniture burned in a fireplace adjoining the kitchen and dining room of the farmhouse. Outside, Leone and Giovanni stood watch, while Rita and Elsa did their best with what food rations remained. Hector sat on Rita's knee. Everyone had his or her own job.

"What did you want me to see?" Jess asked, walking over to Roger, a hammer in her hand.

"Those Venus coordinates I got from Al-Jawf." Roger swiped across the laptop's touchpad. "Look at this. Two hundred and forty thousand kilometers." He pushed a button, and a three dimensional image of Earth sweeping past Saturn filled the screen. "In seventy-eight weeks, that'll be us."

"That puts the Earth going through Saturn's rings?" Jess pulled up a chair.

"Not quite, but almost. The Earth is above the plane of the rings, but it still puts us at risk of striking one or more moons."

"What's the error?"

"About two hundred thousand kilometers."

"Any way to refine it? Get more data?"

Roger raised his chin. "Let me have a look in there?" He pointed at Jess's backpack. "Three days ago you were dying for me to decode it." He patted a disk drive on the table beside the laptop. "I could give it a crack."

"It's not the time."

"Why not?"

"We have other things to think about."

"More than the Earth hitting Saturn?" Roger folded his arms.

A flash of light lit up the room. Jess crouched and spun around, checking where Hector was. The light dimmed. It seemed to come from every direction at once.

"Jess, get out here!" Giovanni yelled from the front of the house.

Looking again at Hector, wrapped in Rita's arms, Jess took off in a shuffling run to the front door. She grabbed Leone's rifle from the umbrella rack before swinging the door open.

A crackling shudder reverberated through the dark sky, shaking the old farmhouse. On the horizon, a dying light faded, but the sound echoed through the ground, vibrated up through Jess's prosthetic and into her bones. A bright orb of light streaked across the sky. It ended abruptly in an expanding glow that pierced the dark skies brighter than the sun.

"Another attack?" Giovanni crouched behind the Range Rover with Leone. "The people who attacked Vivas?"

"Worse than that." Roger stood in the open doorway. "It's a meteor shower."

"Worse?" Giovanni slowly stood up straight.

Another brilliant streak overhead, ending in another distant roar that thundered through the blackness.

"And there's a million more coming from where these came from."

A gray Mercedes truck crouched hidden behind a pile of rock and rubble, hidden amid the swirling snow atop a ridge a half-mile from the farmhouse.

Salman licked his lips. He angled the rear view mirror to try and get a better look at his lip. It was cracked, bleeding. He needed Vaseline, or some cream. Something to protect it from the arid cold. He angled the mirror to the right, catching a glimpse of a truck, its wheels mounted on tractor treads, parked beside a snowmobile. Streaks of light flashed in the sky. A thunderous boom echoed through the darkness.

He craned his neck forward to get a better look at the sky. "A new terror from God?"

"Afraid so, old chap," the blond-haired Englishman replied. He sat next to Salman in the passenger seat of the Mercedes. "Our astronomers told me to expect something like this."

"One can never be sure of God's plan." Salman struggled not to slur his s's. He licked his lip again.

"Were we to be in possession of the data Miss Rollins carries, I suspect we might in fact be very sure."

Salman turned his mirror to look at two of the man's mercenaries—thickly muscled beneath black battle armor. Night vision goggles perched atop their helmets. These military men made his own people—one an injured young boy and the other his cousin—look like peasants. He grunted and picked up a pair of binoculars and focused on the farmhouse atop the next ridge.

The Range Rover came into sharp focus.

And, there, was Jessica.

"Why don't you just take her now?"

"Not all is as it seems, I think," the Englishman replied. "Whoever attacked Vivas—"

"Destroyed?"

"More of a flesh wound." The Englishman grimaced and stroked a bandage covering the right side of his face. "The inner sanctum was unharmed, but the surface buildings...well, at least we don't have to deal with the peasants, anymore."

Salman clenched his jaw and shifted in his seat. "You think *she* attacked you?" He put the binoculars down.

"Someone is protecting her." The Englishman tilted his head to one side. "Or someone is trying to kill her. Not sure which yet. But remember, she led us into an ambush once. We don't want that to happen again. So we wait. We watch. We study the situation. We need to protect that merchandise, it may be more valuable, than, well, I was going to say the Vatican, but that's gone, isn't it?"

The Englishman let an uncomfortable silence settle.

"I have a man on the inside."

"So you said."

"Not just a man, but a man and *two* women."

"How perfectly Italian of you." The Englishman smiled at Salman's scowl. "So, partners?"

"*Si*, partners."

"Lovely. Make sure that man of yours doesn't let them get too far."

"Do not worry. I know where they are going."

"Then we're all settled?" The Englishman opened the passenger side door.

Salman grabbed his arm and pulled him back. "You remember, you have fancy guns and clothes, but you are in my country."

"What's left of your country, I think you mean."

"Don't misunderstand me, English. I have people, everywhere here. You cross *me*, I kill *you* in very unpleasant ways."

The Englishman shrugged off Salman's hand. "You can consider that understood, and that it cuts both ways." He paused before stepping out. "And how do I know it wasn't you that attacked Vivas? As you say, you have spies everywhere. How strange that I came across you, watching my city burn, and now you want to make a deal."

11

THE SOUND OF children playing tinkled over the noise of waves crashing into the sand. A man sitting in a fabric recliner dug his toes into the hot sand of the beach, his nose in a book, and reached for his drink on a small rattan table next to him. Taking a sip, he held his drink aloft and inspected it. Empty. Just half-melted ice cubes glistening inside the condensation-streaked glass.

"Honey, could you get me another one?"

"What was it?"

"Rum and coke, but dark rum. The Cuban one."

"I'll get the waiter," she replied, waving one arm in the air while coming up behind the man, her long blond hair pulled back in a bun under a wide-brimmed hat, dark sunglasses obscuring her eyes.

She was wearing her pink bikini today. It was the man's favorite, and he wrapped his arm around her tanned waist and kissed her hip. Her skin was salty. Sweaty. The sun burned fiercely overhead in a perfect blue sky. The woman tousled the man's hair playfully.

"Did you see this?" the man asked, putting his book down and picking up a folded newspaper from the rattan table. "Jovian meteor impacts in Northern Europe."

"Is it bad?"

He slapped the paper back onto the table. "Worse is coming."

"I thought the worst was over. It's been two weeks, hasn't it?"

"And just fifty weeks left," the man said with a smile.

"Sir? Ma'am?"

A white-aproned waiter hovered over the man's left shoulder.

"Another rum and coke, same as last time, with the dark Cuban," the woman instructed.

"Yes, ma'am." The waiter swiveled in the sand and took off for the bar.

"Why don't you make sure Cassandra and Krista are okay?" the man said. "They're playing with the Buchanan kids near the breakwater, looking for crabs."

The woman shielded her eyes from the sun. She scanned to their right, past the leafy canopy of palm trees to the wooden dock.

"I'll go check. Maybe take them for a walk through—"

"Don't go through the forest back to the condo. *He's* there." The man didn't need to explain who *he* was.

"Then we'll just go along the beach," the woman replied with a smile.

"And we're doing lunch with Susan and Phil, don't forget."

"I'll get the kids ready."

"Perfect."

The man craned his neck up to give the woman a kiss. Behind them, the waiter stopped at a respectful distance for them to finish before he deposited the drink next to the man.

"Thank you, Manuel," said the man, taking the drink.

The ice cubes chinked together as he angled the glass back and took a long sip, feeling the sweet burn of the alcohol hitting his lips. What a beautiful day. He picked up his book and settled into the recliner.

NOVEMBER 7th

Fourteen Days A.N.

12

THE MORNING BROUGHT with it a luminous haze, soundless and still. It enveloped the farmhouse. Visibility was less than a mile. They couldn't even see the hilltops next to them, but it was warmer, the temperature hovering near freezing.

Jess liked to sleep, relished the small moments where she could escape into it. Frightened, angry, excited were all things she experienced when she slept, but never sadness. Sadness was reserved for her waking world, and sadness was the thing she feared the most. She awoke stiff, but it was more from sleeping on the floor on a blanket, something she'd never get used to. When she opened her eyes, she found the smiling face of Elsa hovering over her, pulling on her blankets, asking her if she wanted tea.

Her fingers still ached, but the feeling and movement had returned. Her little finger on her left hand was still purple toward the tip, but that wasn't enough to suppress an excitement that filled their small group that morning. There was an almost festive atmosphere as they packed up to leave, early that morning, shoving what they could into the Range Rover before all nine squeezed in again.

She'd been stubborn, and had refused to change paths, but now Jess felt some measure of relief for the first time since they left *Castello Ruspoli*. At least this wasn't on her head, that they'd been forced this way, and maybe that was a good thing. The idea of trekking a hundred miles across sea ice seemed insane now. If you don't laugh at the hand fate gave you, her father used to say, it was because you weren't getting the joke. Today they'd reach Civitavecchia, Rome's main port, and Giovanni had secured a berth with promises of the gold bars. By this time tomorrow they might be sliding across the Mediterranean on their way to Africa.

The rolling landscape, covered in ice, glistened under a patchwork of pregnant clouds. As they neared the coast, the terrain shifted from the brittle-skeleton trees of the countryside to an urban chaos of flattened buildings and twisted power transmission towers that clogged the hillsides. Smudges of fire-smoke rose needle-like from the valleys, rising and dissipating into the sun-infused yellow glow between black clouds.

They passed people in the towns, but they cruised into the encampments with their rifles raised, meeting the hollow stares of the ragged survivors they passed. They never needed to say it: Don't try to stop us.

As they neared the coast, they saw fewer and fewer until there were no more.

"Just over the next hill," Giovanni said, studying the map spread out in his lap. "We should see water."

Leone was driving again, and he grunted at Giovanni's prediction and downshifted. If the old man wasn't feeling well, he was stoic about it. Next to Leone, though, Jess noticed Lucca's cheeks streaked pink, a thin sweat on his forehead.

The Range Rover slid through the two-foot mush of ash and snow covering the road. The engine was knocking again, the same problem they had two days ago. Just yesterday they'd replaced the spark plugs Massarra brought to them before she disappeared, and the engine was smooth. Today the knocking had returned, but in just a few hours they should reach some semblance of civilization, the evacuation center they'd been talking to over the radio. Elsa and Rita seemed more serious than usual, and even Roger wasn't being his usual sarcastic self. Perhaps the meteor shower the night before continued to weigh on their minds.

Jess noticed Raffa sitting close to Rita, the two of them speaking quietly in Italian. Raffa played with his hands as he spoke, glancing at her, his face slightly flushed. Rita would drop a hand onto his arm from time to time and smile at things he said. A tiny moment of humanity in all the darkness of the last few days, Jess thought. Seeing them together lifted her a little.

She turned to Roger. "So it's like the Perseids?"

As a child, every August her father would make the pilgrimage to the top of Slide Mountain in the Catskills to watch the peak of the Perseid meteor shower. "The Perseids are a cloud of debris from the comet Swift-Tuttle," he'd explain, the same every year as though she wouldn't remember. "The Earth's orbit sweeps through the cloud starting every July, finishing in August." It was her favorite memory; of warm, humid evenings, her father urging her up the trails, the air scented with pinesap and moss and baked rock from the hot sun of the day. Something she'd never experience again, she realized with a stab of regret.

"Sort of," Roger replied, sitting in front of Jess.

Beside Jess, Giovanni fiddled with the controls of the shortwave. He had it plugged into the cigarette lighter of the truck. Hector was squeezed between them, and Giovanni had given him a small radio of his own to play with, an old FM they'd found batteries for.

"But what meteor shower was that last night?" she asked.

"My calculations say they were the Jupiter Trojans. They've never come near Earth before. Or, I guess I should say, we've never gone anywhere near them. Everything's changed now." He held up his laptop and pointed at a collection of dots in front of, and behind, Jupiter's orbit. "See these groups here? They're called the Trojan asteroids."

He put his laptop back down. "They're a collection of leftover debris that were scooped into stable orbits by Jupiter's gravity, sixty degrees in front and behind it, in its Lagrangian points. Problem is, Nomad punched straight through L4, the Trojan grouping. And you see this?" He held up the laptop again. "Gravitational slingshot straight into Earth's orbit."

"Already? I mean, that's way out at Jupiter."

"Jupiter ain't where it used to be, and neither are these. We're fourteen days since Nomad, and Mercury's already shot out past Mars. Gravitational slingshot. Same mechanism that's firing these Trojan asteroids at Earth like a Gatling gun." Roger fidgeted with his thumb, chewing on the nail. "Everyone's heard of the Asteroid Belt, but the truth is, there are twice as many asteroids in the Jupiter clusters."

"How big are these things?" Jess asked. The Perseids were sometimes spectacular, but it was just a light show.

"Maybe a million over a kilometer in diameter."

Giovanni played with the shortwave's dials, but was listening to their conversation. "That doesn't sound too bad."

"Not bad?" Roger didn't even bother to resort to sarcasm. "A kilometer-sized asteroid killed off the dinosaurs. One. The planets have been in more-or-less stable orbits for billions of years, and these Trojan asteroids collected like dust in the corner of a room. A million planet-killers are on the loose. Nomad blew a gust of air through the solar system, and now the dust is everywhere."

"Won't we be able to predict what will hit us? Maybe with this?" Jess patted her backpack in her lap.

"In the sim tool, a thousand of the biggest Trojans are mapped, along with clusters of others. We should be seeing another cluster the night after tomorrow."

"Should we find somewhere to hide?"

"That cluster should hit on the other side of the planet, so I wouldn't worry too much about it, but there will be another two or three days after that. Give me the disks, let me work on decoding them, I might be able to tell more."

"When we get on the ship, we'll do it together, okay?"

"Sure, but——"

"Hey, Jess, listen!" Giovanni nudged her shoulder. He turned up the volume on the shortwave.

"*Station Saline, do you read...*" crackled a voice over the radio. "This is Captain Ballie Booker of the RNLB Jolly Roger."

The Jolly Roger, a British coast guard ship, was one of the first survivors they contacted on the shortwave after Nomad hit. Giovanni grinned at Jess and pressed the radio's *talk* button. "Reading you five by five, Jolly Roger. This is Station Saline. Ballie, it is good to hear your voice, my friend. Over."

"Ah, mate, not as good as hearing yours. I have news. Over."

"What news? Over."

"Those survivors you contacted?" said Ballie Booker's voice over the radio. "The ones on Sugarloaf Mountain, in Florida? A boat picked them up last night, mate!"

The knuckles on Giovanni's hands, gripping the shortwave microphone, went white. The hair on the back of Jess's own arms prickled in excitement. Giovanni's grin spread almost from ear to ear as he looked at Hector, then at Jess. In all of this mess, a small victory.

"You saved them, mate," added Ballie. "And they told me to tell you, *thank you.*"

"That's good news," Giovanni said into the microphone, his voice choked.

Jess took his hand in hers and squeezed the *talk* button. "What's your position, Jolly Roger? Over."

"Ah..." The radio crackled. "...France, we managed to get into La Roche yesterday. Or what we think was La Roche. Tricky business getting in past the ice. Total mess, like everywhere else. Scavenged a little more food, found some diesel. We'll not be stopping again till we steam around Gibraltar. The devastation is bad, mate. Everywhere. And you? Are you on the move? Over."

"We are near Rome. We are heading for evacuation ships at Civitavecchia. Over."

The radio hissed. Jess was about to repeat herself and confirm they were still in touch when the response came: "Say again. Did you say Civitavecchia? Over."

"Affirmative, Jolly Roger. Over." Jess was rusty with her radio voice procedure. She did the basics in the Marines, but never used it much. Giovanni had been teaching it back to her.

More radio silence.

"Mate, that's news to us," came Ballie's voice after another long pause. "On what frequency?"

"Seven-four-four-zero," Giovanni said, pulling his sheaf of papers from a bag by his feet, his survivor logs. He leafed through them, finding the scribbled notes of their contact with the Civitavecchia port authority.

"That's not a maritime frequency. Who were you talking to? Over."

"Port authority of Civitavecchia. Over."

"Noted, Station Saline. I'll pass that information along to the other groups."

Where Giovanni's shortwave was a small portable device, with 200 Watts of transmission power, the Jolly Roger had a maritime emergency transmitter of 5,000 Watts with a hundred-foot-high whip antenna. They were able to keep in touch with more of the survivor groups, on a more frequent basis.

Jess took the microphone from Giovanni. "Jolly Roger, I have a question."

"Go ahead."

"Have you ever heard of something called Vivas?"

"Say again?"

99

"Vivas. Some kind of bunker system for the super wealthy."

The radio hissed quietly. "Funny you should say that, because last night the skip was really in, yeah?"

The "skip" in radio talk meant that atmospheric conditions were good, that radio waves bounced off the ionosphere and ground making it possible to talk over very long distances, all the way around the world.

"We talked to your friend Corporal Zaskin of the Russian border patrol, out in the Gobi desert. He told me they'd found a bunker out there in the middle of nowhere. Private airport full of Gulfstream jets, just sitting on the runway. Totally locked down. Bunch of rich bastards, right? Over."

Jess locked eyes with Giovanni. She pushed the talk button. "Do us a favor, Ballie? Don't report our location to anyone."

"Say again, Station Saline?"

"Do not report our location to anyone. We had a run in with a Vivas group yesterday. It was destroyed."

"Destroyed?"

"Someone attacked it. We don't know who."

"Roger. Will not report your location to anyone else. Anything we can do? Over."

"Not for now. We'll be in touch. Station Saline out."

Jess turned off the radio. "What the hell is going on?" she said quietly to Giovanni.

He said nothing, his face blank.

"And something else," she whispered. "How much morphine did you give me?"

"Two ampules. Why?"

"Did you take any more? For the wound in your side? Because I did an inventory this morning, and half of it is gone from the med kits. And I noticed the Vicodin tablets were missing when I did inventory two days before that."

Giovanni shrugged. "In the rush to get away from Vivas, perhaps it was lost."

"Maybe." Jess held Giovanni's gaze, then glanced around the truck, at Elsa, Rita, but stopping at Roger.

The truck crested a ridge, and through the luminous mist, a line of blue appeared.

"Capo," said Leone, his gruff and usually monotone voice now filled with excitement, *"il mare."* He pointed through the windshield. He pointed at the ocean.

Jess noticed everyone sat upright to get a better look, but Roger slumped lower in his seat, pulling the laptop screen closer.

Giovanni pulled out his map again and inspected it. He traced one finger along the road they were on and then tapped one spot on the map. Looking up, he squinted, leaning forward to get a better look through the window. "The main ports are to the right of the city."

On the plain below, all that remained of the port city of Civitavecchia, that once existed here just three weeks before, was fractured remains of razed buildings, all smoothed over by a coating of ash and ice. The luminous sky they'd been enjoying all day turned dark, a shadow moving quickly through the skies. The blue of the Mediterranean was dotted with flecks of white.

Following Giovanni's arm, Jess took a closer look. Near the edge of blue was a massive cruise ship, twenty stories high. But it wasn't in the water. It was halfway into the city, one end perched atop a crumbled building. It was coated in ice that glimmered even in the dim light.

"That can't be it," Jess whispered.

They topped the ridge, coming to a plateau that edged the city. Leone drove past an airstrip and semicircular airdrome buildings. An orange windsock snapped to attention in a sudden breeze, whipping up the snow.

Her eyes adjusting to the scene below, Jess scanned the edge of the city. The dark blue water came almost to the edge, but an unbroken white strip of varying thickness ringed the edges. Ice. Sea ice was already forming.

"Where are the ships?"

Apart from the cruise liner tipped half on its side in the middle of the destroyed city, she couldn't see any other ships. She couldn't even see any break in the ice at the edge of the water.

13

SEAGULLS SQUAWKED AND wheeled in circles high above. They skimmed the scraped hull of the Ocean Princess cruise liner. Pregnant clouds scudded by, their distended bellies almost touching the ship's superstructure of masts and funnels towering more than twenty stories up.

Jess craned her neck back to get a better look. Some of the birds alighted on the ship's railing, staring back at her. Others swooped down, fluttering overhead, fighting for position to get closest to this group of humans. They were hoping for a meal. So was she. They didn't have much food left.

"It looks deserted," Jess said.

To break a trail and negotiate the mile and a half from the ridge down through the city to the ship took two hours. Civitavecchia, though, was no longer a city. It had become a debris field, a collection of matchstick telephone poles, twisted metal, slabs of shattered concrete and husks of cars piled in clumps and waves. The ship itself looked almost undamaged, apart from gouges and dents across the lower hull. It listed at almost thirty degrees, one side propped up on brick rubble two stories high. Roger had scampered up the wreckage to get a better look, while Leone and Raffa scouted around the other side. Lucca sat in the front seat. He still wasn't feeling well.

"Was this our ship?" Giovanni asked, his mouth agape, staring up.

"Look at the ice." Jess pointed at the edge of the debris pile under the hull. It was covered in a thick layer of ice-and-ash-snow. "I'd bet this washed up when Nomad hit two weeks ago."

Roger came scrabbling and skidding down the rubble toward them. "Maybe we just push it back in the water? Use the winch on the Range Rover?"

Giovanni ignored the attempt at humor. "It might have washed up yesterday." The ground was wet, streams of water running through the debris toward the bay. "Maybe one of those meteors hit the water, brought up a wave? You heard the explosions."

Jess took another look at the ash-snow covering the upper decks. Last night there *was* an intense storm squall after the meteor shower.

"Maybe. But it looks abandoned. Don't you think there'd be someone around? What did they say?" She pointed at a family, a man and woman with two young children, cowering next to the Range Rover. Rita was making them something to eat from the meager supplies they had left. Leone had objected, but Jess had insisted. A gesture of kindness, but they also needed information.

"They came down from the hills when they saw us," Giovanni replied. "They say that nobody comes near the water. Too afraid after what happened, but they came when they saw us. They're desperate."

"And there's more like them coming," Roger scoffed. "We don't even have food for ourselves. I'm telling you, as bad as all this seems, this is just the tip of the goddamn iceberg. A lot of people survived, and now they've run out of food. What are they going to eat? I'll tell you what—"

Jess held a back-up-you're-not-helping hand at Roger. "But did they see anything here?" she asked Giovanni. "Any people, trucks, equipment?"

"No…but—"

"Doesn't sound like much of an evacuation center," Roger quipped. "Not even any people to evacuate."

"He's right," Jess muttered. "If there was a wave yesterday, that sea ice at the edge of the water would be fractured, wouldn't it? And it doesn't look like any ships came in close to here and broke through it. Not lately."

"Which means what, exactly?" Roger's eyebrows raised in mock debate. "That the person we talked to on the radio was lying? Giovanni was the one talking to them, in Italian. What did they say? Why can't we get them back on the radio?"

They hadn't been able to contact the evacuation group since morning.

"Maybe the ship hasn't arrived yet," Giovanni suggested. His eyes narrowed. "And it was you, *Roger*, who first contacted them."

The accused held his hands up. "You talked more to them than me."

"Are we in the right place?"

"They said the port near Civitavecchia."

"Near?"

"I assumed—"

"Are there any other ports?"

"This is the coast, there are ports in every city."

"This is a trap," Roger said, his voice flat. "How do you even know who you're talking to on that thing?" He waved a hand at the shortwave sitting on the truck's tailgate. "This Jolly Roger guy, Ballie Booker, how do you even know he's real?"

"Stop being paranoid."

"Are you kidding me? *Someone* is hunting for you. You said it yourself. That's not paranoia." Roger's face was slick with sweat, his eyes glassy. "Someone with the ability to destroy a goddamn fortress is trying to get to you. In this Godforsaken mess, the powers-that-be, whoever they are, are hunting you down…and it's got to be on account of that bag." He reached for Jess's backpack.

Giovanni pushed his way between them. "What are you saying, Roger?"

"That backpack is cursed. Almost killed me a couple of times already. Let's ditch it."

Jess swiveled herself away, keeping the backpack out of reach. "My father *died* for this."

"And that's something *I*"—Roger thumped his chest—"don't want to do."

"You would be dead if we hadn't rescued you." Giovanni shoved Roger away.

"You want a piece of me, Italian?" Roger threw his weight into Giovanni, tried to push him, but Giovanni didn't budge an inch.

"*Bastardo maledetto*, you want to fight? You little junky piece of shit. You don't think we've noticed?"

Roger's face flushed scarlet. "It's for the pain. You know how much this hurts?" He held his left shoulder with his right hand and turned to face Jess. "You shot me with a goddamn crossbow." He glared at them, but turned and stalked away through the sludge of snow of ice. "Screw all of you. You're going to get what you deserve."

Giovanni watched him go. "Should we contact the Jolly Roger

again? Maybe he can get us?"

"Talking on the shortwave might be dangerous," Jess replied. "Anyone could be listening." The sudden turn of events, from expecting rescue to feeling trapped, had her off balance.

"They'd need to be tuned into that exact frequency at just the right time—"

"And we talk to Ballie more than anyone else, on most of the same frequency—"

"But still, it would be luck—"

"They don't *need* luck," Jess said, her voice rising. "Most of the world has been pushed back into the Stone Age, and some of us have a few scraps like these shortwaves working…but what I saw in Vivas? That's fully equipped modern technology. Data centers. Communications gear. They had goddamn pictures of me in Rome. Where did they get those?" Her voice reached a keening edge.

"Jessica, please keep calm—"

"I can't believe we came this way. We should have kept going south." She balled her hands.

"We had no choice."

A noise startled Jess. But it wasn't an explosion. It wasn't gunfire.

It was children laughing.

Hector kicked a ball of knotted cloth to the little boy of the family they'd just met. They were about the same age, and had the same twinkle of glee in their eyes as they chased each other. A little girl squealed and chased them around the other side of the Range Rover. Their father met Jess's look with a sad smile, and he held the small bowl of rice and chickpeas aloft in a gesture of thanks.

The ball appeared from the front of the Range Rover, Hector and the boy in pursuit. Jess watched them, wondering what memories they'd keep of this time. Would they grow to be old men? Regale their wide-eyed grandchildren of stories of the Great Disaster while sitting in leafy sunrooms?

She wondered what memories children of the Holocaust retained. The generation that survived that became great citizens of the world, witnesses of horror but also of the glory of the human spirit. She wanted Hector to be that old, wise man she pictured in her mind. She just had to keep him alive.

Giovanni took her hand. "I know."

"What do we do?" she whispered. "Maybe drive back?"

"To the castle? Certain death. We need to continue south to the warmth."

"Then it's back to the main highway?"

"The Rover's engine is overheating. We'd need to pass Vivas, or what's left of it. Even so…"

"What about coastal roads?" she asked.

"Very difficult. Mountains. Small roads. Maybe impassable in places."

"But there's a chance, a slim one, that this evacuation center is in the next town."

"We need to take care of ourselves, first. You're soaking wet." A fine mist had begun to fall. "Inside and out. Sweat. Jessica, the cold is dangerous, but wet and cold together is deadly. We need to wash. It's more than a week we've been on the road. Rashes can be dangerous, debilitating. When we fight, you're the leader, but listen to me about cold, about survival."

He was right. In their headlong dash for the south, she'd thought of it as a sprint, but it had become a marathon. A long, slow grind. "Okay, let's set camp and get everyone washed. We can use the climbing gear to get into the ship, see what we can scavenge."

"And I have an idea."

Jess pulled open her parka and caught her own smell. She reeked. "Go on."

"On the plateau before the city," Giovanni continued, "we passed an airfield."

"Yeah, I saw," Jess said. A row of planes with wings flattened under ice.

"Some of the airdromes looked intact. There might be something in them."

"Are you serious? Can you fly a plane?"

"I did my private pilot training—"

"And did you get a license?"

"I don't think anyone will be checking." He smiled thinly. "I never got my license. I only flew with my trainer. But Roger, he's a qualified pilot, yes?"

Jess closed her eyes and exhaled long and slow. "He had a few hundred hours when I dated him. Yeah."

"You're the one that said you needed him. Go talk to him."

Jess held a hand up at the dark clouds churning just hundreds of feet overhead and imagined trying to fly through them.

"It's a low ceiling, but we've heard of propeller aircraft flying at other survivor camps," Giovanni added.

"I don't know…"

"Someone is looking for you. This Ufuk Erdogmus. He must want your father's data. Do you want to let him take it? Or do you want to find out what's on it yourself? We need to get away from here. Fast."

"If we get a plane up, how can we find a place to land?"

"One step at a time. It is an idea."

"We'll go look in the morning," Jess conceded after a long pause. "Right now we need to make camp."

"Let me help with that." Jess stepped through the snow to help Leone, who staggered in from the darkness with what looked like a dining table balanced on his broad shoulders.

The old man grunted and lowered the table so they could carry it the last twenty feet together, to stack on the pile of other collected scraps next to the crackling fire. A pot of water was perched above the flames, set on an improvised chimney of bricks built to reflect the fire's heat. Two tents had been erected to each side of the fire, with the Range Rover forming a barrier between them. Inside the truck, Giovanni was helping Hector get cleaned up, using the hot water they prepared. Tonight was washing night. It was also his turn to read the nighttime story. Everyone else was out foraging for anything flammable but non-toxic to burn.

Leone paused for a moment, then turned to go back out and search again through the wilderness of destruction, but Jess gently held his arm. "Sit with me?" She motioned at two camp chairs unfolded next to the fire. "I need a rest. Just for a second?"

She was tired, that was true, but she was more worried about Leone. His breath wheezed in and out, his face slick with sweat, but the old workhorse never let up. She guessed he was in his mid-seventies, but he worked harder and longer than anyone else. He seemed more wild bear than human, sometimes, but he was a gentle giant. And she'd never seen him sleeping, not once this past two weeks. He always literally had one eye open, always watching over them.

The old bear grunted again, looked into the darkness, then back at Jess. "Okay."

"Tea?" Jess offered as he sat. She took his scowling nod as a *yes* and filled a cup from a kettle she just filled. "So, no pipe today?" She'd noticed his signature item, usually clamped between his teeth, was absent.

He took the proffered cup. "Pipe, yes. Tobacco, no. Left in other truck." An awkward smile of broken teeth. "Stupid. No think."

"Ah, but we had to leave in a hurry." That had to be frustrating. Jess imagined that if she smoked, right now would be about the worst time to try and quit. Or be forced into it. "Maybe we find some."

"Maybe." The old man took a sip of tea and stared into the fire.

The hulk of the abandoned ocean liner loomed above them, the firelight casting dancing shadows onto its hull. In the dim light of day, it seemed a perfect place to camp, almost like a cave, but with night Jess felt an irrational fear that it would tip over onto them. She pushed the thought away.

"I wanted to thank you. For saving my life, back at the castle," Jess said, breaking the silence. It was the first time she'd been alone with Leone. "I know you were looking for Hector when you found us on that ledge, but you rescued me too."

The fire crackled and popped.

"I was also looking for you," Leone said after a pause, glancing at her.

"And I wanted to thank you for doing your best"—Jess took a breath—"to try and find my mother and father." Such a simple thing, to thank someone, but the effect of saying the words seemed to radiate warmth into the cold air around them. "Do you have any family, Leone? Daughters? Sons?" She'd never asked before.

The old man stared into the fire. "A son, yes. My wife, she died many years ago."

"And where is your son?"

"Also dead." He stared straight ahead.

"I'm so sorry—"

"No sorry. Very proud. My son was Italian army, went to Lebanon in eighty-three. Was in bombing at Beirut barracks."

"He died there?"

"Was injured. Came back to Italy. The Baron, Giovanni's father, took care of him."

"And what happened?"

"How do you say…long story? But the Baron did everything to help." The wry smile faded from Leone's face. "And I failed him." He returned to staring into the fire.

"Who?"

A heavy pause. "Giovanni's father. Nico killed him. I failed the Baron."

Jess hadn't thought of it like that. Giovanni's father had died more than a year ago from a protracted illness, but it turned out it had been Nico, poisoning the elder baron. Another fresh wound in this damaged world.

"I will not fail again," the old man added. He swigged down the remainder of his tea and handed the cup back. "I *do* have a family, and it is Giovanni, my Baron's son, and Hector."

From the darkness, two more shadows shuffled into the light. It was Lucca and Raffa, dragging a huge tree branch behind them. Seeing Leone, they dropped it, their faces lighting up. The old man got up from the chair and advanced on the boys, throwing an arm around each.

"And these two, these are my family," Leone rumbled, his face breaking into a craggy grin. "So, yes, I have family."

Jess settled back into her chair, squeezing the hot mug of tea in her hands, and watched the horseplay as the teenagers tried to squirm out of the big bear's embrace. Their smiles were infectious and she found herself laughing. Ripples of laughter echoed off the ship's hull, for a moment drowning out the silence around them.

NOVEMBER 8th

Fifteen Days A.N.

14

"LOOKS AIRWORTHY TO me." Giovanni patted the underside of the Cessna, sliding his hand along the wing as he walked the length of it.

The metal exterior was dented, shiny new rivets clear evidence where a new strip of metal had been placed over another. Jess gave him a stern look. She hadn't slept the night before, camped out at the base of the cruise liner through the night, but she remained alert. And skeptical. "This thing looks as though its best days were before I was born."

They stood shoulder to shoulder under the flapping white-plastic dome tent. Aluminum girders stretched in arcs above their heads, the rolling garage door open just enough to walk through crouched over. Two of the other domed plastic buildings along the airstrip were also intact, but empty of aircraft, while at the edges of the field a collection of single and two-engine planes laid scattered, all with some crippling damage, and all covered in layers of ash and ice. But the Cessna under this domed structure looked pristine, or at least, not destroyed by Nomad.

"These things are workhorses. Probably thirty years old, but I can't see any damage."

Raffa spoke quickly to Giovanni, nodding and gesticulating, and opened the pilot-side door. He climbed inside and dipped beneath the instrument panel, unscrewing part of the cowling.

"What's he doing?" Jess asked.

Giovanni paused, then said, "He thinks he might be able to, how do you say, *hotwire* it?"

"In here?"

"We'll pull it outside. Starting it is the only way we can find out if the engine works."

"If Raffa can get it going."

"Help me push." Giovanni knelt to grab the door handle and pushed the door to the hangar fully up. Raffa jumped out and pulled the orange chocks free from the wheels.

The Mediterranean was not visible from this ridge overlooking

Civitavecchia, yet she felt the sea looming next to them. She half-expected it to swell again, drown them in freezing water. In the morning she was happy to break camp and get away from the shore. She understood what the ragtag groups, that came to them begging food, meant when they said they feared the water.

She feared it now, too.

The airstrip was on a plateau a thousand feet up in altitude and a mile back from the sea. After discovering the intact Cessna this morning, they decided to make camp in the hangar next to it. Leone took charge and organized a second camp for the people that appeared from the mist. They were as thirsty as they were hungry, and Rita seemed keen to help.

Or keen to have Raffa see her helping them, Jess thought gently.

She was about to join the men in pushing the plane out of the hangar when Roger came swaggering around the corner, smiling. He was clear-eyed this morning.

"No need, my friends." He held his arms up. Keys jangled in one hand. "I broke into the offices at the end of the runway and busted open the lock box." He inspected the nametag on the keys. "And this is a 1981 Cessna 182RG, if I'm not mistaken?"

"I have absolutely no idea." Jess frowned at Giovanni—as though to ask who's-this-guy?—before realizing: "Holy Christ, it's more than a decade older than me."

"Lucky thing, too," Roger pointed out. "The 182RG has a range of a thousand miles with a hundred and seventy knot cruise speed. That's about two hundred miles an hour of wind speed. I found the manual with the keys. I think I'll take her for a spin."

"In the air?"

"Why not?"

"For one; the runway is full of snow," said Giovanni.

"I just walked it going to the buildings. It's covered in ice, but most of the snow has blown off. Maybe an inch or two of hard pack still clinging. I kicked aside all the big debris." He pointed at the Cessna. "And it's got oversize tires for rough field takeoff and landing. Cold like this, I only need to get up to 55 knots. I'll float her up and around and do a bump and run."

"You seriously want to *fly* this thing?"

"Another hour and we won't be able to." The clouds were thickening, fat snowflakes starting to fall. "No other way to really know if she's airworthy. And you want to get out of here, right?"

"I'm going to come with you," Jess said.

"That is not a good idea." Giovanni held his hands out, miming a wall. "No way."

"Because it's not yours?" Roger said.

"Because it's too dangerous."

Roger took a deep breath. "I'm sorry, okay? Let me make it up. I'm good at this. Trust me."

"Trust *you*?"

A squall of wind brought swirling snow-devils of flakes into the hangar. "We ain't gonna be flying tomorrow, maybe not the next day, either. You know a bit about this, Giovanni, right? About flying?"

He waited for a nod before continuing, "If this thing flies, then we spend the snow days doing flight plans. And anyway, it's my neck." He held up one hand, jerking his head sideways as if it was caught in an invisible noose, his tongue dangling loose from his mouth.

"The sooner we have a plan the better," Jess said. "If you think you can, go ahead."

"This is reckless." Giovanni turned, shaking his head, but he motioned for Roger to get into the plane. "But you take it up by yourself first. Jess, you don't go on the first run."

"All right then."

Stepping onto the wing strut, Roger swung himself up into the Cessna's cockpit. "Even a full tank of gas," he observed as he scanned the gauges. He put the key into the ignition. "Everyone, stand back. Okay, magnetos and solenoids on…"

The plane's engine wheezed, then emitted a high-pitched whine. The propeller began to spin, a loud *tock-tock-tock* knocking from the engine, and then a growl, the propeller whirring into a blur before the knock-knocking again and the propeller froze in place.

"…okay, let's try that…"

Tock-tock-tock knocked the engine and the propeller spun around in jerky circles again before the engine growled to life, this time the roar deepening and soaring in pitch. Roger gave a thumbs-

115

up and closed the airplane's door, pausing to strap himself in before gunning the engine again. A cloud of dust, snow and debris rushed into the back of the hangar from the prop wash, sending Jess and Raffa and Giovanni coughing to escape ahead of the aircraft.

The Cessna followed behind them, the engine almost deafening at this close range. Jess clapped her hands over her ears. Grinning at them, his thumb up again, Roger angled the rear rudder and turned the plane onto the runway. Everyone emptied from the hangar-camp a hundred yards away, with Elsa and Rita holding back Hector, who tried to run to Jess.

The engine whined to a higher pitch and the Cessna began to bump along the runway, gaining speed. It bounced and lurched from side to side, hitting chunks of ice and lumps of snow. More than once, Jess thought a wing tip was going to hit the ground, but Roger kept it centered, and with two bounces it jumped up into the air, twin tornadoes of snowflakes rippling off its wingtips. The Cessna's nose jerked upward, then straightened out. The air grew still, the noise subsiding into the whistle of the wind brushing snow across the ice, the Cessna disappearing into the gray-white fog of snow.

Jess became aware of her breathing, that her labored breaths were sending puffs of white vapor into the air. Her heart pounded. She could hardly believe Roger managed to get into the air, it seemed impossible.

"You think he's coming back?" Giovanni said quietly.

"Where else would he go?"

No noise now, just the flapping of the torn hangar fabric. Then a faint whine, like a wasp's, to their left.

"There!" Jess pointed toward the sea.

Through the twisting clouds of snow, the Cessna appeared and disappeared, the buzz of its engine growing louder again. They all turned, as if attached by an invisible string to the airplane in the sky, mesmerized. The small plane swung around in the distance, gaining altitude, then lined up with the runway, it's engine coming down in pitch, the wings swinging from side to side in the cross wind. It roared past them and bumped once, twice, three times off the icy runway before it settled into a rumbling roll.

The Cessna turned on the runway and made its way back

toward them.

Roger leaned out the window, thumb up, a wide grin on his face. "Jess, you want that flying lesson now?"

"What's your man up to, I wonder?" the blond-haired Englishman said, passing the binoculars back to Salman.

"Gaining their trust," the old Italian replied.

He took the binoculars and focused on Roger and Jess getting out of the Cessna. They gave each other a high-five. The snowfall was thickening and had allowed them just enough time to make another flight.

From this perch in the second floor of a building, what was once a bakery, across the road from the airfield, he was having trouble seeing through the two hundred yards of distance to watch Giovanni and Raffa push the airplane back into the hangar.

"I thought your man was supposed to keep them down at the water?"

"He was to keep them in this town."

"Not what you told me yesterday. And now, they have the capacity to fly away." The Englishman fluttered his fingers in the air. "Do you think someone else in that ragtag assemblage can fly an airplane? Why did your man take it up?"

Salman put the binoculars down. He took one hand out of a glove to test the cracked skin over his cleft lip. "I told you—"

"That does look uncomfortable, old chap—"

"I grow tired of you."

"As I do of you." The Englishman dusted off the lapels of his woolen overcoat. "And I'm equally tired of this cat and mouse."

"They go nowhere in this snow. They are trapped—"

"Unless they decide to fly away."

"Nobody is flying away."

"They better not be, on that we can agree."

"Why don't you make your contacts again? They have flying machines, yes?"

"You're not so sure, are you? Which is why you have me as a partner. I can make copies of whatever Ms. Rollins has in that bag.

Create backups. Safety, my friend, is why you need me."

"As soon as the snow stops, we do this my way," Salman said, his voice low and menacing. "We go, and we take them."

"Not your way. Too blunt. No, no, no. You don't put a frog into boiling water. You heat it up slowly. It struggles less, unaware of the creeping danger."

"So what is your way?"

"Divide and conquer, old boy." The Englishman smiled a greasy grin. "But the frog still boils."

15

A THUNDERCLAP SPLIT the heavens, a tearing, cracking sound followed by a roaring boom. The hairs on Jess's arm prickled as the interior of the hangar strobed white in staccato bursts, electricity rippling through the air in the Range Rover. The rumble echoed outside, fading, the slap and tremor of the wind tearing at the torn flaps of the hangar's stretched fabric. She held Hector in her lap, and he gripped her tight, his breathing ragged.

"It's okay," she cooed, kissing his forehead. "It's just the thundersnow. We're safe. Try to sleep."

She adjusted the nest of blankets in the back seat to cover him. They'd parked inside the second hangar, a hundred feet from the one with the Cessna in it, in an attempt to escape the maelstrom raging outside. The new snow was already two-feet deep, the last time Jess checked, with snowdrifts as high as she was next to the hangar's door. That was an hour ago.

"What if we fly straight to Palermo?" Giovanni stabbed one finger at the map of Italy spread haphazard across the driver seat and steering wheel.

He leaned over the seat to get a better look. A dim red light seeped from a headlamp attached to the Range Rover's sun visor. The red light setting conserved battery power, but it was hard on the eyes, and made distinguishing colors almost impossible.

"That's five hundred kilometers over open water. No way." Roger had a pad and stack of books in his lap, a pen in his hand. Notes and calculations were scribbled across the paper. The map was in kilometers, the airplane specs in knots and nautical miles.

"You said the 182RG has a range of 1500 kilometers."

"1550 kilometers with 93 gallons of grade-three jet fuel, at a cruise speed of one-seven-three knots." Roger tapped the manual.

"So that's what, two hours in the air?"

"You ever done any cross country flights? We can't do IFR. For one thing, there are no airport transponders working. Or at least, I'd doubt it. This is going to be all visual, and water doesn't have a lot of fixed visual reference points."

"What about these islands?"

"You want to try and find islands by dead reckoning? We need to fly city by city, one reference point at a time." Roger held out two fingers and rotated them in the air.

"But we might not even be able to recognize cities," Giovanni pointed out.

"Big piles of rubble miles across sitting on the coasts, covered in snow. Easy to see from the air."

"But going that way adds hundreds of kilometers of distance."

Thunder cracked and boomed outside again, the flashes of lightening revealing the tents huddled outside the truck.

Roger snorted and leaned back in the passenger side seat. "Do you know why you don't fly over water in a single engine plane?"

"In case the single engine fails. I'm no idiot."

"When you fly over water, you always keep enough altitude to be able to glide back to land if the engine fails. From fifteen thousand feet, with the glide ratio of this Cessna, that'll give you…nine nautical miles. Ten statute miles, sixteen kilometers."

"But if we have to land anywhere"—Giovanni swept his finger along the western edge of Italy's coastline—"we're dead. If that engine fails, we're not getting airborne again."

"Maybe. Maybe not. But do you want to be *dead* dead? Because that's what will happen out here." He pointed at the water on the map. "Along the coast, I guarantee I can land that thing, and then we'll just be back to this." He did his best to smile ironically.

"We fly over land," Jess whispered, trying to add something to the conversation. This wasn't her field of expertise, one of the reasons she insisted on Roger taking her up for a flight, even if it scared the hell out of her. "We minimize risk."

"Except we can't avoid this last stretch." Roger pointed his pen at the tip of Sicily, then moved it across the map to a town called Keliba on the coast of Tunisia. "That's a hundred miles of open water."

"Eighty."

"No, it's a hundred." Roger waved his pen back and forth from one point to the other.

"You just said we could glide almost ten miles from full altitude. So ten miles out, we can glide back…and ten miles from the coast on the other side, we could glide and make it. So only eighty miles in between that's a water landing."

Roger wagged his head from side to side and conceded the point. "You catch on quick."

"And soon that open water may be solid," Giovanni said. "Sea ice is forming fast."

"But we can make it?" Jess kept her voice low. Hector squirmed in her lap. Outside, the wind gained urgency, slapping the loose flaps of hangar tarp in rattling bursts like machine gun fire.

Roger leaned forward, his face coming from the shadows into the dim red glow. "Good news is that it's cold."

"And that's good?"

"For a small airplane like the Cessna. The air is denser, gives more lift, more to dig into. Lowers the stall speed, and makes it easier to take off and land in short distances. Usually less turbulence too, although in this case"—he paused and listened to the thrum of the wind across the hangar's metal frame—"I'm not sure if that's true. And there's less chance of the carburetor freezing. Cruise speed of one-seven-three knots is three hundred twenty kilometers an hour. That's fast for a single-engine. So that's all good news."

Giovanni picked up the map. He angled the plastic ruler they'd found in the Cessna's glove box onto the map surface. "Two hundred kilometers to Naples, two hundred more to Paola, then three hundred to Palermo. From there it's three hundred more—"

"—mostly across open water—"

"—to Tunisia." Giovanni frowned at Roger. "That's a thousand kilometers. Three hours at three hundred kilometers an hour."

"If all goes according to plan."

"So what's the bad news?" Jess asked.

"Sure, airspeed is two hundred miles an hour, but we'll be fighting that." He pointed up. The wind howled.

"It's coming mostly from the north, isn't it?"

"Maybe. Maybe not. Wind tends to shift direction from surface winds to winds at altitude. Sometimes ninety degrees. And those thick clouds that're blocking out all our sun? Maybe two thousand foot ceiling, at best. More like a thousand most of the time. Not enough to climb over these coastal ranges."

"So then you climb into the clouds for a bit."

"You know what's in those?"

Jess shook her head. "What?"

"I don't know either, but I bet it's full of ash."

"I thought you said that just stopped jets from working in it."

"It'll drop a jet, for sure, but I bet it'll cause havoc with the pistons and injectors if we fly this thing through it long enough. And no VFR if we climb into—"

"VFR?"

"Visual flight reference," Giovanni said.

Roger nodded, smiling. "Very good. Means we're eyeballing it the whole way with very little in the way of instruments to help."

"What about the compass?"

"You had a look at one lately? Not sure south is south anymore. I've been watching mine, looking at this map today. I think Nomad messed with the Earth's magnetic field. It switches from time to time, you know. North to south and south to north every few tens of millions of years. I think another gift from Nomad is a pole reversal. And it's not like we'll be getting any weather reports. We hit bad weather, we gotta put her down."

"So we can't do this? Is that what you're saying?" Jess couldn't help her voice rising. Give her a mountain to climb, she could get up it, one step at a time, and then even jump off it. But airplanes were never her thing.

"We can do it. Like Giovanni said, three hours of flying and we're out of here to somewhere warm. Or, warmer at least. I'm just highlighting the danger."

"Maybe we can we use the parachutes?"

"Excuse me?"

"The parachutes we packed. They're still in the roof rack. I'd just feel a lot safer flying if I had a parachute on."

A rap on the window startled Jess, and she sat upright. Hector mewled in her lap. Raffa's face loomed outside the window, his own headlamp switched into red mode, the light glinting dully off the window.

"*Si?*" Giovanni asked through the glass. He'd have to turn on the Range Rover's windows to roll them down.

"Lucca?" Raffa pointed to the back of the truck. His face was tight with concern.

"*Tutto bene*," came a weak voice from inside the truck. Lucca lifted his head and attempted a smile, but all he managed was a weak grimace.

The poor kid had been throwing up all day. Jess had given him another dose of Ciproflaxin antibiotics, but it didn't seem to do anything. Jess hoped whatever he had wasn't infectious, but she'd insisted that they make space for him to sleep in the back of the Range Rover. It was warmer, quieter, and she was sure it felt safer than sleeping outside in one of the nylon tents.

"I can do it," Roger repeated, now looking straight at Jess. "I can get you to Tunisia. But my arm"—he held his left shoulder, where Jess had accidentally shot him with the crossbow bolt at *Castello Ruspoli*—"it hurts. Please. Just a little."

"No."

"Some Vicodin. Something."

"Give him nothing." Giovanni swiped one hand in the air. "Nothing, you understand? I'm going outside to heat some water for Lucca." He opened the backside passenger door and stepped out. Freezing cold air rushed in before he could slam the door shut. The blue-white light of an LED floodlight winked on outside the truck, illuminating the cavernous interior of the hangar.

"Please?" Roger winced as he held his hand to his shoulder.

"This isn't a negotiation. You stole from us, from what little we have to keep us *all* alive."

"I'm no good to you in pain…"

Jess took a deep breath and shivered in the sudden cold. "Get me to Tunisia, and I'll get you everything I can. You can dope yourself up to hell."

The wind whipped the loose fabric of the hangar, shadows danced across the ceiling.

Roger slumped back in the front seat, squeezing his body against the door, pulling his arms and legs into a ball under the sleeping bag. "Must be what, minus 10 out there?"

"Maybe." Jess closed her eyes and pulled Hector closer.

"You know what's funny?"

She didn't respond.

"We were worried about global warming, but the Earth was still in an ice age. Did you know that? Everyone said the last ice age ended ten thousand years ago, but that's not true."

Now Jess exhaled, trying to express her displeasure, but Roger didn't get the hint. Or maybe he did.

"Technically, the Pliocene glaciation began about three million years ago," he continued, "and we're still in it. The big ice sheets covering Europe and North America receded ten thousand years ago, but we still had polar caps."

"And that means we're still in an ice age?" Jess decided to play along, since he wouldn't shut up on his own, and since she needed him to fly.

"For most of the last five hundred million years, there haven't been any ice caps. The oceans were a hundred feet higher. That's the Earth's normal. And that's what we were trying to stop." He laughed, small and quick, almost a hiccup of a giggle. "We thought we were triggering a mass extinction with all our carbon dioxide, but Mother Nature beat us to the punch."

"And you find that funny?"

"I'll tell you what I find funny. You ever hear of Snowball Earth?" He waited. The wind howled. "Eight hundred million years ago, the ice caps spread all the way from the poles to the equator. One giant ball of ice, the entire planet. For two hundred million years. That's what I think is happening out there, so all this running around—"

Roger stopped mid-sentence. The intensity of the rat-tat-tat of the flapping fabric intensified, and in the stark white-blue light of the LED floodlight, a black hole appeared and grew in the wall of the hangar directly in front of the Range Rover. Giovanni and Raffa, knelt together beside the butane stove, stood quickly. A figure emerged through the black hole in the wall. Jess's body stiffened and she wrapped her arms around Hector.

From the corner of her eye, she saw Roger grapple at the door handle. He opened the door and spilled out, a blast of cold rushing in. He didn't even shut it behind him.

"Who's there?" Giovanni yelled. "*Chi è?*"

The person advanced, their head encrusted in snow and ice. It wasn't a man. Even under the layers of clothing, the body was small. A boy? The hood and scarf fell from the figure's head as they

124

advanced. A shock of black hair. Piercing blue eyes.

"Massarra?" Jess whispered, doing her best to put Hector down to one side on the seat. She grabbed her parka, pulled it on before opening her door to step out. She noticed Roger hovering near the back door of the hangar, ready to bolt.

Jess jumped around the front of the Range Rover. Even with the hood down, the face was encrusted in snow, but Jess knew those eyes anywhere.

Massarra wiped the snow from her face. "You've been followed," she said before collapsing onto the hangar's oil-streaked concrete slab.

NOVEMBER 9th

Sixteen Days A.N.

16

"IS THAT THEM?" Jess pointed at a small dot, barely visible in the mist.

She sank into the wet snow as she tried to get more comfortable. Her stomach growled. She had given her breakfast ration to Hector, telling him not to tell Giovanni.

"That is *him*, yes." Massarra adjusted herself on the outcropping of rubble and handed the binoculars back.

Today was warm again, well above freezing, with a south wind bringing a beige mist whiffing of sewage. The haze around them merged into the clouds, back lit by the sun into a glowing umbrella that seemed to follow overhead. They were soaked from trudging through snow, following the path Massarra had seen the man disappear the evening before. Down into the city. It was warm, but Jess knew the temperature would drop as soon as the north winds began again. All this wet snow would turn into a skating rink of ice and jagged metal and fractured rock.

Jess focused the binoculars.

A man came into focus, clad head-to-foot in tight-fitting black clothing. A tent was just visible under the snow, pitched in the hollow under the hulking mass of the cruise liner, almost exactly in the same spot where they'd parked the day before. The pile of equipment she'd discarded was visible a hundred feet to the man's left, just at the edge of the seawall, the plastic sheet she'd pulled on top flapping in the breeze.

"It looks like he's alone," Jess said.

The man pulled something from his blue nylon pup tent. He wrapped up whatever it was, then placed the package into a sled attached to the back of his snowmobile.

"Alone?" Roger asked. "Are you sure?"

He squirmed in the snow next to Massarra, who moved away from him, her face pinched. Jess was surprised when he volunteered to come on the trek down to the water, and she'd noticed Massarra watching him, an unreadable expression on her face. Now he fiddled with his gloves, pulling one off to play with his finger, and kept glancing at Jess.

"I think so. Let's wait here and see if anyone else shows up, or if anyone else is inside that tent. Are you sure that was the man you saw? It was dark, snowing…"

"I didn't see the man, but the machine is the same. It was parked in the snow, by your airplane hangar."

"And did he see you?"

"No. I am certain of that. He left with his headlight blazing on the machine. You did not see? You did not hear?"

When Massarra surprised them the night before, and collapsed after telling them they were being watched, Jess and Leone went straight outside to do a reconnaissance while she rested. Massarra had murmured about wanting to go with them, to show them where, but she was barely responsive and Jess had refused. Massarra couldn't even stand and was shivering violently.

They left immediately and were out for nearly an hour, but hadn't seen anyone.

Then again, trying to see anything in the storm was almost impossible. Jess couldn't understand how Massarra had even survived out there, much less how she had found them. Giovanni had done his best to inspect her while they were gone. No frostbite. Just exposure, exhaustion and mild hypothermia.

They'd wrapped her up in blankets and laid her down in the back of the Range Rover, and turned on its engine to warm up. The back of the truck was fast becoming a convalescent hospital, with Lucca back there as well. All through the night the storm raged, while Massarra shivered and mumbled. Giovanni said it was Arabic. Leone kept watch in the driver seat of the truck, with his back to the window so he could see into the cabin. He was like that when Jess had finally dropped off to sleep, Hector in her lap, and he was still in the same position, the same place, when she awoke some hours later. Always watching over them.

In the first thin light of the morning, the wind tearing at the hangar died down. Massarra roused and wolfed down what food they could scrounge to give her, gulping down great mouthfuls of chicken broth Giovanni boiled from cans they found near the ship the day before. She explained, between mouthfuls, how she drove the Humvee south and then west around Rome's ring road.

She had abandoned it two nights before and set off on skis, following the roads to the coast and following it back. Sixty kilometers in two days. Giovanni appeared skeptical. He said very few people could trek sixty clicks across snow that fast.

How did you find us? Jess had asked her. The airplane, she'd answered, I saw the airplane.

A lot of people must have seen it.

"Do you think he's dangerous?" Jess asked, offering the binoculars back to Massarra.

"May I have a look?" Roger was still playing with his hand.

Massarra brought the binoculars up to her eyes and began to scan again.

Jess nudged her. "Let him look." She adjusted her backpack, still carrying her father's laptop and data.

"The only ones with machines like that are Vivas," Massarra said. She passed Roger the binoculars without looking at him. "And the brown arm band?"

Same as the guards when they had driven into the town around the bunker. "When you said I was in danger in Vivas, that we had to leave...why?"

"Because you were in danger. It was destroyed."

"By who?"

"I do not know. I just knew there was danger."

"That's a bit vague, isn't it?" Roger moved away from Massarra as he said it.

She ignored him. "So there are no boats?"

"Unless that was it, no." Jess pointed at the snow-covered hulk of the cruise liner dominating the view.

She was thrilled to have Massarra safe with them. Thankful. But there was also a lingering doubt. Fear was never far from any thought. How did this slight woman, less than a hundred pounds, do what she said she did? And why would she come all the way back here to find them?

The obvious answer was the boats, the promise of an easy voyage south. But there were no boats. If Massarra was disappointed, nothing in her expression betrayed it. She stared straight ahead, silent.

"I think we should get back. I don't think there's anyone there with him." Jess took the binoculars from Roger to have another look.

The man seemed alone. He didn't speak to anyone. He didn't seem to be in a hurry to go anywhere. Did he know they were here? As the sun rose behind the clouds, the wet yellow smog dissipated, but the man didn't look their way, nor up at the airfield a half mile up the road. Was he even looking for them? Or was he, too, searching for the mythical boats?

If he was from Vivas, then he had to be in radio contact. If he found them last night, then he would have contacted them. But why wait here? Wouldn't he be trying to hide? Or leave while the cavalry arrived? But he looked unconcerned and wasn't packing up. He sat on the snowmobile and pulled something red from his pocket. He bit into it. An apple.

"That guy's definitely from Vivas. Let's get out of here, and stay low." Jess slithered backward through the wet snow. "Roger, what are you doing?"

He was still fidgeting with his hand, but it wasn't his finger. It was a ring. She noticed the flash of a yin yang symbol on it before Roger pulled on his gloves. He slid down the snow-covered rock pile after her. "Yeah, let's get out of here."

"Only one?" Giovanni stopped shoveling snow, stood upright and wiped his brow with the back of his arm.

He stretched backward, letting loose a pained groan. He was shirtless and sweating in this strange heat. A brown-stained bandage covered his right side, where the bullet back at the castle had grazed him. His bruises were fading, but clearly visible on his torso and under his eyes, in the bright light of this dim day.

"That we could see," Jess answered.

"Vivas?"

She shrugged yes.

"Then help me dig." He bent over and pushed the garden spade he'd found into the three-foot-high slush pile ringing the hangar.

Leone and Raffa followed his lead and went back to trying to move the snow away from the front of the hangar; both of them were armed only with strips of plywood they attempted to use as improvised snow plows. Inside, Elsa bent over a fire of scraps of wood scavenged from collapsed houses just over the fence from the runway. Lucca smiled weakly, sitting in a collapsible camp chair beside the fire.

The family they had met the day before was gone. Leone told them they had nothing to give. Told them to leave. Jess had seen sadness in his eyes as he said the words, shame even. She saw them now on her walk, scavenging in the twisted remains of the empty city, but there wasn't much to find. Only ghosts remained.

"Why don't you use the truck to push the snow aside?" Roger said, watching them work in front of him. "And we're never going to get her up in this." He kicked a pile of the wet snow.

Giovanni grunted as he lifted a shovel full. "First we need to clear a path, then we use the truck." He bent to scoop another load. "And if we don't hurry, this might freeze and we'll never get it out at all."

It took Jess and Massarra almost an hour to climb back up through the wreckage of the town to the airfield. The snow was deep and heavy. In that time, the direction of the wind changed and the temperature dropped. They'd stopped every few minutes to watch the fading dot of the mysterious man-by-the-ship. He didn't move.

"We'll need skis on the Cessna," Roger said, not offering to help with the snow. "How about I take the sleds strapped to the Rover's roof rack and cut wheel holes into—"

"Don't touch them," Giovanni growled, throwing aside more snow.

"But we need skis—"

Giovanni stood upright. "Then why don't you go scavenging and find us something we could use?"

"Like what?"

"You have a degree in astrophysics. Use it to figure out how to make skis."

Giovanni stared at Roger, held his gaze until Roger dropped his eyes and shuffled past him. Massarra followed.

Jess waited for them to be out of earshot. "Should we drive

south? Flying still seems crazy."

"You've seen the roads."

"Massarra just trekked sixty kilometers in two days."

"By herself, carrying nothing, and almost dead when she got here. And if you believe her."

"You don't?"

"We need to get out of here." He returned to digging.

"What about Ballie Booker? The Jolly Roger? He must be around the tip of Spain by now. That's a boat. We're on the west coast of Italy."

"You said it was dangerous to contact anyone."

"But Ballie? Really?"

"You think he could get in past the ice already here? He's driving a lifeboat, not an icebreaker, if that's even who he is."

"What about our friends in Libya? Ain Salah? If we told him what we have, in my father's bag, maybe they could send someone from Al-Jawf."

"It's two thousand kilometers. And do you really want to broadcast that information to the world? We talked about this. I have a bad feeling. We need to get out of here."

Jess exhaled long and hard, shaking her head. "How many can we fit in that thing?" She pointed at the Cessna.

"Me, you, Hector, and Roger flying it."

"So we'll abandon Lucca, Raffa, Leone?" Her voice rose as she listed each person.

"Roger comes back for them."

"You really believe that?"

"I'll kill him if he doesn't."

"But can't you fly?"

"Not like him." Giovanni pushed aside another load of snow and stopped. He threw the shovel into the snow. "And he's right. We need to construct some skis to put on the plane. Raffa can do it, but it will take time. And we need to pump jet fuel from the depot at the end of the runway, carry at least fifty gallons all the way here. There's a lot to do."

"How long?"

"Two days. We need two days." He sighed a bone-weary wheeze. "What about this man by the ship?"

134

"If he contacted Vivas, they may be here at any moment."

"A day in this mess, even for them."

"So we need more time." It wasn't a question. "I don't think he saw us."

"How can you know?"

"What we need is to capture him." Massarra appeared beside Jess, blowing on a steaming cup of soup. "You like some?"

Jess shook her head. "We need to find out what he knows."

"Need to do more than talk." Giovanni retrieved the shovel.

"It could be a trap." Massarra took a sip.

"It's probably a trap, but what choice do we have?"

"We watch him. Massarra and I will watch him. If he comes this way, we'll take him. And Giovanni, get this goddamn plane ready." Even if they managed to ready the plane, they'd have to leave behind Leone and the teenage boys. Could she do that?

Jess closed her eyes.

She was constantly faced by a discipline of necessity. One moment fighting, the next calm. An amount of force or violence was needed one moment, then a gentleness and caring to ease the emotional pain the next. What was necessary? This was the reality of her life. Before it had always been: what do I want, what is my desire? Now it was what do I need to do to survive? What will I be forced to do to ensure the survival of those I love? And it was the same for everyone that surrounded her, for everyone they met. It didn't mean an end to kindness, but it was the beginning of a savagery according to the new discipline of necessity.

She opened her eyes and looked toward the fire. "Where's Rita?"

Giovanni turned to the hangar. "I haven't seen her in an hour, maybe two. I think she is gathering wood."

17

THE DIMPLED GRAY plastic of the old shortwave radio was chipped and cracked. A yellowing lump of cardboard displayed vertical lines of frequency bands. Underneath it, one large knob was surrounded by a family of smaller ones, with a column of switches to the right of that. Each had a red and a black side. Giovanni had scavenged it from a crushed Dash-8 aircraft at the side of the runway.

"It's analog," he explained to Jess. "Survived the radiation blast. Now we have two." He'd propped it on top of an improvised table off to one side of the Range Rover, away from the rest of the group. "This is the main frequency dial." He grabbed the fat knob in the middle and twiddled it back and forth.

"Am I fooling myself?" Jess didn't look at Giovanni as she said the words.

He stopped playing with the dial. "We all fool ourselves, Jessica."

"I'm being serious. Is this *that* important?" She swung her backpack off and dropped it on top of the shortwave.

"You were in Vivas. You said they were looking for you. That means it must be important. Why else?"

"Maybe it was something my father did. Or they think he did. Maybe it's not this."

"And they want to punish him? Humanity has more pressing concerns."

"But—"

"Do you want to wait for them and find out? Because that would be much easier." Giovanni adjusted himself to lean against the door of the Range Rover. "Massarra was the one who said you had to leave Vivas. Did she tell you why?"

"She heard them saying I was to be killed."

Giovanni folded his arms. It wasn't much of an answer.

"She saved me," Jess added. "More than once."

His expression remained blank. "So you are to be killed for what's in that bag?"

"I know I'm risking all our lives."

"You think because it will tell us if Saturn will hit the Earth?" He held his hands wide. "If so, what is the point?"

"Maybe they don't know anything about Saturn."

"Someone wants your father. Very badly."

"But he's dead."

"But you're not. So I think what we're really doing is keeping you alive." A thin smile crept its way onto his grim face. "Which is good enough reason for me."

Static crackled. "Target is moving," said a disembodied voice.

Jess looked at the radio before realizing it was her walkie-talkie. She picked it out of her pocket and thumbed the *talk* button. "Moving?"

"Affirmative," crackled the voice again. It was Massarra. She was ten minutes down the road, watching their man. "He is packing up."

"Tell me when he leaves. Out."

"We can hide," Giovanni said. "We can—"

"He'll see the tracks in the snow if he comes this way."

"I'll come with you."

"One of us needs to stay with Hector, and you need to work on the flight plans with Roger. I can't help with that." Jess grabbed her backpack. It was frayed and worn. She opened the Range Rover's back passenger door and took out another backpack with the medical supplies and emptied it into the seat. "Are we able to fly yet?"

In two hours the feeble light of the sun would fade, leaving the glacial night to return. "We have fuel, and shoveled enough snow and ice away to get out of the hangar. The crust of ice over the snow may be hard enough, but the skis aren't ready."

"I need a straight answer. Can we take off?" Jess unzipped her father's backpack and gently took out the wrapped package of her father's laptop and box with the CDs and tapes in it. "Turn that radio on, we need to speak with Al-Jawf."

He ignored her request. "We might be able to take off, but we can't fly at night, Jessica. That is madness. There are no city lights to guide us, no roads to follow. We'd have no way of landing."

"Turn on the radio," she repeated as she pushed half the

medical supplies into her father's backpack and gave it to Giovanni, putting the rest in the pack that she slung over her own back. Taking a steady look at Giovanni, she took her father's laptop and data box and put them into a plastic bag. She handed the other backpack to Giovanni. Now they each wore one, but her father's data was in a plastic bag she was going to hide.

"Are you sure? We agreed it was dangerous to talk over the radio."

Jess reached past him to click on the radio's power. The display glowed to life. She picked up the sheaf of papers beside it and shuffled through them. "Seven-four-four-two kilohertz, yes?" She clicked off the sideband switch and cycled the main dial, turning up the volume.

Giovanni unclipped the attached microphone, his eyes on Jess. "Station Saline, this is Station Saline. Do you read me Station Al-Jawf?" The radio hissed silence. He clicked the talk button again. "This is Station Saline, do you read me, Station Al-Jawf?" He clicked off the talk button. "End of day is usually a good time for—"

"Station Al-Jawf, reading you five by five," warbled a voice over the radio, with a heavy, Middle Eastern accent. "It is good to hear your voice, my friend. We were getting worried some. Over."

"Ain Salah, is that you? Over."

"Affirmative. We have new sightings for you, last night was clear in the desert. We are sure we saw Venus last night, but the disk is fading. Rains have returned. Did you reach your ship?"

"That's a negative."

Radio silence hissed. "I am sorry to hear this, my friend. There are many boats arriving in Tunis. Perhaps further south?"

"Perhaps."

Giovanni clicked off the talk button and held Jess's gaze. "What did you want to say? Do you want the new sightings?"

She opened the plastic bag, the one with her father's laptop now in it. She inspected the metal case of CDs and tapes, wrapped in foam. In the middle of the pile was her father's circular star chart, the one he taught her to use as a child, to identify constellations. He always brought it with him when they were supposed to meet. He never missed an opportunity to stare up at the heavens with her.

She closed the bag.

"Station Saline, are you still there?" came Ain Salah's voice over the radio.

"Jess?" Giovanni whispered. "What are we doing?"

She took the microphone from him. "Mr. Ain Salah, my name is Jessica Rollins. I'm traveling with Giovanni."

"Ah, copy that, Miss Rollins." His voice sounded confused.

"Tell me your situation there, Mr. Salah?"

The radio whistled for a few seconds. "Many people are coming from the north."

"What's happening in Tunis?"

"Very dangerous. African Union forces have come here, are trying to help."

"Government forces?"

"What is left of them. Many problems. But we are doing our best."

"Do you have aircraft?"

"Excuse me?"

"Airplanes. Do you have airplanes?"

"Some old transports. Some that have come from the north, some from the east. But the situation is very chaotic—"

"My father is Benjamin Rollins, Mr. Salah."

"Say again?"

"Dr. Benjamin Rollins. *The* Benjamin Rollins, of Harvard University."

Jess looked at Giovanni. They hadn't revealed her name before. Before the Nomad disaster, her father's name had been all over the news and Internet, claiming that he knew about Nomad more than thirty years earlier. Conspiracy stories and death threats had flooded the airwaves and news channels. He became perhaps the most infamous man on the planet. Maybe that was why they hunted Jess.

The radio hissed an accusatory blank static, and she was about to repeat herself when—

"I know of your father, Miss Rollins."

"Mr. Salah, what you have heard is not true. We're in possession of critical information. We are in Civitavecchia, just west of Rome, and I need to know if you have some way to come north."

"Miss Rollins, as I said, there is chaos here. I do not think—"

"This is not for us, you understand. This is important. Let me explain…"

Ain Salah clicked off the shortwave radio. He stood and rolled up his shirtsleeves, then wiped one hand across his chin. Could this be true? What this woman told him? How could he be sure that she was whom she said? But then, who would lie about something like that?

He paced back and forth in the communications room, a small concrete bunker with metal shelves overflowing with stacks of notepads and dust-coated, aged electronics.

What difference could it make if what she was saying was true?

A squall of rain hammered against the window. A stream of people slogged along a road of mud outside, through a gap in a chain link fence topped with barbed wire. The Sahara desert. The word literally meant desert in Arabic. So it was the *desert* desert.

But it was a desert no longer.

Massive lakes were already forming in the basins, and not the salty oases that dotted the Sahara before, but deep, fresh water reservoirs. Water. Too much water, it felt like. The rain stopped for a moment, and a break in the scudding clouds revealed a fat orange sun, a reddish glob behind a waxy sky. He watched the tired and filthy procession along the road, their backs bent, carrying what possessions they could. Refugees.

As a Coptic Christian who grew up in Cairo, he knew something of oppression, of living in fear. Not that long ago, it was refugees from here, from the south and east, that had swarmed into Europe and the West. Now the tide had reversed horribly. Those who survived the terror in the north and braved the freezing water of the Mediterranean had landed on these shores and wound their way through the soaking sands. Beside the stream of refugees was a truck, a khaki tarp spread over a metal frame with a gold-and-green African Union insignia on its door.

Ain Salah stopped pacing and stood still. "Mustafa," he yelled.

Shuffling in the next room. The metal door creaked open an inch. A young man appeared, the scraggly beginnings of a beard clinging to his cheeks.

"Get me General Ugava."

"Now?"

Was it worth the risk? It wasn't Ain Salah's decision. "Why else would I ask?"

"Sorry, I am sorry, Ain Salah. Of course." Mustafa's head disappeared back through the door.

Beyond the barbed wire, rows of metal holding tanks of the refineries loomed through the mist. They had precious little food, but oil, they had a lot of oil. That made this place strategically important. The pipelines were burst, so there was no way to get the oil out, not for now.

But he was sure oil would remain important in this new world. As would this information the young woman told him.

Past the rows of metal tanks, he could just make out the airfield. An Otter had arrived from the north, it's pilot in debrief right now with the General. Perhaps this was to be a lucky day for Miss Jessica Rollins.

18

WISPS OF FOG eased their way over rubble piles and misshapen skeletons of buildings. A graveyard, but not just for people. The fog was layered, horizontal bands staggered against the red-orange sky, but near the ground it collected in hollow pools, soothing the fractured cityscape. Somewhere behind the clouds, the sun was setting.

Jess imagined she could see it, imagined its hot warmth on her face, tried her best to ignore the sting of cold against her cheeks. She balanced an open ration package on her knees next to the walkie-talkie, waiting for the call from Massarra to tell her if their interloper was coming this way.

A set of eyes watched her from the shadows of a corrugated tin roof leaning against a crumbling wall of bricks. A foot of snow, crusted in yellow ice, frosted the tumbledown structure.

"You can come out." She motioned with her hand and held out the ration tin.

The eyes moved back and forth in worried circles before a snout emerged tentatively from the gloom.

"It's okay," Jess said gently, holding the ration tin further out.

The dog took three tentative steps toward her before retreating. It re-emerged with a small boy, the one that played with Hector down by the ship. His cheeks were ruddy, the dog scrawny. They both hesitated.

"Is that your dog? *È il tuo cane?*"

The boy nodded. His eyes darted back and forth.

"It's okay. Leone isn't here." She knew that he meant well, that he was just trying to protect their own dwindling supplies, and she saw the pain in the old man's eyes, his stolid determination to protect Giovanni and Hector. Even if it meant going against his nature and piling suffering upon others.

"Take it," Jess urged. She put the pack of rations on the ground and retreated to her plywood seat.

The boy darted forward and picked the food up, in the same motion taking out a cracker that he fed to his dog.

"Jessica, do you read me?" whistled the walkie-talkie. It was Massarra. "He's coming this way."

Startled, the boy withdrew into the shadows of the tin hut.

Jess thumbed the *talk* button. "On my way." She shouldered the AK. "Hide," she said to the boy. "*Nasconditi.*"

Behind her, Raffa stood quietly and followed. Giovanni had insisted that she take the teenager, but he wasn't a child anymore; his expression taut, his rifle slung across his back. They were two hundred yards down the main road leading from the hangars, halfway to the waterfront. She didn't want this fight, but the day was clear, or as clear as days came now.

If this scout came past the airfield, he'd see the tracks in the snow. Had he seen the airplane two days before? She didn't know.

She didn't know a lot of things.

Were the Vivas people coming this way? Was it destroyed? What did they want with her? They only needed another day, and they could be away south. Jess had them dug in defensively at the hangar. Everyone was given a weapon, even if just a knife.

Keeping low, Jess and Raffa did their best to jog along the edge of the road, slipping on patches of ice, crunching across the granular hard-packed snow. In the distance came the whine of a snowmobile's engine. Reaching the wide boulevard by the water, she held up one hand to stop Raffa. Sweat trickled down her back. Her chest heaved. The engine noise warbled but grew louder.

"He's coming your way," crackled Massarra's voice over the walkie-talkie.

Jess thumbed the *talk* button. "Do you have a shot?"

"Yes."

"Not yet."

Jess turned the volume all the way down and pointed at a snow-covered gazebo to one side of the main road. She flicked her fingers at it, gesturing for Raffa to take position there. She hunched over and limped to a snowdrift by the seawall. Her prosthetic dug into her rubbed-raw stump. The snowmobile's whine pitched higher. Each breath pulled a rush of cold air into her lungs. Adrenaline flooded her bloodstream. A single snowflake drifted in front of Jess's eyes and hovered in space.

"Massarra!" screamed a voice.

A man, dressed in khaki, appeared through a hummock of rubble between two buildings a hundred yards from Jess.

Crack. Crack. Gunshots echoed.

Bursts of ice and snow erupted next to the man as he jerkily ran forward. He yelled something. Jess couldn't make it out. Another shot. The man fell face-forward and skidded to a stop.

Behind Jess, another roar, but not from a snowmobile engine. A car swerved along the road she just had just come down. It was white, with skis on its front. A Volkswagen Beetle. Its engine gunned and it slid sideways trying to negotiate the curve to the boulevard, skidding and crashing into a debris pile of metal rods and tumble-down brick.

"Raffa, get back, go back!" Jess yelled, pointing up the road.

From the corner of her eye, she saw what looked like Massarra running toward the man in khaki. Another burst of gunfire, the tat-tat-tat of an automatic. Ice fragments exploded around Massarra. Jess looked toward the snowmobile. The man was visible now, his weapon centered over the handlebars, the engine revved high. A buzzing whine echoed above it all. Two more engines. Dots appeared in the distance, from behind the hulk of the beached cruise liner.

More snowmobiles.

The door of the Volkswagen swung open.

"Go!" Jess screamed at Raffa.

He took one last look at Jess and turned to scramble across the snow.

The fire crackled and popped, sent up a spray of red embers. Giovanni threw another stick of wood, the leg of a chair, onto the pile and held his hands out to warm them. His pistol lay against crates beside him.

Roger sat to his left, with his back to the Cessna. He had his foot propped up on the improvised plywood ski Raffa had attached to the landing gear. Hector sat on the floor to Giovanni's right, leaning against his leg. Lucca was curled in a pile of blankets near the fire. He had a bad fever, and the antibiotics didn't seem to be doing anything for it. Elsa had found sausage in a larder in one of the houses on her scavenging. Giovanni had a wedge of particleboard balanced on his knees as a cutting board, slicing the sausage into chunks.

He offered one to Roger, saying: "So our flight plan is good enough for—"

"Coming your way," hissed the walkie-talkie by Giovanni's feet.

He stood, knocking the board on his knees onto the ground. A roar erupted outside. Elsa stood by a tear in the hangar fabric, a pistol in her hand.

"*Cosa c'è?*" Giovanni ran to Elsa. She pulled the fabric wide enough for him to see a flash of white. A car rumbled past on the road outside.

"Leone!" Giovanni yelled, pushing past Elsa to get a better look. It was a Volkswagen Beetle. "Get—" He turned, his hands out, urging the rest of them forward. But his words slid away into silence.

Rita stood next to the Cessna, her feet planted wide. Her red hair was pulled back, her face scowling. She had a rifle pointed at Giovanni. "*Dammi la borsa.*" Elsa pointed her pistol at him as well.

"The bag?" Confusion, anger and fear jockeyed inside Giovanni's head. Rita wanted his backpack? Why?

The roar of the car's engine faded, replaced by the crackling pop of the fire. Leone stood in the hangar door behind the Cessna, a swirl of flakes settling around his feet. He glared at Rita, then at Elsa, his lips curling. "*Stronze …*"

"Just give them whatever they want," Roger shouted. He was still beside the fire, his hands up. Hector sat on the concrete beside him, his small eyes on Giovanni.

Gunshots echoed outside. A voice screamed. Hector jumped to his feet and ran squealing at his uncle, who sprinted forward and scooped the boy into his arms.

A deafening burst of gunfire reverberated inside the hangar.

Giovanni fell to the floor and pulled Hector beneath him. He skidded to stop next to the fire, not feeling anything. Glancing back, he saw Elsa's body jerk into the air. Blood spattered against the hangar wall.

Rita screamed, a guttural shriek of terror and rage. She fired her weapon, but not at Giovanni.

Lucca had taken Giovanni's pistol. He was the one who shot Elsa. The down blanket he was wrapped in exploded in a mist of feathers, but he'd already rolled away under the Cessna, leaving the gun on the ground. Leone stepped in front of him, bringing his pistol around, but Rita kicked her way through the embers of the fire, her rifle pointed squarely at the Baron and the boy.

At first she tried desperately to pull the backpack from Giovanni's back, but then, seeing that he wouldn't let go of it, she grabbed hold of Hector's wrist and dragged the screaming child around the still-burning coals. She held him tight, and, her chest heaving in and out, pushed him to the ground. "*Scusa*," she cried, but brought the rifle around, the muzzle tip shaking, and pressed the end of the barrel against the boy's head. She glanced toward Elsa, who hadn't made a sound since being shot.

Giovanni scrambled to his feet. He saw hesitation in her eyes, but also wild rage. Her sister was just shot. This woman could do anything. He pulled the backpack off slowly, holding one hand up in the air in surrender. "*Prendilo,* take it. But why? Do you even know what this is?"

"I do, and I'll take it," Roger said, his voice calm. "And we'll take this too."

In his left hand was the plastic bag with the wrapped package of Jess's father's laptop, and the bundle of data CDs and tapes.

Jess crouched against the seawall. Another shot rang out, and the man on the snowmobile closest to her slumped. The machine veered off to one side. She looked up to where Massarra was, next to the crumpled man in khaki, and saw a rifle muzzle flash. *Crack.* Another shot. This one at the two snowmobiles approaching from the distance. Snow sprayed into the air near Massarra and she rolled out of view. Jess looked back at the Volkswagen. A man pulled himself out of the open door.

Not a man. A boy.

He limped forward.

She saw his face clearly. It was the same boy she'd shot in

Bandita.

The scavengers.

What the hell was going on? Nobody was firing at her. Not yet. But everything was converging on her.

She glanced over the sea wall. A fifteen-foot drop into a mess of tumbled rocks and ice. There was a jetty a quarter mile away, toward the beached cruise liner, which was still intact. A light snow had started. Jess looked to the horizon. A thin line of blue in the distance, but ice stretched hundreds of yards from the shore. She looked back at the kid, the one she shot. He had his gun up, but he didn't fire at her.

Jess took a deep breath, swung her legs over the wall, her AK still in her right hand. Her left hand tried to grip the concrete but slipped. She gasped and fell through space, crunching in the rocks after a second of free fall, and splayed backward. Her prosthetic came loose. Her rifle clattered away from her into the rocks.

She tried to suck air back into her lungs as she propelled herself away from the wall on her back through the snow and ice. The kid's head appeared, a bobbing black dot on the seawall, fifteen feet overhead. He didn't know if she still had her weapon. She pointed her arm at him. His head darted back.

Jess rolled onto her stomach and cursed. She needed to lead them away. She needed to give Giovanni—

Shots echoed, but not close this time. Muffled; the sound of this gunfire drifting through the snow. From the top of the ridge. From the hangars.

Giovanni's chest heaved in and out. Spittle covered his chin. He licked his lips and bared his teeth at Roger. The traitor's face remained impassive. He held out his right hand. "Give me the backpack," he repeated. "I need to be sure. It's the only way."

"You piece of…" Giovanni glanced back at Rita, her foot pressed into Hector, her shaking gun still pressed against his head. "Okay, okay." He handed the pack over.

Roger took the bag and added it to the collection in his left hand, reaching back with the other to take the pistol from the ground where Lucca had scrambled away.

"*Stupida cagna*," Leone roared. He darted forward, a mad bull rush straight at Rita.

Her eyes wide, she swung her rifle up from Hector's head and fired.

It didn't stop the old man's charge. He bowled into her, knocking her from her feet. Roger turned to look at them. Giovanni grabbed the knife from the floor swung it in an arc at Roger, who flinched back to avoid the blade burying itself in his cheek. Giovanni lunged and brought the blade down hard, straight into Roger's outstretched hand as it reached across the plywood ski for the pistol. The razor-sharp blade went straight through the middle of Roger's hand and sank deep into the plywood.

Roger screamed, his voice high and shrill. He dropped the bags from his left hand.

Hector had already scrambled away and thrown himself into the blankets by Giovanni's feet. Roger's scream curdled. He clawed at the blade, cutting his fingers to shreds as blood poured out.

Rita was back to her feet and had her gun square on Giovanni. Leone crawled on the floor by her feet. She lowered the rifle toward him, but again she hesitated. The old man slumped against the concrete.

"No more. *Fermare.* Take it." Giovanni kicked the bags Roger dropped across the floor. "Just take it." Hector mewled at his feet.

"Wait!" Roger shouted to Rita. "You can't activate it without me."

Keeping her rifle sighted on Giovanni, Rita picked up the bag. She backed away toward where her sister lay in a pool of her own blood. A thin wail filled the air. "Elsa?" she sobbed

No reply. Just the soft whistle of wind outside.

Rita looked back at the men as she continued to back away toward the flapping tear of fabric at the side of the hangar.

"No, wait!" Roger wailed, his blood-soaked hand flailing and slipping on the knife's handle.

Taking one last look at her sister, Rita disappeared through the hangar wall. An engine snarled to life. It revved high. Ice crunched beneath metal as the machine pulled away.

The engine noise faded.

Leone groaned.

Raffa appeared through the same tear of fabric that Rita had just exited, his chest heaving. "Giovanni, *dov'è* Lucca? Rita?" he said breathlessly.

The hangar door behind the Cessna opened a crack. "*Sono qui,*" coughed his brother, slipping through the door and staggering forward.

Giovanni picked up Hector and spun him around, checking him front and back. No blood. No wounds. The boy squirmed from Giovanni's grip. "*Dove è* Jessica?"

Shaking his head, unable to answer the boy but as desperate to know as he was, Giovanni ran to the inert Leone, blood pooling beneath him.

Jess hobbled over a pressure ridge of ice. Water slopped in the crevasse. The snowfall had thickened. Plump flakes fell soundlessly. The orange-red sunset was deepening. Darkness crept into the fog and snow. How far had she come out onto the ice? A hundred yards? Two hundred? She wasn't sure. Each breath burned her lungs, every step flared pain into her stump. Her prosthetic wobbled and got stuck in the snow again and again.

But she pushed on. She pushed outward.

The boy's head appeared again on the seawall. Two more heads had appeared next to him before they disappeared into the snow-gloom. Somewhere to her left, a single snowmobile engine droned. Its noise faded in and out. More muffled shots. But now Jess had only one thought. Get them as far away from Hector, and from Giovanni, as she could.

Bent over, she skidded on the ice.

It wasn't covered in snow now. It was slick, smooth. Black. She took another step. A bubble of air slithered past underneath, the ice splintering in cracks. She hesitated. Her body shook.

"I would not go any further," said a voice behind her.

She stopped, shivering, and turned.

A man appeared through the churning snow. His hair white, a slash across his lip. "Stop, Jessica."

The boy appeared beside him. He limped forward.

"Who are you?"

"Who I am is not important. But you knew my nephew, Nico."

It took Jess a second to register. "Are you friggin' kidding me?"

"He was misguided."

"What the hell do you want with me? What is wrong with you people?" She stood up straight, defiant, and edged further out.

"I mean you no harm."

"Then get away from me."

Almost reluctantly, Salman raised his arm and showed her the pistol in it. He squeezed the trigger. Jess flinched, but the bullet wasn't aimed at her. It impacted the ice ten feet behind her.

"I am not my nephew. I have no interest in the Ruspoli. I will not harm the boy, or you, or your new lover. I just want your father's laptop."

"This?" Jess slung her backpack off and held it in the air. "How did you know?"

The man shrugged. "Ask your friend Roger."

The snowflakes fell around them in Jess's furious silence. "What's so valuable about it that you'd risk your neck chasing me out here?"

The man shrugged again. "You might be able to answer that better than me."

"Fine." Jess threw the pack across the ice, as far to her left as she could.

The boy hobbled over to pick up the bag.

"I need you to come as well," Salman said.

"Screw you." Jess took another step back, but planted her foot, ready to run forward. She tensed and lowered her stance.

The ice cracked in a wet pop and Jess felt her right leg fall into the freezing water. The man and boy backed up in alarm. Her other leg slipped into the water, submerging her up to her waist. She flopped forward onto her stomach, stretching her hands onto the ice, her gloves sliding against the slick surface. "Help me," she wheezed.

The water stung, as if she rolled naked through a field of nettles. She gasped, her diaphragm tightening, forcing all the air from her lungs. The sheet of ice she clung to cracked and tipped up, angling itself into the air. Jess slid back, desperate to hang on.

Her body plunged into the water up to her neck, her skin shrinking around her body, her brain shooting signals to the capillaries in her extremities to clamp down. With a final desperate scramble, she pulled herself six inches back onto the ice.

For a second it held her.

Snowflakes settled.

Then the ice cracked.

In her mind, Jess saw the small boy's face once again, her little brother so many years ago, his eyes wide as he held onto the ice. As he slipped away. She plunged into the dark water, her head submerging. Jess fought to swim, but the water flooded her parka and boots. Stuck in molasses.

The dim blur of light above faded, the cold water like tiny, sharp needles. She struggled in the blackness, fighting the need for oxygen, but there was no use. She screamed soundlessly, frigid water filling her lungs. The needling cold faded, replaced by a warm fuzz that crept along her fingers and into her chest. The dim blur faded. A spasm overcame her as her lungs tried to push out the water.

Her heart thumped slowly. Once more, then twice.

But not a third time.

19

SALMAN WATCHED THE black pool surrounded by frosted ice. A breeze rippled wavelets across the water, but nothing stirred beneath. He realized he was holding his breath, and finally exhaled to let his lungs draw in the icy air. Snowflakes floated onto the rippling surface and melted, becoming one again with the ocean from where they came.

He'd wanted the girl, but now she was beyond reach. Gone.

But he had the laptop. He had the package. That he was sure of.

And he had Roger.

Off to his right, a hundred yards away, a man stood on top of a snowmobile. He watched Salman through binoculars. A gunshot rang out, ice bursting into mist beside the man. He swung his rifle from his back and fired it.

Not at Salman.

At a small figure sitting on the seawall. The figure disappeared from view. One shot. Two. The bullets ricocheted off the concrete seawall.

"*Sbrigati,*" the old man said to his boy, who limped back to him as fast as he could, the backpack in his hand. "We must hurry."

The snowmobile's engine whined to life, and the man steered it around, away from Salman. His silhouette faded into the snow.

Salman grabbed the boy by his collar and led him back toward the seawall, but at an angle, away from whomever it was who now hung down from the ledge. He had what he needed. Now he needed to get away.

Leone was alive, but for how long? Giovanni had no idea. He had a bullet wound that needed more attention than he had time to give. Right now, he had to find Jessica. They needed her. He needed her. He dressed the wound as best he could and stood over the old man. How long had he served his family loyally, looked after those he loved? How could it have come to this?

Giovanni jumped into the Range Rover and gunned the engine as he shifted into reverse. "Watch him!" he yelled, leaning out of the truck's open window to jab a finger at Roger, who was tied with frayed yellow nylon rope to a strut of the Cessna.

Cursing, Giovanni lifted the clutch and the truck squealed over the smooth concrete of the hangar floor to rocket through the open door, up the snow-and-ice embankment to lurch into the air. He jammed on the brakes, flipped into first gear, and spun over the snow.

Over the noise of the engine—gunshots. Down by the water. Raffa told him that the last time he saw Jess, she was climbing over the seawall. He saw the Volkswagen drive past, he said, but that there were also snowmobiles, the same as at Vivas. Giovanni heaved the steering wheel, swinging the truck into the narrow street sloping down to the water. Fresh tracks in the snow. He followed them, the truck bouncing up and down, left and right.

Up ahead, through the snow, the Volkswagen appeared.

Two men crouched behind it. One of them stood. Not a man, but a boy. He pointed at the water before the other man pulled him back. Giovanni pushed on the brake. The truck slid through the mush, fishtailing. The man and the boy edged around the Volkswagen, keeping it between them and Giovanni.

He didn't see Jess with them.

Off in the distance, past the seawall, someone scurried across the ice. Giovanni revved the engine, released the brake, and the truck weaved forward. He slammed sideways into the seawall. The truck ground to a stop against the concrete. He threw open his door, and was halfway out before he paused, breathing heavily.

The small figure had stopped on the ice, paused in front of a black oval a hundred and fifty yards out. Giovanni turned in his seat, grabbed the spool of yellow nylon cord and what was left of the medical kit and his pistol. He jumped from the wall, slammed into the ice and rocks twelve feet below, rolled to his feet and ran.

He strained to see through the swirl of snow.

Was that Jess? No. The figure was too slight. It was Massarra, her rifle up, aimed at him, but she dropped it in recognition. She waved, pointing at the black oval of water in front of her. His stomach tightened. He knew.

"In the water?"

"She's gone."

Giovanni skidded to a stop ten yards from the edge of the cracked ice. He threw the nylon cord onto the ground and grabbed one end, unspooling arm lengths with each pull. "How long?"

"Five minutes, perhaps more."

"How?"

"A man chased her here. The one in the car."

Giovanni swore under his breath. He should have come with her. "Anyone else? Vivas?" He kicked the spool of cord behind him and pulled off his parka.

"I shot two. Two escaped."

His pants and boots came off next. "And who was the man in the car?"

"I don't know, bandits, the same ones that—"

"You and I both know that's not true." He didn't look at her as he said it, but concentrated on tying one end of the yellow cord around his waist. One knot. Two. He tested it, pulled hard, and shivered in the cold. Wet socks weren't any protection against the cold ice.

Massarra didn't respond to his accusation. She stood silent.

Giovanni squeezed his eyes shut and took two deep breaths before opening them. He held out the nylon cord. "Three sharp jerks, and you pull me back." He locked eyes with her. "You understand?"

She returned his gaze and took the offered cord, then backed away, snaking the line through her hand. She wrapped the end around her waist and nodded.

The bay was shallow here. Not more than a hundred feet away, a shoulder of breakwater rocks hummocked through the ice. He squeezed his hands into fists, tensed all the muscles in his body and took three quick breaths. Gulping in a final lungful of air, he stepped forward, planted his foot and dove headfirst into the oval of water.

He felt like he was hitting a glacial wall, but his body slid through, the sting familiar, that needling pain of ice water against the skin. He'd swum in arctic temperatures before, although only as a stunt. A relief from the heat of a sauna, or a laugh with friends. He'd studied its effects, the tightening of the diaphragm in the chest cutting off air, the suffocating panic and slowing of the muscles.

He fought it. But he knew he couldn't fight it for long.

Down he swam, one stroke, two, before he opened his eyes. A nearly impenetrable gloom. He could barely see his own hands. Three strokes. Four. His outstretched arm touched something. A cloud of debris boiled up around him, a soup of muck and mud. The cord pulled around his waist, and, careful not to tug it too jerkily, he pulled to get more slack.

His lungs burned.

The cold seared his skin.

He pushed sideways off the bottom, his feet skating over the slick rocks, his arms stretched wide, fingers out as whiskers feeling in the darkness. Something. He wrapped his hand around it, pulled himself inches from it. A metal post, sunk in a concrete pylon. He pushed away at ninety degrees, trying to move in a grid.

Come on. Come on.

He looked up at the bleary smudge of light and tried to resist the convulsions in his chest, but then kicked off the bottom. A second later he gasped in a lungful of air as his head broke the surface.

"Do you have her?" Massarra screamed.

She pulled the cord tight and jammed him into the edge of the ice.

"Let go!" He slapped the water, sucking in air, trying to control the shivering.

He dove back under.

Was there any current? His mind was sluggish. The cold seeped into his skull.

No.

The particles of mud churned around him but didn't seem to float away.

Already he had trouble moving his arms. He couldn't feel his fingers. Still he clawed through the water. Not more than ten feet deep. His hand hit the rocky bottom, but he didn't feel it. Just the sensation of his hand not moving forward, his arm jammed back

155

into his body. This time he kicked off to the right.

The mud whorled around him, but there was a patch of yellow. He scrambled and scraped his way toward it, pulling on rocks, digging at the water. Jess's face loomed from the darkness, her eyes closed. Her skin blue-white. Her mouth open in a frozen scream. Giovanni pulled her close and did his best to wrap his legs around her waist, with one arm around her neck.

He tugged three times on the nylon cord.

And waited.

Shivering hard, he pressed his face against Jess's cheek. Hard and cold as ice.

He jerked again on the cord, and this time it ripped away out of his hand. Water rushed past him. His head knocked into something. The ice. He was at the edge of the ice. He reached out—in slow motion, his body a sack of wet cement—and wrapped his arm around the edge and pulled. The thin layer of ice broke and his head popped up.

"I have her," he gasped, rolling onto his back.

With the last of his strength, he pulled Jess's body up, her head breaking the surface of the water beside him. Her lips were purple-blue, her skin pale-marble.

"Pull, pull!"

Eddies of blowing snow skidded past. Massarra had the nylon cord wrapped around her waist, her body forty-five degrees to the ground. She heaved with everything she had. Giovanni felt himself slip up against the ice, and he hauled Jess's body over himself. The next pull from Massarra popped them both onto the snowy surface. She dug her feet in, yanking and dragging them onto the ice.

Shivering almost uncontrollably, Giovanni staggered to his knees. "Start the Range Rover," he stuttered, his teeth chattering. "Get the heat on."

Massarra nodded and let go of the rope. She disappeared from view in the thickening snowfall. The orange-red glow of sunset had faded into a deep gloom. Darkness descended, but Jess's face shone white. He rolled her onto her side and stuck a finger into her mouth to feel for any obstructions. Water poured from her dead lips. He waited and shivered in the dark, then rolled her back.

He put both hands together and pressed them into her chest.

Once, twice, three times. He leaned down to breathe air into her mouth. He repeated this a half dozen times, until he heard the growl of the Range Rover's engine starting up. Faint beams of its headlights pierced the darkness. Giovanni pumped Jess's chest one last time before forcing himself to his feet.

He grabbed Jess by the hood of her parka and dragged her stiff body across the snow.

20

"IS SHE DEAD?"

"You'll know if she's dead."

"How the hell would I know?" Roger grimaced and tried to shift position. He was hog-tied against the strut of the Cessna.

"Because I'll slice the liver from your body and feed it to that boy's dog while you watch."

Giovanni didn't turn to look at Roger as he said it, didn't bother to try and menace him further. A dog doesn't bark before it bites, and he wasn't barking anymore. Just looking at Roger made his stomach turn. He was afraid that he'd kill him, but he knew they still needed this pathetic excuse for a human being, at least until they got the truth from him.

"I was trying to protect her, I told you—"

"Enough! Shut him up, *fallo stare zitto!*"

Raffa got up from the bench next to the fire in the middle of the hangar. Blade in hand, he stalked toward Roger, who flinched away. Raffa knelt to grab an oily rag from the floor and stuffed it into the traitor's mouth. Lucca sat at the hangar's front door, open a crack, on guard but seeing only the darkness outside.

Leone groaned. Hector worried over him as he lay wrapped in blood-soaked blankets next to the fire. Off to one side of the concrete floor were two bodies. One was Elsa; the other, an old man Massarra had dragged up from near the seawall, already dead. She hadn't said anything yet, hadn't explained, but she hadn't tried to run away, either.

Right now, Giovanni's singular mission was Jessica. Everything and everyone else was secondary.

He lowered his cheek to her mouth, and rested one hand on her neck. A weak pulse. She was breathing, but barely. They'd constructed an improvised stretcher from plywood, softened it with a rolled foam sleeping pad, but he only covered her with a thin blanket.

"Should we not move her closer to fire?" Massarra asked.

The old man she'd dragged up here, Giovanni didn't recognize.

She seemed unable, or unwilling, to leave him, hovering close to his bullet-riddled body. The anguish on her face was real, if about the only real thing he knew about her now.

"Rewarming too quickly can be fatal." He knew the core temperature of victims of hypothermia continued to drop, even after they were brought into warm environments.

Cold blood from the surface tissues were rich in lactic acids, and bringing that into the core of the body too quickly added more stress to an already over-stressed situation. He'd heard of fisherman plucked from arctic waters who had thanked their rescuers, were wrapped up in blankets and urged inside for a cup of tea, only to drop dead, one by one, from reheating too quickly.

When he got Jess into the Range Rover, he'd done his best to warm her gently, pressing her chest, pumping her heart to get blood into her brain, breathing new, warm air into her lungs. But the extreme hypothermia brought with it the risk of afterdrop, the difference in temperature between the core and extremities shocking the heart back into fibrillation. She had a weak pulse, but at least, thank God, her heart had started again.

She was young. She was strong. And now, gently, gently, was how he needed to bring her back to life. But how long had she been dead?

Maybe her body was limping back toward living, but was there brain damage? She might never awaken. Her skin was still cold to touch, her lips purplish-blue, but some color had returned to her waxen face.

"Bring me another blanket."

Raffa pocketed his knife and fetched a pile from next to the truck. He'd said nothing since Rita disappeared, but Giovanni noticed him glance over at Leone every so often, and flinch each time he did.

They moved Jess another two feet closer to the fire, swinging her around to warm her other side. Roger had already managed to spit out the rag stuffed in his mouth.

"Who were those men in the Volkswagen?" Giovanni asked him again, grunting as he put the head of Jess's stretcher down. It was still painful for him to lift anything, and he wasn't getting stronger as he healed from his own injuries. If anything, in this cold, with the constant dehydration and strain, the lack of food and sleep, he was getting weaker.

"You idiot. I was protecting you from them, and from those bitches, Elsa and Rita. They would have killed you in your sleep."

Old Leone had never stopped watching them, Giovanni thought. Invisible beneath his pile of sodden blankets next to the fire, the old man hacked up a phlegmy cough. He and Jess formed a vee around the crackling embers. The old man never trusted anyone except Jessica, Giovanni realized, and he should have trusted his instincts.

Raffa sat cross-legged next to Leone, anguish creasing his face. He whispered soft questions, asking if he wanted water, something to eat. No, no, was always the answer.

"You want answers, ask Massarra," Roger continued. "Tie her up, stick knives in her. Those men didn't capture her. She wasn't with us. She's lying. Ask her what she's doing here." He spat blood-speckled sputum onto the concrete.

Giovanni held a hand to Jess's cheek. She felt warm now, warmed by the fire, her breathing more regular. He wanted to get some fluids into her. "Is that true, Massarra?"

She hung back at the edge of the hangar, beside the dead man she'd dragged in. She still had her rifle in hand. "Mr. Roger was not captured by those men, that much I can tell you."

"I was!" Bloody spittle sprayed from Roger's mouth.

"Not what I saw, not back at the castle. And I watch for a long time."

"She admits it! She was spying on us!" Roger strained against his ropes. The tendons in his necked flared, his face mottled red.

"But I, Mr. Roger, am not the spy," she replied in a cool voice. She sat on her haunches, balanced on the balls of her feet, balanced by holding her rifle upright against the floor in front of her. Giovanni hadn't tried to take it from her, and she hadn't offered it up.

"How did they know about the bag, Roger?" Giovanni stroked Jess's hair, then felt the pulse on her neck again.

"I told them."

"Why?"

"Because I needed some reason that they shouldn't kill me.

When I went outside with Jess's father, I was thrown down the mountain in an explosion. That man, Salman, found me. Nico had called him, asked him for help. Told him how much gold you had."

"Then why didn't they come for the gold?"

"They wanted to kill all of you. I told them there was something much more important."

"And why, exactly, would that be more important than gold?"

"That data…" Roger's voice faded.

"You're telling me some *goomba* thinks a bag of CDs is worth more than gold?"

"He can sell it, that's what I told him."

"To *who* exactly—"

"Tie her up," said a small, weak voice.

Giovanni turned from glaring at Roger. His eyes and mouth opened. "Jessica! My God." He dropped to his knees and held her head gently in his hands. "Do you know who I am?"

She took a moment and breathed as deep as she could. Her chest rattled and she coughed. "Baron Giovanni Ruspoli."

"Where are you? Do you know?"

"In hell, as far as I can tell," she wheezed.

Giovanni half-giggled, half-sobbed. "How do you feel?"

"That's a stupid question. Get me water." She raised a shaking hand and pointed at Massarra. "And tie her up."

Massarra stood and shouldered her rifle, but she didn't budge and didn't move away. In fact, a smile flitted across her lips, seeing Jess awake.

"She saved us, both of us."

"Do you have it?"

He held Jess's gaze. Her eyes were bloodshot; angry veins swollen red around her blue irises. He shook his head.

She didn't reply, but her chest hitched, a spasm that ended in coughing fit.

"Jess, Roger gave it to them. He was with them, the men that chased you."

"I told you," Roger gurgled. "I was trying to save—"

"You were not helping anyone but yourself!"

"Please, tie me up." Massarra stood over Giovanni and Jess. She'd put her rifle on the floor. "If that is what Jessica wishes."

Giovanni shook his head. "You keep watch, help Lucca."

"She's not who—" Jess coughed.

"We need her right now."

Massarra offered a tiny bow and retrieved her rifle. She walked to the front of the hangar.

"Are you kidding me? You have *me* tied up, and you're giving her a gun?" Roger squirmed against his ropes. The wing above him had a gaping hole in it from one of Rita's shotgun blasts. "Jess, how long have I known you? You *know* me."

"No, no, no!" Raffa's voice rose in a crescendo. He held Leone's head in his arms.

"What is it?" But Giovanni knew from the way Raffa's eyes grew wide in sad fear.

"He is not breathing," Raffa sobbed.

The teenager buried his face in Leone's chest, holding Hector together with him. Lucca skidded across the smooth concrete on his knees, already having sprinted from the hangar door. He wrapped his arms around his brother and the body of the old man. Their bodies rocked back and forth, punctuated by sobs. From the hangar door, Massarra watched them, her face pinched. She returned to staring into the darkness outside.

Giovanni shifted on his knees toward the mass of bloody blankets. He put a hand to Leone's neck. No pulse. There wasn't anything he could do. The old man had lost too much blood.

With a groan, Jess propped herself up on one elbow and looked at Roger. "Any reasons these people have for keeping you alive are dwindling fast. And I *don't* know you. Now tell us *everything*."

The trapped man's eyes darted back and forth, from Massarra, to the heaving, sobbing mass of the boys and Leone, to the snarl of Giovanni. "They knew about Nomad."

"Who?"

"I don't know. They just called it The Organization."

"The organiza...what do you mean, *they knew about Nomad?*"

"I mean for years."

"*Years?*"

"Decades. They knew it was coming."

Giovanni stood, his hands balled. "Who? The American government? They knew about Nomad but didn't tell anyone?"

A wet laugh percolated up from Roger's chest, small hiccups that turned to sobs while he smiled and leered. "All those conspiracy nuts telling you about government cover ups? That the end of the world was coming? They were right. The Organization stamped out the louder ones, but the wingnuts they let sing. They had a lot of time to prepare."

"And you worked for them?" Jess held onto Giovanni's leg and propped herself up higher.

The traitor scoffed. "Stupid question. We don't have much time. They'll be coming back. You need to untie me."

"How long did you work for them?"

"Maybe three years. They recruited me at the university. My dad was naval intel, remember?"

"You said you hated your father."

"I did. I do."

"So us, you and me, that was all…" Jess's voice grew thin.

"That was real, Jess. I didn't mean to—"

"You're disgusting," Jess spat. Her body trembled. "So you were spying on my father? Why?"

His chin fell into his chest, the laughs subsiding into sobs. "I'm no professional. They just told me to watch him, to get close to him."

"And you knew all along about Nomad? And didn't tell us?"

"I didn't know. Not back then. It was all *need to know*, and they didn't think I needed to. I thought I was doing my patriotic duty. I thought they were CIA. I found out different at Darmstadt. It was a shock to me, too." He fixed Jessica with the intensity of his gaze. "Those men, they'll be back soon. We need to get out of here."

"Who did you speak to in Darmstadt? Who was your contact?"

"I had a handler. Head of security called Maxim. That's all I know."

"And why did you leave Darmstadt?"

"Your father had come to find you."

"And you wanted to go with him? If they knew about Nomad, they must have had somewhere safe to go."

The beaten man nodded. He broke off his stare. "Please, Jess, untie me."

"Where did they go?"

"You don't understand."

"Where did they go?" Jess's voice intensified. Then she bellowed. Roared. Her father was dead. He had discovered Nomad, but they hid the secret from him.

Why? To blame it on him, while they hid like cowards, even as he sacrificed his life to try and save what was left of humanity.

"They gave me a beacon," Roger said, his voice barely a whisper. "When I left Darmstadt, my handler gave me a beacon that I could activate to get rescued. They told me to watch your father, to find out what data he had. They told me to find you."

Giovanni looked at him incredulously. "Rescued to where, exactly?"

The beaten man hesitated but relented. "There are three or more of them, and they're big, ten thousand people each. One in central Europe, one in America, one in China, and others I don't know where. Together, they're called Sanctuary."

21

TRILLS OF SONGBIRDS echoed through the dense foliage. High overhead, the sun burned bright in a clear blue sky. A flash of color in the greenery, and a parrot exploded through the leaves, squawking at the intruder in its midst.

"Mr. Erdogmus, it is time." A thickly muscled man in a black ballistic vest, a large handgun strapped to his hip, parted a palm frond to one side.

"Thank you, Maxim. You can leave me now."

"As you wish."

The man disappeared back into the jungle.

Ufuk Erdogmus breathed deeply, inhaling the scent of the black, loamy earth beneath his bare feet. He raised his face to the sun and felt its warmth, then clicked his watch, turning back on his data feeds. He liked to come here and disconnect.

"You can leave," croaked the parrot, twenty feet overhead. "You can leave."

"I know, I know." Ufuk leaned over, seated on a wooden bench—*his* wooden bench—and swept bits of dirt from the soles of his feet, put his socks on and then his black patent leather shoes.

This was his refuge, his private sanctuary *within* Sanctuary. Of course, any resident of Sanctuary could come to wander through the Forest, just as they could swim in the Ocean. But when he was here, people knew.

Do not disturb.

They knew his importance, and left him to himself.

While tying his shoelaces, he stopped to inspect a troop of ants marching single-file, each balancing a fragment of twig or leaf over its head. Insects were surviving, out in the cold, amid the dark, the ash and snow. Insects had survived a dozen mass extinction events, sometimes even thriving while other species were extinguished. But these hardy creatures would have a hard time with what was coming. Hundreds of millions of humans, possibly billions, had persevered through the initial blow that Nomad had dealt the planet, but a long, slow death-march was coming.

He stood, wiped the sweat from his brow, then adjusted his tie and brushed off his lapels before following the path Maxim had taken, pushing aside the palm fronds as he went.

Dappled sunlight fell in patches on the ground. A breeze brought a little welcome relief from the heat, and the sound of children at play drifted over the burbling of a stream he was stepping by. Breaking through the last of the vegetation, a wide expanse of green grass opened onto a sandy beach.

The children were splashing around the edge of a hundred-foot-wide patch of water they called *Ocean*. A wall of apartments curved up into the sky beyond that. People sat on the balconies enjoying the Sun. Two hundred feet overhead, the curving ceiling of the Dome swept over the top of the apartment complex, the projected images of clouds scudding across the blue sky. Ten thousand souls were sequestered here, underground, in this gilded cage.

Or gilded tomb.

He had his own apartment in the complex. The most exclusive, of course. Not a penthouse, not near the top. Down at the bottom, where the illusion of the sky and sun projected onto the Dome could fool him, when he let his imagination run rampant. There he could dip his foot into the Ocean, listen to children play, and remember what the world once had been.

His watch beeped, warning him that the meeting had commenced.

He keyed a quick response, asking them not to start before he got there, then quickened his pace, stepping off the green grass into a corridor leading under the wall of balconies. The heels of his shoes click-clacked across the polished white marble. Two uniformed men, armed with automatic rifles, nodded as he passed them. He held his pass out to another man, sitting behind a desk further down the hallway. A glowing monitor faced away from him.

"Hand on the screen, Mr. Erdogmus."

He didn't need to be told. Ufuk complied and pressed his hand against it, which allowed his DNA to be sampled at the same time his fingerprints passed muster. He gave his pass to the man.

"And what was your mother's father's name, Mr. Erdogmus?"

"Philip."

A pause. The door to the left of the desk slid open.

"Thank you, Mr. Erdogmus."

Ufuk smiled and nodded, taking back his pass. Something you are, something you have, and something you know—multi-factor authentication. He'd personally insisted on systems like this when he helped design Sanctuary. Security wasn't something to be taken lightly. Not back then, and not now. Not ever. And now he might have to overcome his own security protocols. He might have to take control.

But one thing at a time.

The door slipped closed behind him, sealing him inside. He strode along the interior corridor. A voice echoed from an open doorway ahead.

"Goddamn it," he muttered, quickening his pace.

"...another attack by extremists has all but destroyed the Vivas facility outside of Rome," said the voice.

Ufuk turned the corner, stopping the presenter, General Marshall, in mid-sentence.

"Ah, Mr. Erdogmus, glad you could join us," Dr. Müller said, standing from his seat at the back of the expansive conference room.

A thirty-by-ten-foot polished cherry wood table dominated the middle of the room. Framed pictures of nature scenes—a mountain top, a forest stream, a lush white orchid draped from a tree branch—lined both walls. A cup of coffee steamed in front of each person seated at the table, military uniforms on half of them, even though the Sanctuary council was a civilian executive.

At either end of the room were large projection screens. Maxim, the head of compound security, stood at the back, behind Dr. Müller, while General Marshall stood in front and glared at Ufuk.

"I asked if you could wait—"

"I remind you, private citizen Erdogmus, that your attendance at these meetings is a courtesy," the General said.

The billionaire flashed the military man a tight smile. The *General*—Ufuk always wanted to laugh when he heard the title thrown around. Before Nomad, Marshall had been in charge of a European Union battle group, the Gendarmerie Force, but no EU battle group had ever been engaged in operations. This *Netherlander* was a political appointee, a second-stringer who even the Dutch armed forces had tried to get rid of. Worse, his Gendarmerie was a military police force aimed at controlling civilians. But laughing would be a mistake. Insecure people tended to lash out.

"Is that Vivas Romana?" Ufuk asked as he pulled a chair from a row of them by the wall and dragged it up to the table. On the projection screen behind the General, smoking wreckage of huts and twisted metal struts of corrugated tin.

"As I was saying, it was attacked by Islamic extremists three days ago."

"Extremists? In *Italy*?"

"They mounted the attack that destroyed the Vatican before Nomad arrived. They had to have a sophisticated cell operating within Italy. It seems they are now operational again." The General switched to a new view of the destroyed surface of the Vivas installation. "And we have reports of an army of extremists amassing in the Western Desert of Egypt, on the border of Libya. They are close to the African Union encampment at Al-Jawf."

"Have you talked to them? To the survivors at Vivas?"

"We must not break protocol," the General said thinly. "No communication with individuals or organizations outside of our network for one year. No exceptions."

The mantra they had forced everyone inside of Sanctuary to repeat over and over again, the psalm of security for the saved and the faithful. Something Marshall seemed to enjoy reminding them of. Even with the European Union reduced to the dust of yesterday, its politics seemed alive and well.

"Violation of this protocol is grounds for court martial," the General added.

"I'm not military."

"Then expulsion, which is worse," Dr. Müller said from the back of the room. "Mr. Erdogmus, like you, I am here as a courtesy, and I too share your..." He grimaced and smiled at the same time. "...discomfort with our reliance on our military colleagues. But these are dangerous times. The *most* dangerous times." He paused. "You didn't contact Vivas, did you?" He held up a hand to hold back General Marshall. "I know protocol, but you do have covert operations, yes, General? To recover persons activating beacons?"

He turned to look at Maxim, who shrugged non-committedly.

"I didn't contact Vivas," Ufuk replied. "That would be foolish. And why would I contact them? I have no interest—"

"But you do have an interest in finding Dr. Rollins, yes?"

Ufuk remained silent.

"As do I, Mr. Erdogmus, as do I," continued Dr. Müller. "To find the truth."

"Rollins is dead," the General growled. "Because of that man's actions, extremists destroyed the Vatican. His betrayal began a cycle of violence that has continued even now, into what little remains out there."

"I don't know that that's true."

"Why did he leave Darmstadt in the dead of night? Like a thief, stealing data from the ESOC headquarters?" The General planted his feet wide and cast an accusatory glare in Dr. Müller's direction.

"It's obvious. To find his wife and child," the old scientist countered.

"But we offered to retrieve them," the General pointed out. "Enough. You do not need to defend him. It's irrelevant now." He took a breath. "Please, can we continue with the business of this meeting? Mr. Erdogmus, the reason we invited you—"

"My space launch facility in central Africa will be operational, as far as we can tell. But—"

"That is all we needed to know."

"Military GPS is still not functioning?"

The General shook his head after a pause.

Ufuk stood and half-bowed. "Nomad gave us all quite a bit more of a shock than we expected. Even with the models. But I'm on it. And I'm going to record the rest of this meeting, with your permission." He dropped a small device onto the table and propped it up on a stand. "You can query any questions into it, and I will respond. Thank you for having me at your meeting." He turned and exited the room.

Dr. Müller watched Ufuk walk out. The man was on very thin ice, but then, the cocksure Erdogmus knew that. They needed him,

169

and that was his power. "These extremists massing on the border of Libya, are they within striking distance of Mr. Erdogmus's space launch facility?" he asked the General.

"We have very little tactical information," answered one of the General's staff, a young man. "Our satellites were knocked out. We need to get some birds in the air."

"Have we established comms with Sanctuary America?"

"Seismic events on the American continent exceeded operational parameters."

"So they're gone?" Ten thousand of the most senior Americans, Dr. Müller knew, were in that installation.

"Might still be buried. It's only been two weeks."

And these installations had been designed to stay buried for years, Dr. Müller knew, each with their ten thousand occupants living in luxury below ground. One year of complete radio silence, with no contact except with other Sanctuary installations. Not even with the network of fifty Vivas installations. Tales of the Sanctuaries had whirled around. Everyone with money had heard of them, or at least the rumors of them. Those who had made it inside knew they just had to hang on for a year. After that, the protocol was to open Sanctuary doors, once the worst of the Nomad event had passed and the Earth stabilized.

The rebuilding would begin.

They'd saved vast libraries of genetic material, frozen embryos, veritable Arks of the Apocalypse.

"What is Erdogmus's fascination with Rollins?" asked the General.

Dr. Müller frowned. "Maxim, you had a man with him, didn't you?"

Maxim stepped forward from the shadows. "Roger Hargate. He had a beacon, but we still don't know how he acquired one. If he survived, he would have activated it by now. We would have found Dr. Rollins."

"But perhaps...perhaps it is not Dr. Ben Rollins that Mr. Erdogmus is searching for."

"Then who?"

"For *what*, might be the better question, General Marshall."

22

"I HAVE A COPY." Roger coughed.

The hangar was still, with only the wind whistling over its frame to soothe Lucca's intermittent sobs. Raffa had left Leone's body and now stood by the door, staring out into the darkness. He hadn't said a word since Leone died. Jess lay flat on her back in the improvised stretcher. The fire crackled, and she watched its light flickering and shifting against the domed ceiling. So *they* knew Nomad was coming.

But who were 'they' exactly? Did her father know?

Not possible. No way. He would have told her.

Her sluggish mind reeled. The room spun. She wanted to vomit, but forced back the bile. "What did you say?"

"I have a copy of your father's data," Roger repeated. "Not all of it, just the CDs and what was on his hard drive. It's on a memory key, in my jacket pocket. That's why I gave them the bags. I had it copied—"

"You're lying," Giovanni snarled. "I saw the look on your face. You were…how do you say…*gloating*. That was your face. If I hadn't stopped you, you'd be gone. You thought you were clever."

Clever. The word echoed in Jess's mind. Her father always told her that clever was the first cousin of wisdom, just with all the guts knocked out of it. Or was it the other way around? Was it better to be clever, or to be wise? It depended on the situation, she decided. Wisdom could get you killed for the right reasons, but cleverness could keep you alive for all the wrong ones.

"Go check his jacket." Jess shakily propped herself up again.

Giovanni rooted through a pile near the truck and found Roger's coat, and after a few seconds of rummaging, produced a matte black memory key. "Is this it?"

"It was our insurance. I was leaving it with you." Roger's voice rasped, dry and cracked. "I was doing it to protect all of you. They get what they want. You get to escape. Now they think you're dead, Jess. It's perfect. Just let me go. They'll be coming back for me—"

"How do we even know what's on here?" Giovanni frowned at

the memory key in his hand. Their only other laptop had been in the Humvee. In the rush to escape Vivas, he hadn't had time to retrieve it, along with a lot of other things he wished he had now.

"You have to trust me."

Giovanni snorted.

"You have to let me go." Roger writhed against the cords. "You don't understand."

"If they come back, we will be ready."

"You should be tying her up," Roger whined, flicking his chin toward Massarra. "Why was Vivas destroyed? Who attacked it? She came from nowhere."

"Not nowhere," Jess said quietly, trying to put the pieces together. "We met in Rome. She brought us back to the castle."

"So you met by accident?" It was Roger's turn to snort. "I was told to stay close to Ben, see what he knew and where he was going." He paused. "They told me the Rollins family had connections to terrorists."

The blood drained from Jess's face. "Who told you that lie?"

"So then who's the dead guy she dragged up here?"

Jess had no idea what he meant.

Giovanni rolled to his feet, the memory key still in his hand. "Now *that* is a good question." He walked toward the body laid out near the wall. Before he could get near, Massarra crossed from the door and blocked his way. He shoved her aside and knelt to put an arm under the dead man, firmly but gently raising him up. Massarra hovered but retreated.

"Do you recognize this man?" he asked Jess.

She squinted. Something about his face. An old man. Where had she seen him? In the photograph in Vivas. And in the car with her mother. "Is that your uncle, Massarra? You said he'd died."

Massarra didn't reply. Instead she stood, watching them, hands by her sides.

"You know him?" Giovanni propped the dead man up higher.

"I met him in Rome, when my mother and I got trapped outside our apartment."

"You see?" Roger said excitedly.

"And he was in the car with us when Massarra drove us to the castle," Jess added. "And the pictures in Vivas. They had pictures of me with him, from some security camera, they said. That's when she appeared and told us we had to leave."

His face beet-red and sweat-slicked, Roger leered at Massarra. "And *poof*...Vivas was destroyed. Tie *her* up. Find out who *she* is."

Massarra crossed back to the doorway, never taking her eyes from them.

Giovanni put the dead man down and dusted off his sweater arm. "I trusted you with my life," he said to her in a flat voice.

Her eyes moved back and forth from Giovanni to Jess, then to Roger and the crumpled, blood-soaked mess of Leone and the boys. Her body flinched, as though to go out, but something held her in place.

She closed her eyes, and her body sagged. "Abdullah-shah, the man I said was my uncle, he was a member of the Levantine council. A cleric. I was his protégé. But he was more of a father than uncle."

"Israeli intelligence?" Jess struggled to make sense of the pieces, but the sideways-sickness in her stomach intensified.

"Doesn't sound Jewish to me," Roger sneered.

Massarra hesitated in the doorway, halfway into the darkness outside.

"Please, don't leave," Jess implored.

If this woman disappeared, she'd never know the truth. The small woman seemed more of a wraith now, her image wavering in the firelight, somewhere between this world and the lands of the dead outside.

Jess needed to drag her back, into *her* world, to find peace. "I lost my mother and father for this. I beg you."

She should be angry, Jess knew, but she wasn't. She had been lied to, by almost everyone around her. Did that include her mother and father? Even Giovanni? Circles felt as though they turned within circles. Was Massarra just another level of deception? Why save her—more than once? Maybe it was her mind, still slow, or perhaps the daunting darkness of having died and come back to life, but Jess didn't feel anger.

Only sorrow.

For her family, and for the world that had been lied to. Now she needed answers. Something terrible had been put upon her family, upon everyone's families. A lie, a deception beyond all deceptions, and beneath it all—greed. If not for money, then for power and for control. Ultimately, for life. But she didn't see any of that in Massarra's eyes.

"A great wrong has been done," Jess said, her voice quiet. "Help me make something right of it."

Massarra edged back into the light.

"What's the Levantine council?" Jess said. "You can trust me, Massarra. I won't let anyone here hurt you."

"You will not understand."

"Please."

The small woman closed her blue eyes and seemed to gather herself from the inside. "We were—*we are*—a political organization representing certain…" She paused. "…groups within the Middle East and beyond." She paused again. "Islamic groups."

"But who are these groups? Do you mean—"

"Terrorists!" Roger squealed. "I told you."

Massarra looked at him, her face riven by disgust. "Not terrorists. We are a peaceful, purely political organization. We also work with resistance movements, the Kurds, the governments, even with the Israelis. The answer to our problems was not going to come from the outside, by bombing or fighting. And it was not going to come from Western politicians. The Levantine movement was started to begin again the discussion of what Islam means, the peaceful side. We wanted to bring our people together. To stop the fighting, but on our own terms."

"So you knew me?" Jess asked. "In Rome. You knew who I was?"

"Of course. We were sent to meet you."

"Sent to *meet* me?"

"Our meeting was not by chance. Is this not clear?"

"Who sent you?"

"As I said, the Levantine Council."

"It was you that attacked me and my mother in the apartment that night? You were controlling Nico?" Jess gripped the edge of her plywood stretcher, her knuckles white.

"That was not our doing." Massarra's eyes flitted to Roger.

He laughed. "I had nothing to do with whatever happened in

Rome."

"Somehow, I still believe everything from her mouth," Giovanni said, "yet nothing from yours."

"And speaking of Rome," Roger continued, ignoring him, glaring at Massarra, "remind me again, what happened to the Vatican?"

"It was destroyed."

"Hundreds of thousands killed. Incinerated. By Islamic extremists. *Her* friends."

"Perhaps," Massarra said quietly, "perhaps not."

"Are you kidding me? Who else? ISIS claimed responsibility—"

"In fact they did not. That agenda was pushed upon them by media, by your governments."

"But they didn't deny it."

Massarra pressed her lips together, balled her hands, but said nothing.

"I have a question." Giovanni raised one hand like a schoolboy. "What is so important about the Rollins family, that we have"—he frowned and shrugged at Roger—"something like the American CIA, and a secret society of Islamic clerics hunting them down, chasing them into this frozen wasteland beyond the end of the world?"

The faintest of sad smiles flitted across the Muslim woman's face. "Isn't that obvious?"

"Enlighten me."

"The Rollins family, if you will excuse me, Jessica, has become almost mythical. They are the discoverers of Nomad, of the great destroyer. The great evil that wrecked the world. Have you not listened to the radios? To the broadcasts before Nomad?"

Jess had, and she lowered her head. They blamed her father. They had to blame *someone*. "But he didn't know."

"That is not what you told me, around the fire that night."

"Around the fire?" Jess frowned. "I never said—"

"You said your father lied."

"I was talking about him lying to me."

Massarra held her hands together. "But if you remember, the Levantine councilors asked you about Nomad. Asked you if your

175

father lied."

"I thought they were your uncles."

"You said he lied."

"You know I didn't mean it that way."

"At the time, we didn't," Massarra replied gently.

The words floated through the air and swirled into a maelstrom in Jess's mind. "Wait, are you saying…that you were sent there to find the truth about Nomad, and your council thought that I said my father lied about Nomad? That he knew about it for thirty years?"

"I am sorry, Jessica." She bowed her head. "I was given a task. I didn't know what it would mean."

In the silence, the wind ruffled the hangar's fabric. A low, burbling cackle began, rising in pitch into a hissing giggle.

"And her friends bombed the Vatican," Roger cried out, gasping between sobs of laughter. "They destroyed it because you said your father lied."

Jess curled into a ball on her stretcher, pulling her legs into her stomach.

"You guys better untie me," Roger cackled. "You don't know what's coming. Let me go."

Jess tried to fathom what she'd learned. She misspoke, and that carelessness killed hundreds of thousands of innocent people. People coming to pray. People coming to pray for protection from something her father had discovered.

"Let me go!" Roger screamed. "Or you're all going to die!"

NOVEMBER 10th

Seventeen Days A.N.

23

FIRST LIGHT DRAGGED a thin dawn over the frozen earth. A suffuse gray reached down from the blackness to gradually reveal the rubble of the city around them. Jess sat, huddled under a mass of blankets, against the front of the hangar and watched Raffa and Giovanni and Hector. They stood, solemn and quiet, around the grave for Leone that Raffa had tried to dig into the hardscrabble earth below the ice and snow.

In the end, an impossible task.

A wooden cross—two beams lashed together with a length of cord—leaned at an angle from the pile of bricks and chipped cement they piled on top of Leone. The best that they could do.

Already, Jess missed the old man. He'd watched over them—their guardian angel—never taking his eyes off Elsa or Rita, nor Roger or Massarra. She'd considered him paranoid, had chided him about it, but he had paid for her jokes with his life. With their watcher gone, the mantle fell to Jess. She'd brought them all on this path, on this crusade of hers.

To end up here.

She'd never felt so weak, so ill, and she hadn't slept. She'd kept her eyes open the entire uneasy night. Roger groaned the whole time, half-conscious, alternating between apologies and threats. Delirious with fever from an infection, she guessed, or withdrawal, or dehydration or starvation—and he'd lost blood. Any of these conditions could account for his reaction. Plus he was an asshole. Giovanni refused him treatment, refused to deplete their stash of antibiotics and medicine on him.

Jess did not object.

None of them were healthy. The combination of malnutrition, stress, lack of sleep and the noxious, pervading atmosphere was eroding their immune systems. They coughed and wheezed, their eyes watered, their skins were both pale and flushed with rashes. Unable to sit upright without assistance, Jess had insisted on being helped to the front of the hangar, to say goodbye to Leone.

Standing in front of the grave, Giovanni crossed himself. Raffa stood beside him, and they spoke for a while, the teenager's face growing darker as they did. Eventually, he nodded and turned away as Giovanni trudged over the uneven ice to join Jess. "How are you feeling?" he asked her.

"Like death warmed over. That's in a good moment."

His face puckered.

"I was trying to make a joke."

"Jokes are good." He sat next to her and offered a ration pack, but she refused. Only a handful left. He insisted. "You need your strength."

"What did Raffa want?"

"He asked about Rita," Giovanni replied. "He wanted to know what happened. How Leone was shot."

Jess nodded. Raffa and Rita had been growing close. She'd seen it. Snatched moments of affection these last few days. He must have felt utterly betrayed. "So now what?"

She opened the pack and took out the crackers, offered one to him. He refused. She insisted. The early stages of starvation had begun. Five days since they'd had to escape from Vivas and leave their food behind. Five days now that they'd been on less than half rations, and soon there wouldn't be anything left at all. They'd have to scavenge to eat, or more likely, survive off whatever fat they had left on their bones.

"We can't fly."

"What if we patch the wing?"

"The Cessna can still fly. I'm saying *I* cannot fly that thing."

"What about Al-Jawf? Ain Salah said he might be able to arrange a flight."

"We'd need to be truthful, tell them we only have a copy of the data. *Maybe* a copy." He sat in silence and watched the crumpled ruins of the town reveal themselves through the morning mist. Not a fog, but fine suspension of ice crystals. Twelve below and dropping. "We can't stay here. If what Roger is saying is true—"

"They will be back for him. But not for us."

"The one advantage we have is that they think you're dead."

"*Advantage…*" Jess sniffed. "And I *was* dead. I should be dead. I was responsible for the biggest mass murder in human history." Jess pulled the blankets up to cover her face.

"What Massarra describes is just the excuse, and she says her people had nothing to do with the Vatican bombing. Besides, and I know that it's not the best consolation, but of those who died, how many would have survived Nomad?" He pulled the blankets away from her face. "And you didn't die, your heart just slowed down."

"You said it stopped." Jess took a deep breath, but couldn't feel air fill her lungs.

Was she dead? Was this hell? Had she become a shadow, cursed to wander this underworld, never dying, hearing the screams of all those she'd cast into doom? She watched the hummocks of rubble laid out into the distance, the mist swirling around them, the ghosts of the dead speaking to her in the wind scratching ice crystals across the snow. A witch, that's what she was, what she'd become. Cast the bones, see the future, that's what she'd been trying to do with her father's data.

Giovanni pulled one of the blankets around himself and joined her in staring into the distance. "So what did you see then, when you were dead?"

She closed her eyes and let herself slide back. The shock of the cold, the terror of her fingernails scraping across the ice, her desperation in begging even her attacker for help. The water filling her lungs. But then. No fear. Just sadness. "My mother, my father…you…nothing…"

"Nothing?"

"Because everything is here. Everything I love is here." Raffa and Hector still knelt beside the grave of Leone.

"There is hope," Giovanni said, his voice tender. "Just knowing places like Sanctuary and Vivas exist, humans will survive, and I want to—"

"Not if Earth hits Saturn. We still don't know what will happen in a year and a half."

"But if Earth was to hit Saturn, do you think whoever is chasing you would bother? Doesn't that prove it will not happen?"

"A million evil men now rule the world," Jess muttered.

"What?"

"Nothing."

"Listen to me." Giovanni squatted in front of her. "They think you're dead. So, we set a trap. Leave Roger here—"

"No more. I wanted to protect my father's legacy, our name, but he wouldn't want this. He'd want me to protect my family. And my name is a curse. They think I'm dead, so I'll stay dead. We change my name, change yours. We run south. The two snowmobiles we retrieved from the Vivas men who Massarra shot, they work?"

"And we have fuel, yes."

"You said we could do a hundred kilometers a day on them."

"Packed light."

Jess laughed, a hacking, wet cough of a laugh. "We don't have much left. Fuel is heavy though."

"We can't go inland from here. Not past Vivas. And over land to the south—"

"Too much up and down, too many obstacles," Jess completed the thought for him. She liked it when they made plans. "And we need to stay away from any other people, as much as possible."

It was something they'd talked about a lot. Three weeks past Nomad, whoever had survived in this wilderness, they would have scavenged the remains of what was left. But whatever they had, and whatever they found, would run out soon.

Quietly one night, Giovanni had pointed out that the biggest source of protein left was frozen human corpses, hundreds of pounds of meat littered almost everywhere they went. It was disgusting, disturbing, but true. And once that line was crossed—

"We can't get on the radio and talk to Ballie Booker and the Jolly Roger, if they even survived," Jess added. "Or Ain Salah at Al-Jawf. We need to do this ourselves."

"And whoever from Sanctuary is trying to catch you, they destroyed Vivas, if what our Muslim friend is saying is true."

Jess inhaled deep and turned to look at Massarra. A hundred yards across the airfield, at the edge of a copse of bare, frozen trees, the small woman stood praying over the gravestones she'd piled atop the body of Abdullah-shah.

She was still an enigma.

She'd lied, but somehow in a more honest way, and like Jess, she was seeking the truth. That was why she came back, she said, why she tried to lead the Vivas attackers away and braved the frozen wasteland to find Jess again. Someone had set this trap, having Jess in Rome, having the Levantine councilors meet her there, and Massarra was determined to discover who it was. In her last words to Abdullah-shah, she'd promised she would find out who had deceived them.

Someone within Sanctuary was responsible, Massarra was certain, now that she'd learned of its existence. It made sense to her. They were trying to kill Jess, to kill her father, and erase any trace of his data. Why, Massarra didn't know, but now she wanted to get inside Sanctuary herself.

And somehow, Jess was sure this fierce woman would make it in.

Jess was on a different mission now. When she'd died, when the blackness had engulfed her, all she longed to do was spend more time with the ones she loved. Now she had a second chance. Her mother and father were gone, but Raffa and Lucca, Hector and Giovanni were here.

"We run. It's what I've always been best at. Running."

Jess began to pull away her nest of blankets. Whatever energy she could muster, it was time to leave this place.

"Two snowmobiles, Raffa and Lucca on one, you, me and Hector on the other. We'll rig fuel sleds for us to pull. We'll go fast, along the edge of the water."

All of this might have been a blessing in disguise.

Without the snowmobiles, they wouldn't be able to skim along the smooth snow and ice at the water's edge. The jet's gas would work as a high-octane fuel for the snowmobiles. Her attackers thought she was dead, and they had the data they wanted. She was free. They were free to run to safety.

And they might still have a copy of her father's information.

"Roger said that in two days, another cluster of Jovian asteroids would intersect the Earth," Giovanni, pointed out. "We need to be away from the water."

"That's in two days. If an asteroid hits us, game over. And we watch the skies. If we see flashes in the sky, we head inland immediately."

"We might not see the flashes."

"We'll see the water recede if a tsunami is coming. So we ride along the edge of the water, and camp on land, as high up as possible."

Giovanni bent over to wrap his arms around her and help her to her feet. "One problem."

"Roger."

"And Massarra. Two problems."

"Let them have Roger. And Massarra can take care of herself."

"But then they'll know that you're alive. And that you have a copy of the data."

Thick plumes of white vapor filled the air between them on each breath.

"So then give him the memory key."

"That won't stop them. And you can't trust Roger..."

He was right. Jess cursed under her breath. Roger. The man was half-dead anyway, so what would pushing him over the edge into the eternal matter? And he'd spied on her father. He even revealed that he'd told Nico, when he was captured, about Sanctuary. Begged him to let him go. It was why Salman had chased them into this frozen wasteland, to get the data, to get the prize.

Massarra was another matter.

She claimed she had come back to find Jess, to find the truth, but also because she believed Jess was undertaking a mission ordained by God. She had sworn her life to Jess. It should have sounded nutball, but it didn't, not coming from her lips. The woman could be an asset, with her connections into extremist groups, but she could also be just as much a liability. She wanted to get inside Sanctuary—somewhere Jess wanted to stay away from as much as possible.

"I'll let you decide," Giovanni said, his face just inches from hers.

She took two deep breaths. "Okay. But, Giovanni, if it were up to you?"

"I would kill them both."

184

24

"IS YOUR MAN still alive?"

The Englishman balanced a jagged-edged hunting knife on the tip of his index finger.

Salman shrugged, his expression somewhere between I-don't-know and I-don't-care. Tent fabric flapped in a stiff wind. White clouds of vapor puffed out with each labored breath. "Perhaps we go inside?"

He tested his cleft lip. Raw-red and cracked. Unconsciously, his tongue darted out to wet it, and he wiped his face with the back of one dirty hand.

The Englishman laughed. "Oh, no, my peasant friend. Our arrangement does not earn you that."

In the night, they'd returned to the area next to Vivas, on a plateau overlooking it. But they hadn't entered, despite the Englishman contacting his colleagues. The passages underground had been re-opened. Just a scratch, that's all the attack had been, the Englishman said, with some civilian casualties on the surface. His men had erected a camp on the ice, and made their meeting space a ten-by-ten makeshift structure.

"I am not here to earn your table scraps," Salman spat back. "But the extremists that attacked Vivas, are they not in the hills?"

The Englishman laughed again. He turned the knife around and slammed its point into the wooden table between them. "You can't believe everything you hear on the radio, can you?"

He flipped his blond hair back with one hand.

"I think our broadcast, the one saying we had Jessica Rollins, was what got us in trouble. I believe there are warring factions within Sanctuary. Someone wants her dead. And wants this." He used the knife to poke the collection of CDs and tapes spread out on the table, next to the laptop they'd stolen from Jessica.

"The girl *is* dead."

"I know she's dead!" The Englishman got halfway up out of his seat, spit erupting as he yelled, his face mottling red. He pointed the knife at Salman. "You got her to give you...what? A bag of medical

185

supplies? And then drowned her?"

"She fell in. An accident." Rita, standing guard behind him, tensed and took a step forward.

The Englishman held up his hands, easing her back. "My man says you shot the ice."

"I didn't mean—"

"If someone in Sanctuary wanted her dead, then equally, *ergo*, there is someone in there who wants her alive. I am an equal opportunist, if nothing else. We still do not know to which faction we need to ingratiate ourselves."

"Why do you care?" Salman grunted. "You have Vivas. Why not hide there, leave this to me?"

"You think I do not want to get back inside Vivas? Have a hot bath? I want to get inside Sanctuary. If they are warring, something must be wrong."

"These Jovians?" The Englishman had explained how his experts predicted the swarms of asteroids, how the Earth wasn't finished getting its ass kicked yet.

He put his blade down. "I've heard that the Sanctuaries will open their doors after one year, to begin the process of rebuilding civilization. But I fear this may not be the case."

"How long can Vivas survive?"

"A year, perhaps two…"

"So you need them."

"Perhaps I should leave you out here. We've run simulations of the Collapse, you know." His smile was thin. "It is already starting, somewhere, out there. Ravenous humans, eating the only source of protein left—other humans. Did you know that human biomass exceeds that of any other living organism on the planet, pre-Nomad, even arctic krill? We were eating the planet, and now we consume ourselves, instead. A certain poetic justice, no?"

He wasn't really waiting for an answer from Salman, and the Italian didn't share his sense of humor.

"Now we gamble," the Englishman continued. "Activate the beacon. Tell them that we have Dr. Rollins's data. Lie, and say we have the girl, and that we need access to Sanctuary."

"What if they refuse?"

"They know I have the resources to copy and distribute the

data. But we cannot broadcast. We need to speak to whomever Roger was supposed to talk to on the other end of that device. Make sure it is not in broadcast mode, you understand?"

Salman held his hand out. Rita deposited a slab of black plastic, emblazoned with a white yin yang symbol. Roger's emergency beacon.

"How quaint," said the Englishman, "to use the yin yang as a secret symbol. Do you not see it?"

The Italian's face remained blank.

"The two small dots, they represent the two black holes of Nomad, circling each other in tight orbits, the lines radiating away outside of this are the gravitational waves. It's not a yin yang symbol. It's a graphical image of Nomad itself. Didn't make that connection, did you, my little peasant?"

Salman's face creased, the veins in his neck flaring out. "If you insult me one more—"

"You are in no position to make demands."

"Only I know the code to turn it on."

"A gift from your man, the one that you abandoned. Anyway, yes, yes,"—he flicked his fingers—"get on with it. Begin the gamble."

The red faded from Salman's face, but the angry creases remained.

Hunching his body away from the Englishman, he hid the beacon as best he could, and flipped up the cover. He keyed in the number sequence, as Roger had shown him, back at the castle when he'd activated it briefly, and spoken to someone on the other end. But the beacon's light didn't activate, the glowing blue that signaled it was on. He tried again, but it didn't work. Nothing happened.

Salman held it in the air. "It's not working."

The Englishman leaned over the table. He took the beacon and turned it over, inspecting it. "Why in God's name didn't you retrieve your man?"

"Because he was not needed."

"Do you see this?" The Englishman pointed at the beacon's main button. "That is a biometric device. I am quite sure it samples DNA and takes a fingerprint. We need Roger to activate this goddamn thing."

Salman gritted his teeth. "If he's still alive."

"Why wouldn't he be?"

"Why would he be?"

Roger's face puckered crimson red. "Let me go!" he screamed.

"Why are they coming back?" Jess asked again.

"Let me go, and I'll tell you," he whimpered.

Still hog-tied to the strut of the Cessna, his arms and feet were bound behind his back. More than twenty-four hours now. It had to be excruciating. The cut in his left shoulder had opened up again, as had the knife wound through his hand. His face was covered in scabby lesions. He was a mess.

"How about a trade?"

His glassy eyes circled around, unfocused, his head bobbed unsteadily. "Let me go. They want you, Jess. I was trying to protect you. I still can." A muted hysterical laugh burbled up from his chest. "It's our only chance. I saw the post-collapse simulations. Do you know what's coming?"

She ignored him. "Morphine."

"What?" His fish-flopping head straightened up, his bloodshot eyes meeting hers. His pupils focused.

"Jessica. No. Absolutely no." Giovanni's voice echoed from across the hangar.

He'd emptied the Range Rover, and opened the boxes, to spread their remaining supplies and tools out on the concrete floor. Hector helped him. Massarra had already retrieved one of the Vivas snowmobiles to drag up the body of Abdullah-shah, so Raffa was outside inspecting its mechanics. Lucca went down to the waterfront, by himself, to get the other one. Jess had complained that it was dangerous for him to go alone, but Giovanni insisted, said they needed to get out of here as quickly as possible.

She didn't argue.

Jess hobbled across the hangar floor. Her prosthetic leg was coming apart. Her stump bled into the harness when she moved around too much. It was excruciating, and, she feared, infected. But there was no time for that. She gritted her teeth and retrieved the medical pack Giovanni was putting together, from what they had left.

But it wasn't for her.

"Just kill him." Giovanni reached to take the medical pack out of her hands. His face had broken out in angry red sores as well.

She wrenched the med pack free and pulled out a vial of morphine.

The Italian relented, seeing it was no use arguing.

"You tell me something, I give you something," she said in a singsong voice, turning to face Roger. She dangled the vial between her fingers, and did her best to saunter back across the concrete, forcing a facade of confidence to cover the lancing pain in her leg.

Roger's eyes hungrily following the vial in Jess's hand.

"They need my fingerprints and my DNA to activate the beacon. The code alone won't work."

"So you gave them the code?" She popped the cap off the syringe she'd taken, and inserted the needle into the vial of morphine.

"Give me some."

"Tell me about the code."

He shook his head in shivering gasps. "You first."

She gripped his arm. "Hold still." She didn't need to cut off circulation to get his veins to surface. He was already straining. She slid the hypodermic in, and squeezed the plunger a quarter inch.

Roger groaned in pleasure.

"Tell me about the code."

"Six, six, four, two, eight, one…"

"Like a dial pad?"

He nodded. "More."

"And you activated it before? Back at the castle?"

He nodded again, this time more emphatically. "But I didn't talk to anyone. I turned it off. I just needed to show them."

"And who does it call?"

"More!"

Jess squeezed another quarter inch of the plunger. "Who does it call?"

"Set to channel one, that's all I know. Maxim. The head of security."

"What about the other channels?"

He shrugged limply, his eyes drooping shut. He perked up. "The last channel is broadcast. All frequencies, wide spectrum, unencrypted."

"Anything else? I've got a full dose for you, but I need to know everything."

"My ring." He held up his hand, showing her the signet with the yin yang symbol. "It's a locater. In case we lose the beacon."

"How does it work?" Jess whispered, putting her cheek next to his.

"A mechanism in it taps against my finger. The stronger the tap, the closer the beacon. Works up to ten miles away. Top of my finger, means in front. Bottom, behind. Then left and right. Simple. Give me more."

"Is the ring tapping, right now?"

"No. More."

"It's not tapping?"

"No."

She squeezed the last of it into his vein. He shuddered in pleasure.

"How does the beacon work? Can Sanctuary find them? How do they locate them?"

"Hard...hard to..." The junkie moaned, but he didn't finish his sentence.

"Roger! Wake up." She shook him, but his eyes didn't even flutter.

An engine whined outside. A snowmobile. Jess tensed, but realized it had to be Lucca. Her heart hammering in her chest, she grabbed Roger's hand and pulled the signet ring off. She put it onto her own finger.

"Nothing," she said to Giovanni, who'd stopped to listen.

No tapping.

The beacon wasn't anywhere close, but that didn't mean that their enemies weren't on their way.

"You could just fill up another of those syringes and finish it," Giovanni suggested.

Jess didn't reply. She watched Massarra, sitting cross-legged on the floor near Hector. Her implacable calm was in stark contrast to the whimpering mess that Roger had become. Maybe it was because he was painfully tied up, but Jess doubted it. She imagined Massarra would bear almost any pain with dignity. She'd even offered to take Roger's life herself, sensing Jess couldn't bring herself to do it. Jess didn't need to be a mind reader to know it was something Massarra had wanted to do for a long time.

And Massarra knew her life endangered Jess's.

She understood that letting her live created risk for Jess. But she didn't leave. She said she put her life in Jess's hands, that if she wanted to kill her, then this was God's will. More than anything else, she wanted to enact revenge, get into Sanctuary and hunt down whoever started them on this path.

Jess just wanted to run.

"We'll have to cut off his fingers," Giovanni said, pulling Jess out of her daydream. "Or burn the body, that might be easier. We can't leave his DNA around."

Jess started to shake her head, but then nodded. "We burn the bodies."

Raffa strained to pull the corpse, wrapped in bloodied blankets, across the concrete floor. This hangar was empty. Jess was ready to burn down the one with the Cessna in it, but Giovanni said to use the one a hundred yards away. No sense in burning down a perfectly good aircraft, he reasoned, when all they needed to do was torch the bodies. With a grunt, Raffa hauled the body next to the other bloodied corpse in the middle of the concrete. Sweat poured from his face, spotted pink from the effort.

"Good work." Jess patted him on the back. "Now go back, help load the sleds."

The teenager, his face already gaunt, smiled and turned to jog out of the hangar.

Leaving Jess alone.

She opened the canister of fuel and soaked the rags and blankets covering the dead bodies. Half of it splashed back onto her. She cursed her clumsiness and did her best to empty the remainder, soaking a rolled-up newspaper with the last of it.

Stepping back, she pulled a lighter from her pocket. She clicked it on.

"Ah, God…" Should she say a few words? There was nobody else here. "Please take these souls at your mercy," she whispered, lighting the gas-sodden newspaper. Flames licked to life around it.

And it felt like something needled her.

She looked at the burning newspaper. Was it prickling her somehow?

No. It was her finger.

The ring.

Roger's ring.

Tap…tap…tap.

Blood drained from her face, a tight fist of fear knotting her stomach. "Shit."

She threw the burning paper onto the rag-covered corpses and a blue-yellow flamed whooshed across the floor, sucking the air from her lungs.

"They're coming," she said aloud, more to herself than anyone who was nearby. She hopped to the door as the flames burst into the air, rushing against the roof fabric of the hangar.

Pain exploded in her stump.

She reached the doorway and waved her arms over her head.

"They're coming!" she screeched, this time with every ounce of air in her lungs.

25

AIR HORN BLASTS from the tugboats bayed in the distance. Through a cascade of hanging vines and blooming begonias, the boats were visible on the bloated gray waters of the Mississippi, busy bees pushing towering ocean-going container ships into port. Ufuk Erdogmus adjusted himself on the wrought-iron chair and checked his watch, then looked at the Café du Monde menu.

"An espresso, please," he said to the waiter.

"Of course." The young man, clear eyed with blond hair and slight of figure, took back the menu and smiled curtly.

Ufuk watched him weave his way through the crowd of patrons and past the line of customers waiting to get in. Even heaven must need good waiters, he mused, but this help staff knew their lives depended on the good graces of the powers that be.

In this world, heaven existed below ground, whereas hell was up above. Checking his watch again, he returned to staring at the ships in the distance. A projection—an illusion—but a convincing one, if you suspended disbelief. A breeze carried in the scent of salt water. Also manufactured, although the sweet fragrance of the begonias was real.

The illusion of space was critical to maintaining the sanity of the thousands of inhabitants crowded together. Escape was neither permitted nor possible. They were in prison for the full term of their sentence. The official line was a year. Then they'd open surface contact, so said the manual, and begin the process of rebuilding civilization.

Ufuk doubted it would only be a year. Not with the devastation he'd seen.

Everything down below was shiny, the air clear, but an almost-closed system like this...how long could that last? A bigger question—what *version* of civilization would they be rebuilding?

And the biggest question of all—who would be in charge?

The solar system had been thrown into chaos, the Earth bombarded daily as it plowed through the cloud of debris thrown up by the passage of Nomad. Most deadly for now were the Jovian clusters, but in eighteen months, the Earth would brush past Saturn.

How close remained a matter of debate.

Few of their satellites had survived Nomad, and they struggled to stabilize their orbits. All were heavily degraded in one way or another, and provided no better than a patchwork solution that enabled only intermittent communications and information about the outside world.

General Marshall dropped himself heavily into the seat across the table. "I'm a very busy man, Mr. Erdogmus." He still wore the blue uniform of the European Union central command, but the military here was more of a mercenary nature, although the General hadn't admitted as much to himself yet.

"I found the remains of Dr. Ben Rollins."

The General's gray mustache twitched, the scowl on his face retreating for an instant before returning in force. "We have allowed you special—"

"Only drones and robotics. No people. I did a DNA sample. It's definitely Dr. Rollins."

"Good riddance."

The waiter returned with Ufuk's espresso, and the General waved him off before he could ask him if he wanted anything.

"He was buried at a castle in Italy, not far from here," Ufuk continued. "I suspect that his daughter remains alive."

General Marshall's face puckered up as if he'd bit into a lemon. "Mr. Erdogmus, I am not sure a public café is the right place for this sort of discussion."

Ufuk picked up his espresso. "Surely, there are no secrets here, are there?"

"And I am not sure this is a proper use of our resources—"

"*My* resources."

"You are breaching protocol, Mr. Erdogmus."

"With all due respect, I know you have Special Forces teams operating outside of these walls. And who gave authorization for an emergency beacon to be given to Roger Hargate? He was low level, and my sources say he had a serious drug addiction—"

"You are walking a very fine line, Mr. Erdogmus. You do not have authorization to carry out any operations other than those

194

relating to your facilities in North Africa. And if you have recovered any of Dr. Rollins's personal effects, I remind you—"

"Of course. I will send over everything to you personally, as soon as it arrives." Ufuk finished the last of his espresso. "Thank you for your time." He reached out to shake the General's hand. "I'll have an update on North Africa soon."

The General watched Ufuk wind his way out of the cafe, then motioned to the waiter. "Filtered coffee, black."

"How many emergency beacons were there in Italy?" asked Dr. Müller, pulling up a chair next to the General.

"Six that we've accounted for, almost forty across southern Europe."

"Have you located Hargate's yet?"

"We still don't know how Hargate got one. I think Mr. Erdogmus is playing a very dangerous game. He had access to equipment such as this?"

Dr. Müller nodded slowly, his eyes narrowing. The waiter arrived again, and he smiled, shaking his head that he didn't want anything as the cup of coffee was delivered. "I've looked into Mr. Erdogmus's computer systems."

"And?" The General picked up his cup to take a sip.

"Very difficult. He's good at what he does."

"That's why he's here, why we give him so much latitude," the General sighed. "Tell me, you worked with Ben Rollins. Why wasn't he part of the Sanctuary team?"

"You can thank Mr. Erdogmus for that. Psychological profiling."

The General's eyebrows raised.

"As I said, he's good at what he does. But..." Dr. Müller hesitated. "I found information that Jessica Rollins, Ben's daughter, was at the Vivas facility just before it was attacked by extremists."

"Not surprising."

"More to the point, I also learned that Mr. Erdogmus was in touch with them. Looking for her."

"That's a serious accusation."

"Do you have any teams in the area?"

The General put his coffee down. "They've been evacuated."

"Good. The next Jovian cluster will hit tonight, centered on the Iberian Peninsula."

"Any big ones?"

"I'll say this." Müller signaled to the waiter that he wanted to order something. "It's not a good night to be outside."

Jess gripped Giovanni as tightly as she could, pressing Hector in between them. Their snowmobile rocketed into the air coming over a ledge of ice, then crashed into a snowbank. It veered wildly before Giovanni regained control, almost throwing them off. She squeezed her arms around his waist, but she slipped and had to grab onto his shoulder.

"Stop for a break?" she yelled over the roar of the snowmobile's engine.

He eased off the throttle. "What?"

"Take a break?"

Giovanni looked over his shoulder, trying to find the other snowmobile with Lucca and Raffa. He raised his left arm, his hand balled in a fist, the command for *stop*. He released the throttle and the engine noise died down to a guttural stutter.

They came to a stop and the snowmobile settled into the pink snow. It stretched in undulating waves into the distance, coated in an inches-thick granular layer. Giovanni said it was like driving in the desert. If you stopped, your vehicle would settle deep into the sand, but keep up a good speed, and the surface layer of crust was enough to keep you from sinking. So he kept them going hard, all day, almost without stopping.

Three hundred yards to their left, the coastal mountains rose straight up from the water; typical for this area of Italy. Beautiful terracotta terraces of vacation homes once lined the palm tree laden hills here, but any evidence of this past life had been erased. The hills now presented a steep, smooth surface of pink ice.

"Are you okay?" Giovanni killed the engine and stepped off the snowmobile. The oval of his parka hood was a white donut ringing

196

the ice-ball of his face, with protruding dark goggles. He pulled his facemask down and shoved the goggles up, his breath shooting white plumes into the air.

"I'm fine, I just...I need a break."

But she needed more than that.

She couldn't feel her foot, couldn't feel her legs, in fact, or her hands. The cold was brutal, made worse by the rush of wind as they burst across the ice and snow at the water's edge. Every minute of the ride was a struggle to stay upright, her bones rattled by the constant vibration.

Hector shivered violently in her arms, and Giovanni picked him up.

"We camp here for the night." He waved at Lucca and Raffa, signaling to pull up next to them.

"We can go...go...farther." Jess stuttered. She squinted into the distance. The sharp hillsides stacked up one after the other before disappearing into the mist.

The sky was the same flat gray as it'd been for the past three hours since they left. They'd raced through the town and away from the black smudge of a fire she'd lit in the hangar. Her ring had stopped tapping by the time they made it onto the edge of sea ice. By now their attackers had to have found the bodies. They'd have no reason to chase them anymore.

"This is enough for today," Giovanni said firmly.

Jess reached up to knock a chunk of snow from his cheek, but it wouldn't come free. Giovanni pulled off one mitten. With his bare hand, he felt his face and rubbed the white spot. He did his best to smile. "My old friend frostbite. No worry, it is just a small one."

"Sorry," Jess muttered. She did her best to make sure his face was covered when they inspected each other. He took the brunt of the wind.

She still felt ill, as if her veins were filled with paste, but Hector, shivering in her lap just a second ago, burbled with excitement seeing Raffa and Lucca getting off their snowmobile, twenty feet to their right. He trundled through the snow, almost as deep as he was high, to greet them. Raffa hadn't spoken much since they'd left. He had gone about his tasks quietly, forcing weary smiles when either

197

his brother or Hector spoke to him, but otherwise keeping to himself.

"I'll heat up some water," Giovanni said. "See what I can do for food. Why don't you dig?"

He'd been taught basic polar survival on his expeditions. Dig a hole in the snow to pitch tents, cover the floor with anything that might insulate it, then cover the top of the tent with a layer of snow. A rudimentary, but effective, igloo. With some body heat, it would warm up inside, above freezing, even if it was forty below outside. And tonight was going to be cold. Snow lightening flashed over distant mountaintops inland.

"We made good distance today," Giovanni said as he followed Hector to the other snowmobile. "Maybe a hundred kilometers. Two or three days and we'll be in Sicily. I've heard it's nice this time of the year."

Jess snorted and shook her head. "Something to look forward to."

She wiggled her toes in her boot. Still no feeling. It was going to be painful when they defrosted tonight. *If* they defrosted. Doing her best to hop-step through the snow, she made her way to the sled, attached by a ten-foot cord, to the back of the snowmobile. She unstrapped the cover and pulled it back.

Massarra and Roger stared up at her, tied together.

She couldn't kill them, but she couldn't release them, either. So Giovanni and Raffa had dragged two corpses, one man and one woman, from a house at the edge of the airfield. Jess set them alight. Nobody would have a forensics kit to sample their DNA. The simplest explanation would prevail.

Maybe there was something worse than death for these two, anyway. Jess almost cracked a smile, seeing them huddled together in blankets like lovers. They hated each other, and even that didn't sum up the vitriol she sensed oozing between them.

"Fuck you, Jess," Roger croaked, seeing her face.

"Not much chance of that anymore," she muttered, and then louder: "Massarra, are you okay?"

"You could untie me from this pig." The woman's face creased in disgust.

"Only if you promise not to kill him."

"I make no promises."

Jess knelt and untied their feet, and unbound Massarra's hands. Giovanni wouldn't approve, but he was fifty feet away, already busy throwing shovelfuls of snow over his shoulder.

"You two, get up and walk around a bit. Get some circulation going." At least they had to be warmer than she was. She pulled out the canister of kerosene and the stove, along with the small bag of what was left of their food.

Massarra climbed out of the sled, but Roger didn't budge.

The bag of food had exactly one soggy box of soda crackers and twelve ration packs, each a thousand calories. Enough food for six people for a day. Jess remembered reading stories of the siege of Leningrad, when people started boiling boot leather. Looked like tonight's supper would be soda cracker soup. Her stomach knotted, thinking of food.

Something squawked overhead, a high, thin shriek. A seagull. It swooped low and fluttered to land in the snow in front of Jess. It was emaciated, its feathers matted.

"Sorry, buddy, got nothing for you."

It made a tentative step toward the bag with the ration tins. Jess was about to shoe it away when another thought floated into her brain: seagull soup. The bird must have seen the gleam in her eye. It backed up, squawking even louder, and jumped into the air. Hector saw the bird and squealed in delight. Giovanni had already raised rifle to take aim.

"Leave it," Jess said. "I've had enough of death for now."

The saved soul flapped to the ground in front of Hector, who jumped through the snow to chase it. Giovanni gave Jess a look, but shrugged and put the rifle down to pick up his shovel.

"We're going to die out here, you know that, right?" It was Roger, his eyes glassy, still huddled in the bottom of the sled.

Jess balanced the stove on a compacted wedge of snow. "Don't thank me yet," she muttered, clicking the lighter in her hand. A small flame burst to life, and the ground around her lit up in a yellow glow.

At first she thought it was the lighter, but the glow brightened and shifted into orange. Was it the sun setting? She looked straight ahead, west, but the light was coming from overhead. She swiveled her head to face it, but the sun moved. Sank. The glowing ball fell straight into the horizon, and a flash of light momentarily blinded her.

Then silence.

The brilliance faded, the afterimage of a flash bulb, but there was no sound. Just the seagull cawing. And Hector laughing as he chased it.

One breath. Two.

The fireball on the horizon glowed bright. Then another bright streak of light in the sky, following the first. *Meteors.*

"Get him!" Jess yelled at Giovanni.

She pointed to Hector, at least fifty feet farther out on the ice from Giovanni.

A low rumbling shook the snow. Ice crystals danced across its surface. Jess grabbed the bag of food and the stove and threw them on top of Roger, who still had no idea what was going on.

"Get in the sled," Jess yelled at Massarra, who stood transfixed, staring at the horizon.

Jumping onto the snowmobile, Jess tried the ignition, but nothing sparked. From the corner of her eye, she saw Giovanni hopping through the snow. He yelled at Hector, telling him to come, but his screams had frozen the child in fear. She flipped out the kick-starter and tried to start the engine again, but her foot slipped off. Giovanni reached Hector and had him in his arms.

Behind him, the horizon shifted. Grew. The rumbling roar grew louder.

"Goddamn it!" She snapped down hard on the kick-starter again.

An engine growled to life, but it wasn't hers. Raffa sped forward on the other snowmobile, Lucca holding onto him, snow spraying out behind them. He spun around and gunned it toward Giovanni, but the machine tipped onto its side.

A wall of ice towered into the sky behind them. It seemed to rise in slow motion, but the wave crashed through the last hundred yards in seconds. For an instant, Giovanni and Hector hovered in space, a hundred feet above her…

The ice erupted. She felt herself accelerate, thrown into the ground. A deafening blast of heated air thundered over her. And then free fall.

To her right, the wall of ice and water swept away and climbed as it crashed into the hillside. She rolled to her left, grabbing the overturned snowmobile, the ice shifting at a sickening angle, and strained to see Giovanni. There. A black dot on the white. The other snowmobile. But a dark rift had opened in the ice between them.

A flood of freezing water drenched her and she accelerated up into space again, spinning, churning. Jess hung onto the snowmobile. The return wave grabbed the ice sheet, cracked and carried it out. She kept staring at the chunk of white she thought was Giovanni's. It boiled up into the air. Another wave crashed into Jess's ice floe, tumbling the snowmobile on top of her.

NOVEMBER 11th

Eighteen Days A.N.

26

"EAT. YOU MUST eat." Massarra held out a dented tin cup of steaming liquid.

Jess turned away, rolled deeper into the pile of sleeping bags that still smelled of Giovanni and Hector. Her sled had all the food, what scraps remained. They had nothing to eat, her boys.

If they were even still alive.

Maybe they were already at the bottom of the ocean, blue-faced, their unseeing eyes staring into endless darkness. Like her brother, so many years ago. Drowned under the ice. How many more loved ones would she kill? Ice. Water. Death. These seemed to follow her everywhere, even in her dreams.

With the maelstrom still boiling around them, Massarra had taken charge and staked two tents, end to end, into the middle of the sodden ice-sheet that had become their lifeboat. She'd emptied the sled and pushed it into the tents, offering some protection from water still sleeting over the surface in waves. Thundersnow clouds swept into the bay, quick on the heels of the meteor impact. Cold lightening crackled between dark clouds. A blizzard engulfed them. A foot of snow covered the tents.

The kerosene stove hissed, its flickering yellow flame the only source of light and heat. The ground pitched back and forth on the motion of the waves. Outside the wind howled, driving the snow in torrents against the mad fluttering of the tent walls.

Massarra had done her best to strip Jess out of her wet clothes and into something dry, but everything was damp. The temperature dropped quickly as night fell, dousing them in pitch-blackness. The soaked snow still sticking to the ice had already hardened into something resembling frozen playdough.

"It is for them that you must eat." Massarra proffered the steaming tin again. "Perhaps they are not yet in Allah's arms. It is God's will, a test—"

"Stop it!" Jess bolted upright. Pain shot through her leg stump. Fire burned in her toes as they thawed. "Is your God happy killing billions of people? I don't want your God."

"You love them, yes? Hector? Giovanni?"

Jess forced back tears. Of course she did. She loved all of them. All of the departed.

"Then eat. They may yet need *your* strength."

A wet cackle erupted from the corner of the tent. It was Roger. Massarra hadn't bothered to try and strip him down. He was curled up in a soaking corner, scraps of cardboard and anything else he could pull around him. Jess had no strength to try and help him, and no desire. She couldn't even help herself.

"Drink this," Massarra pressed the cup into Jess's hand.

She felt its warmth seep into her palm.

How many others were out there, just like her, struggling for survival right now? Struggling even harder, perhaps, to find some meaning in just the *idea* of surviving. Why? So many dead, so much destruction—it numbed the mind and senses. But each death was a unique story of love lost, dreams shattered, families never to see each other again.

"If not for you, then for them," Massarra said, her voice low and soothing.

Taking a deep breath, Jess took a sip. A thin soup of chicken soup mix, but the sweetness passing Jess's cracked lips seemed to her the best thing she'd ever tasted. Its heat slid down her throat. When had she last eaten? She couldn't remember. Couldn't even remember eating. All that remained was the pain in her stomach.

"What do we have left?"

"Some soup, five ration kits."

Five thousand calories, that's the external energy they had left to fuel themselves. Plus whatever fat remained on their scrawny frames. Roger burbled in the corner, and Jess forced herself not to think of other options.

"What else do we have?"

"Everything that was in the sled. I think."

The wind moaned, a thousand tiny fingers of driven snow beating against the tent fabric. Jess downed the rest of the soup and handed the tin back to Massarra. She sat up and clicked on her headlamp to rummage through the jumble of bags beside the sled. And there it was. She undid the sealed plastic skin of the digital radio's bag, lifted it up and turned it around before setting it down.

It glowed to life when she clicked the power button.

One thing at a time.

She could still contact people, even if she had no idea where she was. And people on the outside thought she was dead. Somebody in Sanctuary seemed to want her dead, so if she revealed herself, would that be enough to lure them out here, wherever *here* was? Of course they'd be coming to kill her, but—

One thing at a time.

And Roger, they must think he was dead by now. And she had the memory key, for whatever that may be worth. If what Roger had said was true, then Sanctuary must have all the modern, sophisticated technologies of the old world. They could locate her if they wanted to, *if* she wanted them to find her. But how to talk to the right person? Was Ufuk Erdogmus the one hunting her?

Her father had said to find him, yet she'd almost been killed in Vivas when she mentioned his name. *If* Massarra was telling the truth, then this someone was from Sanctuary, if Massarra wasn't just another layer of deception.

And Maxim, this head of security Roger babbled about. She had no idea who he was, and Roger hadn't been able to provide much detail—only about the beacon, which could contact Sanctuary's emergency recovery team. Which also might be a lie or deception.

Who else might be there?

A name floated into her memory. Dr. Müller. He was the one who had dragged her father to Darmstadt. He had seemed to want her father with him. A former colleague of her father's, she remembered.

Logic.

Her mother and father, both scientists, had instilled in her a belief in logic. These details she'd discovered were like chess pieces. Pawns perhaps, but pawns could still take kings—and pawns could become queens.

Afloat on a frozen ocean, entombed in a blizzard, hidden by darkness—how could she use what she knew to rescue Giovanni and Hector? The prospect of death created a certain freedom, a clarity of purpose, a clear line of desperation. Unthinkable risks became acceptable, any gamble better than simply giving up.

She keyed in seven-four-four-two into the digital shortwave

radio, selected the kilohertz band and turned off the sideband frequency switch, then picked up the microphone and handed it to Massarra. "You need to talk."

The kerosene stove hissed, the light of its flame flickering shadows onto the roof of the tent. The gale howled up and down in pitch.

"Tell me what to say." She took the microphone.

"Just keep repeating, 'Al-Jawf, Al-Jawf station, do you read me?' You want to speak with a man named Ain Salah."

"And what do I say if he answers?"

"Tell him that he had said he might get an airplane to Jessica Rollins, but that she's dead. Tell him you have the data."

Once the snow cleared, an airplane might be able to spot them. Wouldn't it? They weren't that far off the coast. Jess knew more-or-less where they were. More or less.

"And who do I say I am?"

"Tell them...you're my traveling companion. Make up a name."

Massarra paused, but then thumbed the *talk* button. "Al-Jawf, Al-Jawf, do you read me..."

"Just kill me, please..." said a weak voice. It was Roger, curled up in the corner of the tent.

Jess took a long look at him, then shuffled over on her knees to loosen the corded knots binding his arms. His face was a mass of bruises and lesions, his eyes ringed by angry pink welts, his cheeks sunken. She touched his slick forehead, and it burned. He was dying, anyway, and wasn't strong enough to hurt them anymore. Still, Massarra gave her a look as she untied him. Jess returned her gaze. Pity, wasn't that a virtue, as well as forgiveness?

After untying Roger, who didn't move from his fetal position, she rolled up her left pant leg and unstrapped the harness of her prosthetic. A putrid stench wafted up, and she gagged. Tenderly, she prodded her raw-red stump. Pus oozed from infected scrapes and scratches. If it climbed into her veins, it would kill her. She had no meds left. They were in the other sled. Gasping, she slid the harness on and pulled her pant leg back down.

"This is Al-Jawf," said a familiar voice, crackling through the static on the radio.

"Ain Salah?" Massarra said.

"And who is this?"

"I am a friend of Jessica Rollins."

Silence hissed on the radio. "I am afraid we cannot be of assistance. We are under attack by extremists. I am not sure how long the African Union forces can keep them out. I am very sorry, but we are evacuating."

Massarra stole a look at Jess. "Where?"

"I cannot answer. I do not know. We will stay on this frequency, wherever we are going." Ain Salah's voice paused. "If we survive."

"May God be with you."

"And with you."

The Muslim woman looked again at Jess. She shrugged, anything else?

"It's your goddamn friends," Jess spat, hitting the power button to turn off the radio. "Why are they fighting? For what?" She glared at her.

"I cannot answer for God's plan," the small woman replied quietly, but didn't shift her eyes or look away.

Now there was nowhere to go—no southern oasis of safety—even if she could recover Hector and Giovanni.

Or maybe she had it the wrong way around.

Maybe they Giovanni would save her. If they were still alive, he had to be thinking the same thing she was. Maybe they would both run aground. Maybe all she had to do was wait. They still had fuel, still had the snowmobile, assuming its engine wasn't flooded with water.

But where would they go? South. Still south.

Massarra took Jess's hand. "What about the boats?"

"There are no boats. There never were any." Another one of Roger's lies, she'd found out. One that had trapped them.

"Not those boats. The jolly boat."

Jess's mouth fell open. The Jolly Roger. Last they talked to Ballie Booker, he was rounding Gibraltar. By now he had to be deep into the Mediterranean. But those meteor strikes, they were west. Exactly where Ballie and the Jolly Roger should be. But that boat had survived Nomad.

She turned the radio back on, keyed two-one-eight-two and

pushed the "U" sideband frequency. She handed the microphone back to Massarra.

"Ballie Booker, he's captain of the Jolly Roger. Try to raise him."

Massarra clicked the talk button. "Jolly Roger, Jolly Roger, do you read."

"Who is this?" a voice answered immediately, loud, clear, no static.

Tears stung Jess's eyes. "Giovanni?" she blurted out.

NOVEMBER 13th

Twenty Days A.N.

27

"ARE YOU THERE?" Massarra whispered into the microphone.

Silence.

"Yes," came the reply, Giovanni's voice, but almost unrecognizable. The radio hissed static, the signal was getting weaker, but that was only half the problem.

He was getter weaker, too.

"It is still snowing," his voice continued, "and very cold. Fifteen below, at least."

Jess rocked back and forth, fidgeting her hands together. She leaned forward to open the flap of the tent. No snow. Just a slate-gray sky.

Two days of floating on this Godforsaken sea.

"Ask about the boys," she whispered.

"And Hector?" Massarra said into the microphone.

"He is fine—" Giovanni started to say, but was interrupted by a tiny voice: "*Jessica ci sei?*"

Muffled voices on the other end of the radio, the older man softly, "*No, no, Hector non possiamo parlare con Jessica,*" and then the child, "*Ma io ho fame.*"

Jess understood: *I'm hungry.* She held back tears. She was desperate to speak with Hector, tell him she was fine, that everything was going to be okay. But she couldn't risk her voice over the radio. Not yet. And she couldn't lie to the boy.

After a pause: "*Lo so, vai a giocare con Raffa.*" Scratching and ruffling. "We are cold and hungry, but not bad. More of problem is water. I'm melting snow in cups, but...and Lucca has a very bad stomach last night."

"Bad stomach?"

"Diarrhea." Another pause. "But we are okay."

He said the words, but Jess heard the strain. In the cold, calories were a problem. The human body needed much more energy to sustain itself in the cold. Arctic explorers consumed thousands more calories a day, Giovanni had explained to her once. Her boys had no food. And no water.

Dehydration was even more of an enemy.

They were covered in snow, but eating it lowered the body temperature and induced cramps. The snow wasn't just snow, but filled with tiny particles of ash, which could be toxic. Even if it was only an irritant, diarrhea would dehydrate them quickly.

The motion of the waves rocked the tent fabric.

Jess clenched her fists and looked at the compass in her lap. She wasn't sure if north was north anymore, but all compasses at least registered the same thing. Their slab of ice seemed to be floating southeast, according to hers, where Giovanni's was headed more to the west, according to his compass. They'd been caught in a current, or a wind, or something. Last time he'd gone outside, his ice sheet was surrounded by open, dark water.

In the night, they'd tried Al-Jawf again, but with no response.

The extremists must have overrun the camp, or something else, but there was no contact. They had sporadic contact with some other survivor camps, but nothing close by. Jess kept the communication frequency with Giovanni the same frequency as they talked with the Jolly Roger, but so far they hadn't heard anything from the boat, either.

No help coming.

"Massarra, we will talk later, yes? In three hours."

"Radio off," Massarra confirmed.

Batteries were another problem.

Where they started with hundreds of them, to power their LED headlamps and more, they'd been scattered and lost. They had only a handful left, and they weren't the right size to power the radios. Giovanni had jury-rigged some to power the old analog radio he was talking on, but how long that might last was anyone's guess.

The rocking motion of the ice changed. They'd hit something. It had happened before. A lot of other icebergs were floating in the water. Massarra got up and pulled on her boots to investigate. In the corner, Roger groaned. He was extremely ill. They were all sick. At least they were warm, with the kerosene stove, and could melt snow with it.

"Do you want some water?" Jess filled her tin cup and offered it to Roger.

"I want to go home," Roger whimpered. He wept in tiny sobs.

He'd been delirious most of the night.

"Jessica! Come outside."

"What is it?" Her heart rate kicked up and she reached for the rifle.

"Land."

She reached for her boots instead, and a second later jumped up through the tent flap.

Glistening white cliffs shimmered below an ashen sky. The water's edge was just visible as a crumple of snow and ice, not more than a few hundred yards from where their ice floe had log-jammed with other flat slabs into a patchwork of white. Outside the tent, it was bitterly cold, and Jess shivered. "Do you think we make it?"

"The ice will crust. Maybe a few hours."

In the night, Jess had heard the seagull crying. She'd had a feeling they weren't far from land. Now a terrible decision she'd been hoping she wouldn't have to make. She almost wished they hadn't run aground.

All night, on the radio, Giovanni had asked Massarra to make sure they continued south, continued on their mission. Asked her to promise him. She hadn't, and neither had Jess. She'd been on the verge of revealing her identity on the radio, rambling about her father and Sanctuary, on the wild assumption that *someone* had to be listening. Maybe that someone would come and get them. A long shot, but better than no shot.

But now she could get to land.

Now she had to decide.

"There is something I want to say." Massarra stood with her back to Jess.

"I can't leave them."

"I know you blame me for terrible things, and I cannot answer your accusations. But the fight we are fighting now, we are on the same side. We fight the people that hid the existence of Nomad, from you and your family, and from the world. If we let them win, they will enslave what's left of this world. We need to find a way to strike at them. To stop them."

Jess let seconds slip by as she absorbed the words. Finally she said: "I just want to get Giovanni and Hector and the boys. Your fight is not mine."

Massarra remained silent.

Jess grabbed the tent flap and pulled herself back inside. "Roger, hey, wake up."

"Huh…"

"Think we can still fly that airplane?"

"What airplane?"

"The one back at the hangar."

A weeping giggle burbled from his nest. "You'll never find them. Even in good weather, with working instruments, doing a grid sweep over the ocean almost never finds anyone. This whole time, there's never been a cloud ceiling of more than a thousand feet. No visibility more than a few miles. There's thousands of kilometers of open ocean—"

"Just show me how to take off, you don't need to come with me."

"Landing is more of the problem."

"Let me worry about that."

Massarra pushed her way through the tent flap and pulled off her gloves. She squatted by the kerosene stove and warmed her hands.

Jess glanced at her, then back at Roger. "Show me how to take off, and I'll make you a trade."

Crews of workers pulled wreckage of sheet metal and plastic into piles on the snow-laden fields. The Vivas beacon was lit again, bright streaks of light stabbing into the fog from the villa atop the hill above it. The workers were shoddy, there were no earth moving trucks. Salman stood and watched the work in silence. No matter what this Englishman said, Salman sensed the damage to Vivas was much worse than he admitted.

This Englishman didn't just *want* to get into Sanctuary.

He needed to.

They'd barely escaped from the coast with their lives two nights before, when the meteors hit. They'd camped near the beached cruise liner. The sea had risen up and swamped the town. The Englishman lost half his remaining men, a toll to add to the three

216

in the poorly executed attack two days before, and those who perished when Jessica Rollins had escaped.

This Englishman wasn't so smart. He didn't know everything.

And he was desperate.

Salman knew desperation, could smell it on a man's skin, spot it in his eyes. The more he became immersed in this, the more he sensed fear. He realized he was a pawn in someone else's game. When his nephew, Nico, had called him and talked of a government conspiracy, he hadn't paid much attention. He'd only listened to the part about the Baron Ruspoli's gold. The more he thought about it now, the more it became clear that others had lured his nephew Nico into this.

That woman, Jessica Rollins's mother, the Tosetti, hadn't been related to his family, hadn't been connected to the old blood feud. Someone had played upon his nephew's obsession, spoon-fed him lies, and lured the Rollins family into Italy to coincide with Nomad. Whoever that was, they were still pulling strings from faraway, while everyone here danced as puppets in a drama written by someone else.

The time had come to get off the stage.

Salman wet his cleft lip and turned to re-enter the tent. He almost gagged from the stench. Spread out on a table in the middle of the space were two decomposing, fire-blackened bodies.

"Within the hour we should be able to determine if one of these is your man Roger," the Englishman said, seeing Salman. "We might even be able to activate that beacon, if we can scrape a fingerprint from one of your samples."

Salman did his best to look impressed.

"But I think it would be best if we kept the beacon, and Dr. Rollins's laptop and data underground, do you not?"

Without the beacon, without the data, Salman knew his life wouldn't be worth spit to this Englishman. How could the man smile at him with that stupid grin and make threats as if he was doing him a favor?

"Of course, yes, of course," Salman replied, effecting his most ingratiating of smiles.

"But I think this is not your man." The Englishman smoothed back his blond hair. "It makes no sense. If they wanted us to know that your man was dead, and not chase them, why burn the bodies?"

"A delay tactic?" That was obvious to Salman the moment they found the blackened corpses, but the Englishman hadn't wanted to press on. A decision that might have saved their lives. If Roger had gone over the water, if he wasn't dead before, he most certainly was now.

"Sir, sir." A boy, not more than sixteen, with shaggy brown hair, came into the tent holding what looked like a radio and handed it to the Englishman. A note was attached.

The Englishman scanned the note. He turned to Salman. "Please excuse me for a moment?"

Salman nodded. "Of course." He exited the tent the same way he came in, but stayed close enough to listen. He might be old, but he had excellent hearing.

Inside the tent, the radio hissed.

"I am here," the Englishman said, his voice muffled.

"This is Roger Hargate, I want to speak with a Vivas representative," crackled a voice over the radio.

Salman's stomach turned.

"I am such a representative," the Englishman answered.

"Prove it."

"I am standing in front of what we thought was your burnt corpse."

A pause. "Is Salman with you?"

Another pause. "He is not."

The brown-haired boy appeared through the tent opening. "Mr. Salman, please, could you move away?"

The Englishman waited for his boy to return. He nodded. Salman was out of earshot.

"What can I do for you, Mr. Hargate?"

"Do you have the laptop and data, and my beacon?"

A smile crept across the Englishman's face. "I do indeed."

"I have specific information that isn't in what you have. I copied it, deleted things. I'm coming in, and I need to speak to my handler at Sanctuary."

"I am very happy to hear that."

"No tricks, you understand? I've hidden the data. If anything happens to me, it will get out. I promise that."

"You have nothing to fear from me."

"And I have a terrorist, one of the extremists that was responsible for the Vatican bombing."

"Excuse me?"

"And the attacks on Vivas. We think someone from Sanctuary is involved. I'm bringing her in."

"Where can we find you?"

"Just give me your location."

NOVEMBER 14th

Twenty-One Days A.N.

28

SMOOTH HILLS OF ice drifted into view in the distance, each ridge slowly coming into focus through the frost-mist. Each one seemed a million miles away, felt like a distance that she could never hope to cover, but Jess held on and gritted her teeth.

She'd spent one last night in that tent on the ice, then abandoned the camp and sled. The wicked storms of the nights at least brought a merciful layer of soft snow to cover the ice. The tsunami had sloshed water onto the shore, and much of it congealed before it could slip back away into the ocean. The landscape looked beaten, softened into submission by each of the poundings it received.

Jess felt sympathy for this once beautiful terrain.

The vibration of the snowmobile's engine burrowed its way into her bones and brain, each ridge of snow she scaled an agony. Her body was far beyond exhausted. Everything hurt. Her stump, most of all. Perhaps she could just cut it off, her brain giggled, but she couldn't. It was already cut off. Stop thinking stupid thoughts, keep in the here, stay in the now. Think of Giovanni, of little Hector, slowly freezing to death out there, somewhere.

Each wave of snow rose up and fell away. The snowmobile raced forward with its three riders. Massarra's hands were bound together, her legs tied to the chassis of the machine. She sat between Jess and Roger, who brought up the rear. She wasn't sure he was strong enough to hold on by himself, so Jess had strapped him in as well, tied cord around all three of them. She did her best to hydrate them all before they left, and force-fed them the last of their food.

Except for one tin of rations.

That she hid in her parka's pocket. She was saving that for her last meal, for a quiet moment of prayer. And she did pray to God, to anyone who was listening. She screamed in her mind, funneled the anger and frustration into keeping herself alert. She played whatever mind games her head needed to keep moving forward.

How far had they drifted?

Twenty hours?

That couldn't be more than a hundred kilometers, could it? They started about a hundred kilometers south of Civitavecchia, when the wave hit them. How far had it carried them, in its roiling madness? She constructed circles within circles on the edge of the boot of Italy's map in her mind.

Mile after mile, she urged the machine onward and watching the flat gray sky.

Would it dim, would night come before she could get there?

The thought circled in her head, and kept her hand pressed back against the throttle. She kept her eyes on the hills, watching for bandits, watching for avalanches. Each smudge in the sky brought her stomach into her throat—getting caught in a thundersnow, out in the open, would surely kill them. As would some fantastical flying machine from Sanctuary, or some other horror she couldn't imagine.

Or a flash in the sky, another meteor.

Or perhaps just falling through the ice into the frigid waters below.

Everything in this world wanted to kill her, *had* already killed her once. She cursed God, threatened Him, begged Him to take her and spare the others.

But there was no answer.

Every time she rounded a point of land, she expected to see the low bowl of Civitavecchia, see some evidence of its skeletal remains, but only another blank canvas of undulating snow would be revealed, and even that would disappear into the mist. She cheated as far as she dared, cutting straight across the bays in a straight line, trying to reduce the distance. Far out in each bay, the walls of ice disappeared, and she became alone, a single point of existence in the mist, driving forward through her pain and fear.

Lost in her head, she almost didn't see the rubble rising through the snow to her right.

Easing off the throttle, she angled the snowmobile toward the sloping hills that were gentler now. She couldn't feel her hands, or her foot. Even the pain in her stump had disappeared. She could barely move. An effort just to steer the handlebars. The hills here looked familiar, but was this the town?

She squinted to see through the ice-mist, easing the gurgling engine onward.

"This is it," whispered a voice behind her.

Massarra.

"But, where…" Jess's voice trailed off.

If this was Civitavecchia, where was the massive cruise liner in the middle of the city?

"Washed away."

Jess gunned the engine and searched for a way up off the ice onto the seawall. Massarra was right, she had to be. This was the town, but where was the boat? Her stomach knotted painfully. How far did the water carry into the city? She craned her neck around and scanned the horizon, but nothing, just the mist joining up with the ice, an indistinct gray soup.

Gray.

It was getting darker. "We have to hurry."

She recognized a hump of snow as the jetty, near to where she'd fallen under the ice, and raced the snowmobile up it and onto the edge of where the concrete wall had been. Metal beams stuck out of the ground, twisted around each other, with debris piled against them. This had to be it.

The snowmobile slid to a stop beside the wreckage.

"Roger, help me." Jess did her best to jump off the machine, disentangling herself from the ropes she'd used to secure her human cargo.

The man mumbled something incoherent. She grabbed him by the throat of his parka, shook him awake. His bloodshot eyes opened. "What?"

"Help me dig."

She'd been surprised by Roger when she coaxed him into talking on the radio. How he'd managed to come to his senses enough to be coherent. Must have been the adrenaline that came from realizing that all hope was not lost. At least, not for him. Not yet. She gave him one more look in the eye, decided it was useless, and dropped to her knees.

One breath, two breaths, Jess pulled some oxygen into her lungs and grabbed the avalanche shovel from the side of the snowmobile. Another of Giovanni's supplies that was left in the sled. He made them all carry one. Good for digging out of snow, but also good as a weapon.

It unfolded and snapped together easily.

She shoved its point into the snow as hard as she could. It wedged maybe a half-foot deep. With all her strength, she pulled away a wedge of snow and raised the shovel over her head and slammed it down again.

The sky grew dimmer, almost by the minute. She threw the shovel into the snow again, this time hitting ice. It had to be here, please God, it had to be. Shovel up. Shovel down. Pain. Spit dribbled down her face and she wiped it with the back of one gloved hand.

Someone dropped into the snow next to her. It was Roger, another avalanche shovel in his right hand. He feebly dropped it into the pit she'd started and scraped away some snow. She waited for him to get his hand out of the way and slammed her shovel back down. The ice cracked and she dropped her shovel to begin picking away chunks of frozen snow and ice. She dug into the softer snow beneath.

And there, an orange flash of plastic.

Just where she'd left it, lashed to the huge metal moorings on the seawall. The bags she'd emptied out of the Range Rover, the collection of odds and ends of gear she couldn't imagine any use for. She heaved away chunks of congealed snow. Three bags, four, they were all there. She didn't have time to dig them out, though, but instead grabbed a length of the cord from the snowmobile and looped it through the bags handles.

"Get back on," she told Roger.

She secured the other end of the rope to itself, started the snowmobile back up. Grinding forward through the snow, it pulled the bags out in a clump behind them. She gunned the engine and headed up to the hangar.

"Duct tape can fix anything."

Roger slapped the Cessna's wing and showed off his handiwork. Strips of gray tape crisscrossed the leading edge of the airfoil where Rita had blown away chunks with the shotgun. A dozen more gaping wounds still needed to be patched, and he limped down off the crate he balanced on and moved it sideways.

He looked like a crazed scarecrow.

Jess did her best to smile encouragement. He was barely recognizable as the man she'd once known; his cheeks sunken, translucent skin flaking away over angry red sores. His clothes hung off him. But there was a manic energy in his eyes. Maybe some of the food and water she'd forced into his mouth in the morning had some effect, but it was probably a sense of finality, some end to the pain.

Or a mission.

Or maybe even forgiveness.

He'd tried to talk to her, tell her how sorry he was, but she didn't want to hear it.

A roll of tape hung gingerly in his injured left hand. Jess had first used the tape to attach a wood stick to the sling holding his arm, so he could hang the tape on it. She was busy using another roll of tape to try and fix the harness on her leg. It had almost completely come apart, so she wrapped duct tape around her pasty white thigh, trying not to imagine how much of the soft flesh might come away if she pulled the tape off.

It just had to hold for a few hours. No more than that.

Under cover of the hangar, they'd untied Massarra. She didn't say a word, but took the rifles and stood by the open door. They didn't bother to try and heat the hangar. It was too big, and they wouldn't be here for long enough. And anyway, Jess didn't want to feel her toes. She was sure they were frozen solid. The pain of defrosting them would be intense. Her hands were bad enough, every effort to use her fingers created shooting pain that brought tears to her eyes.

Jess pulled another length of tape around her leg and cut the strip. Just this effort was enough to get her breathing heavy.

Sweat beaded on her brow.

On the ground at her feet she'd spread out what weapons they had left—two rifles, a half-empty box of cartridges, a hunting knife and two of the grenades.

She looked around the hangar, pausing for a moment.

Somehow, it felt like home. They'd spent days here, Giovanni and Hector and her, huddled together. Now she was alone. The spray of blood against the door where Elsa was shot, the pool of blood near the strut of the Cessna where they'd tied up Roger, all of it reminded her of Giovanni.

When they arrived, one of the first things she did was open the radio and get Massarra to try and reach him. The signal was even weaker, which meant they were traveling in the opposite direction. At least this narrowed the possible search circles. But Giovanni didn't make any sense. He was delirious.

There wasn't much time.

Finished taping her leg, Jess rolled her pant leg back down and stood to test it. She sat down and opened one of the sacks they'd dragged up from the water's edge. She pulled out the parachute and inspected it. Still looked intact. Good enough. Her plan depended on a sequence of things going right. She was amazed the plane was untouched. The water hadn't reached up this high into the hills. But she would have had to come up with some other plan, if none of this was here.

"You're crazy, you know that?" Roger said, watching her.

"Will it fly?"

He climbed off the crate and inspected his work. "It'll take off." He'd already tested the engine, the first thing they did when they came in. It fired up on the first try. Old technology, but reliable. "Just follow the compass heading like I showed you, and keep to at least two thousand—"

"I know."

"Do you want to go over the takeoff sequence again?"

"Get it outside first. Get the engine going again."

"And then what?"

Jess pulled a blade from the ground next to her. "The hard part."

"I'm not sure I can do this."

She took a long look at him, then nodded at Massarra, who watched them from the doorway. "I think you'll be surprised what you can do, Roger, with the right incentive."

29

A GLOWING ORB floated in space. It pulsed from dim to bright and back before coalescing with another. As the orbs merged, the larger grew in size. In the center of the translucent construct a cloud of angry data bees buzzed. Ufuk Erdogmus reached up to calm and ease them into the probability pipeline.

"Was it Roger Hargate?" he asked.

"Ninety percent correlation," replied a disembodied voice. "Subject was under extreme physical stress."

"Torture?"

"Unlikely."

"Frequency bands?"

"Six before the transmission was received. Manual wide spectrum—or an attempt at it."

Ufuk collapsed the three-dimensional holograms containing the latest radio intercepts. In front of him, a detailed image of the western coastline of Italy morphed into shape. The map glittered with dots, each one representing some event or some related collection of information. Some of the dots glowed as red orbs, like the ones he'd just collapsed. These represented a probability of the location of Jessica Rollins. Almost all of them predicted she was already dead.

"And this Iain Radcliff—"

"The Head of Security at Vivas Romana." An image of a blond-haired man appeared in space in front of Ufuk, alongside a graphic detailing everything they knew about Radcliff. He scanned it quickly. Born and educated in the United Kingdom; studied Law at Trinity College, Cambridge. Served as an officer in the British Army for eight years, after which he took up positions at several prestigious private global security firms. The type of individual Erdogmus had learned not to underestimate.

"He has 'the data', that's what he said?"

"And the laptop."

"What's the probability this is what we've been looking for?"

"I doubt you need me to answer that."

Ufuk smiled.

He'd modeled Simon's conversational interface using his own psychological profile. Simon had evolved into a personal assistant, an artificial intelligence he could call his own, but not the only one he controlled. If the number of people he could bring into Sanctuary had been limited, the number of AIs was unlimited, as was his sizeable army of drones and robotics.

Maybe that was why the rest of them feared him.

And they *should* fear him.

Ufuk said after a pause: "We're committed."

"Should we reroute resources from North Africa? And Australia? This will trigger—"

"Do it."

"And disengage with African Union forces?"

Ufuk grabbed the three-dimensional model with both of his hands and spun it around, looked at it from another angle. "Just what are they up to?" he muttered. "Any contact with Saturn yet? With our satellites? With Mars First?"

"You would know."

"Okay…okay…"

"Sir?"

"This is it, Simon. We need that data."

"They will see this as an act of war."

"Then bring everything we've got."

Jess shivered and tried to pull the blanket around the shoulders of her parka, but the woolen fabric was stiff with blood. Under her gloves, her hands were slick with it as well. The effort was too taxing to bother to clean it off. Massarra and Roger were gone, and she was alone.

So utterly alone.

She peered into the gloom surrounding her. Nothing moved. Just deathly quiet. The darkness gathered. No sunset, just the dome of gray around her deepening to black.

She sat on an upturned crate next to the Cessna, now parked outside the hangar. The temperature had dropped to at least twenty below, but the cold was good. It hardened the layer of ice under the snow, and made the air thicker. Easier to take off in, Roger had assured her, easier to fly in. And she didn't mind the cold, not anymore. Like Giovanni had said to her, you can get used to it.

Her foot still had no feeling.

She was afraid to take the boot off to see what was under there, afraid to smell a gangrenous stench. Black-blue swollen toes, she was sure. She'd already lost one foot, so what was one more? She tried to tell herself this, but she felt considerable affection for her last five toes. Would she never paint a toenail again? And when she took off her hat earlier, for the first time in days, her beautiful blond hair fell out in clumps. She must look awful.

Stupid thoughts like these crowded her mind.

She tried to push them away.

She wanted to curl up into a ball, sit still in the coming night and let the embrace of the frost-world take her again into that warm dark burrow of forever. But her father's voice tickled in the back of her mind; seemed to call to her from the mist. Never give up, it whispered. The shame on her family would never be undone, the black mark never erased if she gave up.

She'd pulled his picture from her pocket—sodden, and smudged almost beyond recognition. She wanted to stare into his eyes, somehow let him see what she was seeing, but he'd never been where she was, had never faced what she faced.

He was gone. So was Giovanni. So was everyone.

Utterly alone.

I am the Nomad, she thought grimly. A lonely black hole bringing death.

The radio was in front of her. She faced in the direction of Giovanni, by her best guess, and bowed her head, in a prayer to her Mecca, then pulled off one glove and turned the shortwave on. Its switches and dials glowed to life. She let herself breathe. She checked her watch, and clicked the *talk* button on the microphone. It didn't matter anymore if someone heard her.

"Giovanni," she whispered, and then louder: "Giovanni, do you read me?"

Static hissed.

"Giovanni, please, do—"

"I am here," answered a tiny voice, hidden deep in the crackle of the static.

"Thank God," Jess whispered, gritting her teeth to hold back tears. She didn't want him to hear her crying. "Has anything—"

"Ice does not sink."

"But I mean..."

After a long pause: "We are still adrift."

She closed her eyes. Exhaled. The effort it took him just to speak seemed immense. "How are you? The boys?"

"They are well. I am giving them what water I can melt."

"Giovanni, you need to—"

"They are younger, stronger." He took a deep breath. "Someone wants to speak with you." Shuffling sounds.

"Jessica?"

This time she couldn't hold them back. Tears rolled down her cheeks. "Hector, *come stai?*"

"I am good, *very* good."

She knew Giovanni had told him to say it. Just like that. "I'm glad to hear that." His voice was clearer than Giovanni's.

"I miss you, Jessica." He pronounced it Jess-eee-cah. It always made her smile. "And I want tell you something."

"Yes?" Her hand holding the microphone trembled.

Through the static, she heard voices. Giovanni encouraging the boy.

"I love you, Jessica."

In her mind, she saw them clearly. Giovanni curled up around Hector, his cheeks ruddy red. Lucca and Raffa quietly watching, keeping close. It had to be dark, just the glow of the radio's lights. Their tent sagging under the load of snow. And freezing cold. A tiny speck in an ocean of black, a slip of ice with its human cargo.

"*Ti voglio bene*, Hector," she wept into the microphone.

"Do not do this." It was Giovanni, taking the radio back from Hector. His voice a murmur. The signal was getting weaker. Distance. Or batteries. Or both.

"It's too late," Jess answered, taking a moment to regain herself.

"If not for me, then for him. Save yourself."

She stared at the radio. How much she wished she could squeeze herself into its wiring, spread into space and find herself with them on the other side. "I'm sorry. For everything."

"Don't be sorry."

"I don't know what else to say."

"I believe…" A long, wheezing cough. "I believe Hector said it all. Hold, on. The radio's lights are…"

Static hissed.

"Giovanni?"

Nothing.

"Giovanni?" she said, her voice rising, but she realized it was hopeless. She waited a few more seconds before turning the radio off.

Last rites. Last ritual.

She pulled her final ration pack from her jacket pocket and peeled off its wrapper to spread its contents on top of the radio. Her last supper. Crackers and cheese paste. Cashews. A pack of cocoa. She'd saved her favorite for last. The foil package main course read: Chili with beans.

She didn't have much time. It would be pitch black in an hour.

Blowing on her bloodstained fingers, she tore off the top of the foil pack. She didn't have the energy to warm it with the flameless heating pack. About to squeeze some of the chili into her mouth, something moved in her peripheral vision. She turned. Eyes watched her from the shadows of the hangar.

She wasn't alone, after all.

"It's okay, come."

The eyes multiplied into four.

Jess's mouth salivated painfully in anticipation, but she gave up on squeezing some into her own mouth and held out the pack of chili. "Here, take it." She put it down on the snow next to her.

The dog and his boy solidified from the gloom. The dog darted forward and retreated in advancing circles; the boy came behind. She picked up the parachute, the one she'd recovered from the shore, and put its straps over her shoulders, tightened its buckles. The boy took the chili pack and crackers and beat a hasty retreat to share them with the dog.

The two of them weren't alone.

And she wasn't alone, either.

Taking the radio, she left the rest of the ration pack on the crate, and climbed into the Cessna's pilot seat. She felt better about wearing a parachute, but what would it matter? She waited for the boy and dog to take the rest of the food, smiled at the boy's *grazie, grazie*, and waved them back.

Okay.

Her scribbled notes were duct-taped to the dashboard. She turned on her headlamp. White clouds of vapor dissipated on each quick breath.

Altimeter. It registered just under a thousand feet. Her note said to keep it above two thousand five hundred, to make sure she cleared any coastal mountains. Assuming she managed to get airborne. Airspeed. Zero now, but to get airborne she needed to get that above sixty knots. He'd said to try and get as much speed as possible before lifting off. That it would be a fight over the snow.

What else?

Vertical speed indicator. That she didn't need, not really, but the attitude indicator was critical. She needed to keep it level, once she got up, and that would be hard to tell in the dark. She searched for a knob marked *mixture* and set it to rich, pulled the choke out and made sure the trim was set to ten degrees.

Enough.

She turned the ignition switch, and the instrument panel lit up. The engine whined, and the propeller turned, once, twice, pop, pop, and then in staccato bursts the motor roared to life. The Cessna jerked forward, but then stuck fast in the snow. She turned the running lights on to illuminate a carpet of snow ending in gray mist. This was no time for half measures. She gritted her teeth and turned the throttle to maximum.

The engine's noise was almost deafening. The aircraft surged forward, the wooden skis Raffa had strapped around the wheels cresting over the hard pack and rattling against chunks of ice. Wind whistled past the cockpit. All she could see was a patch of snow, maybe a hundred feet in front of her. The plane accelerated. Twenty knots. Thirty. Thirty-five. She held the yoke, kept it pressed slightly down as Roger had instructed.

The Cessna crashed into a snowdrift, sending up an explosion of snow fragments. It bounced to one side but righted itself, slowing back down to thirty knots. In the gray distance, a smudge appeared. The buildings at the end of the runway.

Forty knots. Fifty. The buildings loomed larger. Sixty. The plane thumped up and down through the snow, but each bounce it seemed lighter. Sixty-five. She pulled back on the yoke, but not too far. The plane bounced once more and sailed upward. The buildings disappeared.

Seventy. Eighty. She turned the throttle down.

She was airborne. Jess hadn't noticed, but she'd been holding her breath. It came out in a single gush and she gulped in a lungful of air. Her hands shook violently, but she held the yoke as steady as she could and watched the attitude indicator. Not more than ten degrees.

Below her, a hazy impression of the wrecked town spread out in the last of the light. Carefully, carefully, she turned the yoke counterclockwise and felt the plane bank. Gentle. Ever so gentle. Not more than ten degrees. The plane buffeted up and down in the wind. She turned toward the sea, and for a moment, let the nose guide her to the water.

Saying a small prayer to a god she wasn't sure she believed in, she turned the yoke further, banking around more.

As the black of night wrapped itself around her, she turned the propeller of the airplane inland. Her headlamp illuminated the bobbling compass in the middle of the dash. Taped next to it was the heading she needed.

Two thousand five hundred feet. Keep it level.

30

EXCRUCIATING PAIN FLASHED up through Roger's left arm each time the snowmobile dipped in the snow or veered left. He did his best to keep his weight off his much-abused left hand and steer with his right, but this was the hand that controlled the throttle as well. His left was duct-taped to the handlebar, a makeshift splint reinforcing the connection. Like everything now, a kludge as things fell apart—the world, their bodies, their minds.

At least he was going back. Completing his mission. Of a sort.

What had he done? What did it matter? The world was destroyed. But somehow it still mattered. He hadn't meant to hurt Jess; all he'd been trying to do was protect her. At least, that's what he'd started out trying to do, but it had all become a mess.

At the start, back in New York more than two years ago when he had been approached by a mysterious man in a clean-pressed suit and asked if he loved his country. It had been a job. A way of making some extra money and doing something patriotic, he'd been told, but he'd fallen hard for Jess, and was about to tell her everything when she took off for Europe. Since then, he'd been trying to find her. And he did. But then everything went from bad to worse. This was his chance, if anything meant anything, to try and feel good about himself again. It had been a long time since he had, and if he was going to die, he wanted to just feel…clean.

That's all he wanted.

On the back of the snowmobile, behind him, Massarra lolled back and forth, semi-conscious. She was bound hand and foot.

Ink-black night surrounded them, his world just the hundred-foot patch of snow his headlight illuminated, the growl and whine of the engine, the up-and-down pounding of the snow. Mercifully, it hadn't snowed again, and after cresting the ridge coming from the sea in the last of the light, he'd followed his compass heading directly inland. Soon after, he found tracks in the snow. Not footprints, but other snowmobiles. There weren't many options for whose they could be. The tracks were fresh, straight along the road inland. He raced along it fast over the underlying fresh snow.

He knew he didn't need to find them.

They would find *him*. He was the returning hero, and they needed him.

Images floated in the periphery of the darkness. Ben's face, accusing him. His mother, her face sad. Flashes of home, of the leafy suburb in Brooklyn where he grew up. If he was hallucinating, at least he was still aware enough to know that. All he had to do was follow the tracks. Stay on the heading.

How long now? Hours. Had to be hours.

Another searing flash of pain.

What he would give for some Vicodin. Morphine. Anything. And now he actually *was* in pain.

Dots of lights danced in his peripheral vision. More hallucinations? He blinked and tried to force them away, and yet they grew brighter. Then louder. He eased off the throttle. The first part of the plan: *they* would find *him*.

"And they say there are no more heroes." The Englishman smiled, his teeth gleaming in the bright overhead LED lamps. "*I'm bringing her in,*" he laughed, imitating Roger's gruff voice over the radio. "You're like some American action hero. Amazing."

Roger stood in front of him, barely able to keep his legs from buckling.

A thickset man in a black ballistic vest held him up. Two more of them held Massarra tight in their grip, one to each side. After being surrounded on the snowy plain leading up to Vivas, they'd been searched—his rifle taken away—and loaded onto sleds and brought here.

Armed guards surrounded them in the ten-by-ten fabric tent. Roger assumed this was headquarters, but for what exactly he didn't know. Why hadn't they taken them to Vivas? Even in his delirium, he'd seen the lights of the central villa shining again, and the glitter of the shantytown around it. The edge of this ramshackle camp was hundreds of yards away.

Roger fought to raise his head to focus and look around.

So this was the feared Vivas team. The man looked like an

English dandy, his blond hair swept back to one side, his arms clasped behind his back. His men, dressed in matching black uniforms with brown armbands, nonetheless looked haggard, tired. Scared. Perhaps beaten. "Where's Salman?" Roger asked.

"Thought it best that we talk first, as you suggested."

"Good."

"Why don't you tell me who this is?"

One of the men holding Massarra lifted her chin. She scowled and spat in the direction of the Englishman.

"One of the terrorists that attacked Vivas. She admitted bombing the Vatican."

"I did not," Massarra growled.

"How did you find this woman?"

"She's a member of the Levantines. They were told to go to Rome and find Jessica Rollins."

The Englishman's eyes widened. "How interesting."

"Morphine," grunted Roger. He held up his bandaged left hand, a club of bloody rags held together with duct tape.

"I heard of your…needs. I also heard from Salman's daughter, Rita, of your friend Giovanni sticking you like a squealing pig. That does look painful." The Englishman frowned, then whispered to a blond haired boy beside him. The boy nodded and exited the tent through a back flap. "We will get you what you want."

"Good."

"But first, tell me about this *special* information, from our dearly departed Jessica Rollins?"

"I told you, only to my handler, from Sanctuary."

"Sanctuary?" The Englishman's face feigned surprise. "Is this a place? I've never—"

"Spare me."

The mock surprise melted away. The Englishman planted his feet in a wide stance. "We've searched your snowmobile, torn it apart bolt by bolt, but we haven't found any electronic devices. No laptops, no hard drives, no memory keys…"

"You think I'm stupid? I hid it. Away from here. With someone who'll sing to the world over the radio if I don't get back to them by tomorrow morning."

"I think you're bluffing."

Roger shrugged. "I'm somewhere beyond caring. They sent me out here on a mission. I'm doing my job. I just want to get back, alive. I've paid my dues. Now where's my morphine?" He held up his club hand again.

The Englishman seemed to listen to something. He pressed his hand to his left ear, then smiled at Roger. "You may be getting your wish, Mr. Hargate." A thin whine warbled. The Englishman frowned and held up one hand, asking everyone to remain still. The whine grew louder. "What in God's name is that?"

For half an hour, Jess had flown in total darkness, the wind pummeling the plane. She fought to keep it level and on the compass heading. More than two thousand five hundred feet, but not more than three thousand. Too high and she'd be engulfed in the perpetual cloud layer and wouldn't be able to see anything.

Then again, she *couldn't* see anything.

She had the running lights off, the instrument lights off, just her headlamp with its red LED glowing. At least the cockpit heater was on, but she feared her foot coming back to life, so she kept it turned low.

The warmth brought with it the smell of metal and oil, and blood, but the heady stench of jet fuel overpowered it all. She had to keep the window open to keep from passing out from the smell of it.

Blackness.

Her Cessna rushed headlong into the dark, the wind whistling off the airframe, but Jess had the strange sensation she wasn't moving at all. Her cockpit was a tiny refuge, dimly lit red by her headlamp, floating alone in an endless dark space. She had to fight the feeling she wasn't moving at all, keep an image in her mind of what she was trying to do, of where she was headed.

The wind rocked the plane.

And the wind was the problem.

The magnetic center of the compass on the dash bobbled in its liquid-filled enclosure. Each bounce and thrust of wind shook it. Sometimes it stuck and she had to tap it to set the magnet free. But more or less, she could follow her set heading. The bigger problem: how strong was the crosswind?

She had to cover about a hundred and fifty kilometers. At a hundred knots of airspeed, that was fifty minutes. That's what she'd scribbled onto her notes taped to the instrument panel. Of course, the head or tailwind could change that by quite a lot. Thirty knots either way could add or subtract fifteen minutes of travel time.

Before leaving, she watched the windsock at the side of the runway. Roger had found one in the hangar and hung it on a post. It was marked off by orange and white stripes. Each stripe the wind inflated meant ten knots, and gave the wind's direction. Last she saw, about ten knots, a steady wind, but not too strong, straight in the direction she was set to fly.

Problem was, Roger had told her, wind at altitude tended to shift direction, often by up to ninety degrees, and could get much stronger. By keeping as low as she could, but still high enough to avoid crashing into a mountaintop, she'd avoid some of this problem, but she would also be subject to more turbulence kicked up by whatever was on the ground. That was fine. She could handle that. But what she didn't know was how much crosswind she'd be getting.

Fifty minutes of flying with a thirty-knot crosswind would push her more than fifty kilometers off her target, but she'd have no way of confirming that. No visual references. No way to see anything on the ground to check if she was drifting left or right. Outside, all was blackness. This was so disorienting. She didn't even have any way to know what way was up or down, except for gravity pinning her ass into the Cessna's seat. Even this wasn't convincing enough to overcome a growing sense of vertigo.

She checked her watch.

Forty minutes of coasting into the unknown. She scanned outside, looking through the front, the side windows, the back. Nothing. Just pitch black.

Was Vivas even intact? Roger said it was, when he talked to them.

A lot was riding on Roger.

Her traitor.

Now her double agent.

Forty-five minutes. She'd been trying to keep calm, but her heart raced. If she passed it, there was no hope.

In the distance, a bleary smudge of white, off to her left. She took a deep breath, tried to calm her heart from banging out of her chest, and eased the yoke over. The Cessna banked toward the light.

Night flying was dangerous. Extremely dangerous.

That was what Roger had said, over and over again. In this wrecked world, there weren't any street lamps to follow, no towns glowing bright, no airstrips lit up with neat rows of lights. Night flying was mostly dangerous, though, due to one thing: landing. Find a place to land, and judging where exactly the ground began, was almost impossible in the dark.

Jess looked over her shoulder.

A motley collection of canisters, anything they could find to hold jet fuel, thumped and clanked together. The backseat and stowage of the Cessna was jammed with as much of it as Roger reasonably assumed the plane could manage to take off with. Night flying was dangerous because landing was dangerous, but Jess didn't plan to land it.

This was a flying bomb.

The cone of light from the villa over Vivas grew brighter. Jess allowed herself a grin for the first time in longer than she could remember. Now she'd give the bastards a surprise they wouldn't see coming.

31

BASTARDI.

Salman ground his teeth together and watched the men in black uniforms trying to not to make it look as though they were watching him. But he knew. If there was one thing Salman knew about himself, it was that he could smell a rat.

And this stank.

He and Rita sat in the front office of a cinder block building just off the main entrance to Vivas underground. High above, the beacon shone from the villa, less than half a mile away.

Rita had been quiet since her return, pre-occupied and unwilling to talk. The loss of Elsa hung heavy in her mind, but there was something else, something she didn't want to talk to him about. She had always been loyal to a fault, always followed his instructions without question. She sat in silence now, staring blankly at one of the gray walls, her expression unreadable.

Salman looked away from her and considered his own position instead. The attack had flattened half of the above ground outbuildings, but he had instructed his scouts to investigate. Most of the damage was from deep-penetrating bunker-busting bombs. Not ordinary bombs. Missiles. He'd spent time as a mercenary in Africa after serving out his first jail sentence as a teenager. Enough time to learn how a bomb would crater the ground, and the difference between a bomb thrown at a target and fired at a target from above.

He heard Roger tell Iain Radcliff, that English rat, that he had one of the terrorists that attacked Vivas. The Massarra woman. He was claiming that she was the one responsible for the attacks here. But no terrorists had attacked this place, at least not terrorists tossing Molotov cocktails from the backs of jeeps.

Someone had bombed it, from above, with sophisticated weaponry, and they had been intent on destroying what was underground. One way or the other, Roger was lying, and the Englishman knew it, but he'd smiled at Salman, telling him how useful this could be. Nothing made sense. Or rather, in another way, it did.

The Englishman was an idiot.

Salman was as good as dead if he stayed here, but he wouldn't leave without his prize.

Too much blood had been shed, and he'd come too far to quit now.

He eyed the Englishman's men around him and then Rita. They had been allowed to keep their weapons; been told they were going to be escorted underground, as Salman had requested. He wagered that they would be going underground, but not into Vivas. He was betting the Englishman intended to bury him.

Such a threat brought out the very best and the worst in Salman.

He'd sent his own boy out to chase the Englishman's, said he was gone on an errand. They were waiting to find him, he was sure, before they did whatever it was they were going to do. His team was expendable, so it was time to go. But how? He needed a diversion. He slouched back, pretended to sleep, but kept one eye on Rita, who kept one eye on him, too.

They'd been together a long time, he and his daughter. They understood each other.

A buzzing whine like a giant mosquito began outside. Salman flinched, fearing another rain of death might be arriving from above, but the buzz grew louder, and slower. Louder still, as if a lawn mower was approaching through the sky. As it passed overhead, the sound deepened. He strained to see out through the windows, but the sky was black.

An airplane.

Who the hell could that be?

Then a smile crept across his face, a new respect creeping into the hardened Italian criminal's heart. "*Stai pronta*," he mouthed silently to Rita, making sure none of the guards saw him do it.

People ran into the icy streets below, their faces looking up. Jess saw them as murky figures, a few hundred feet below her, but she was sure they couldn't see her. They could hear her though, a grinding noise somewhere in the black night.

Now they were the hunted, and she the hunter.

She buzzed over the top of the put-together town, trying to make sense of where she'd been before. Most of it had changed—flattened in the attack, and covered in snow. Two clear landmarks remained: the hilltop villa with its lights blazing, and the jailhouse she'd been trapped in. That was right next to the tunnel leading into the Vivas underground. If she was going to hide her father's data, and Roger's precious beacon, that's where she'd hide it.

But she didn't just need to guess.

The signet ring on her left index finger started tapping again, just when she saw the smudge of light appear from the blackness. Left, left, it had tapped in its simple code, and then forward, forward—warmer, warmer—a game of hide-and-seek. As she swept over the middle of the town, the ring's tapping shifted from the top of her finger to the bottom. Back, it said, colder, cold.

Just like the game she used to play with her father when she was a child. Where is the Easter egg? Warmer, warmer, no, colder, yes! Warmer. You're close! Marco. Polo!

And she was close.

Jess banked the aircraft, shooting straight over a clump of tents just past the periphery of the collection of huts and buildings. She kept an eye on the attitude indicator, making sure to keep her banking below ten degrees. That was another instruction scribbled onto her notes. She wasn't sure what would happen if she did, but she only took chances she could understand.

The tapping on her finger shifted from behind to left.

Good enough.

Swinging the nose around, she picked a target. The easiest target. The villa on top of the hill. She set her crosshair—the nose of the plane—dead onto it, easing the yoke back a little to gain altitude. Easier to dive bomb than come straight at it, and she needed some clearance.

From the seat beside her, she grabbed a roll of duct tape and pulled off a strip, wrapped one end around the yoke and the other to the instrument panels. She pulled off more strips and secured it the best she could.

The villa grew from bright smudge in the distance to gain some definition. Now she could see its roof and walls. Maybe a mile away.

She pushed back in her chair and inspected the taped-up yoke. Her autopilot. She nudged it forward, feeling the aircraft nose down. Her stomach lurched at the change in gravity.

The tapping on her finger stopped, but there was no time to figure what happened.

Time to get the hell out.

One problem with turning on the cabin heater was her foot had started to defrost. Needles of pain shot up her leg. Her foot was on fire, and she yelped in pain as she tried to move it for the first time in an hour.

The plane's nose dipped further.

The villa swept into view.

Less than half a mile, but her autopilot wasn't quite up to the task. The strips of duct tape ripped away from the instrument panel as Jess tried to extricate herself from the seat, wrenching open the passenger side door handle at the same time.

The plane pitched sickeningly forward.

Jet fuel spattered onto Jess from one of the containers. She gagged and pushed against the door, the pressure of the wind outside forcing it back closed. The aircraft gained speed as it dived, the air driving harder against the door. She jammed her foot against the yoke, using it to shove her shoulder against the door and push herself halfway out.

Pain exploded in her foot—and the plane tipped into a spin.

Wind rushed over her face. She was soaked in fuel, reeling from dizziness. The plane whipped around once. The g-force of its spin threw her outward. The lights of the villa swept by, then swept by again. She sensed the ground rushing up. With a desperate thrust, she ejected herself from the aircraft, releasing her drogue chute in the same motion.

The familiar, sweet rush of open air greeted her

She spread her arms and legs wide, thrust her stomach forward. The shuttlecock. The same position and motions that she'd taught to dozens of beginners on their first jump, and she'd jumped hundreds of times. She waited for the tug of the drogue chute to pull out her main.

But she got more than a tug.

Her body rocketed back. Her arms and legs snapped painfully in front.

The impact rushed all the blood into her head, almost knocking her unconscious. Without looking, she knew. The drogue's lines must have tangled in the airframe of the Cessna. It wasn't an aircraft designed for jumping out of. The wind rushing past her, at the edge of consciousness, just one thought—

Look, grab, pull.

It was the only other critical instruction she'd drilled into the heads of her hundreds of jump students. She grabbed the emergency handle and pulled and felt herself spin away into space.

A bright orange burst lit up everything around her, and a split second later the explosion's concussion sent her tumbling, her reserve chute only half open, flames bursting across its silken surface.

A fiery ball of flame blossomed high into the dark sky over the buildings, the impact of the explosion juddering the ground and shaking the cinder block walls.

"We're under attack again," Salman yelled, getting to his feet.

Rita stood with him.

People ran by in the street outside. Bursts of automatic gunfire erupted in the distance, then close by. Two of the men guarding them stepped out through the swinging double doors to talk to the guards outside. The moment the doors swung closed, Salman pulled a knife from his sleeve, stepped toward one of the remaining guards, who was staring out the window, and plunged the blade into the side of the man's neck. He slumped forward without a sound, blood spraying high up into the ceiling and across Salman's face.

The other guard, staring out the opposite window and fixated on the explosion still reverberating across the valley, never noticed. Voices screamed. Rita swung her rifle around and shoved the muzzle under the guard's chin. He tensed for a second, then went limp.

"Good decision," Rita said in accented English.

She took away his weapon and tossed it down the stairs, forcing the man to his knees. In a swift motion, she brought the butt of her rifle down into his temple. The man splayed out on the floor.

Through the window, Salman saw his boy, his nephew, motioning toward the back of the building.

"*Sul retro*," Salman said to Rita, who watched the guards outside on the front steps.

They quietly stole down the back stairs, Salman first, followed by Rita.

Iain Radcliff watched the fireball, twisting and rolling in on itself, roil high into the dark sky. Flames burst and spread across the ragtag of huts in the distance. The lights of the villa shone above it all. He looked at the flames, back at Massarra and Roger, then back at the fireball.

"What the hell is going on?" he sputtered.

The guards in black fatigues around him hesitated.

"Yes, go and find out!" he yelled at the one closest to him.

Two of them peeled off through the back tent flap.

He turned to Massarra. "Is this anything to do with you?"

One of the guards holding her ripped her hair back, and she grimaced but said nothing.

Beside her, Roger was busy unwrapping the mass of bandages from his left hand, pulling off strips of duct tape and bloody rag. He held a syringe of morphine, one that Radcliff had given him, in his right hand as he worked. The last strip pulled free, revealing his mangled hand, a red welt through the middle, but also a jagged wound where his thumb had been.

It had been cut off.

And something else was in his hand under the bandages.

A gray cylinder.

It thudded onto the wooden floor and rolled into the middle of the room.

Radcliff looked at Roger's hand, at his missing thumb, then at the object rolling along the ground toward him. "What the—"

It was a grenade.

The pin had dropped to the floor between Roger and Massarra.

In a second everyone in the room understood. Except that Massarra and Roger understood the moment differently. He swung his right arm and jabbed the syringe needle into the neck of one of the guards holding Massarra, while she ducked down and delivered a knee straight into the testicles of the other. They all fell backward in a tangled heap.

Roger rolled to his feet and grabbed Massarra by the ropes binding her hands and shoved her through the front tent flap. The crunching detonation threw them into the air, over the top of a snowmobile parked outside, bits of flaming debris falling over and around them, hissing into the snow.

32

"SBRIGATEVI, VENITE," SALMAN'S boy urged, waving to them from the shadows at the back of the jail block.

Salman grabbed him by the nape of his coat. *"Dove?* Did you find it?"

"Sì, sì." The boy doubled over and ran into a jagged opening in a cement wall behind them.

They followed him into the inky blackness.

Behind them, in the sky, a loud whirring noise. Not like the small airplane, not slow and unsteady, but fast and deadly. Another explosion rocked the ground. More staccato bursts of automatic weapons.

He could hide it, burrow it away until they forgot that it existed.

This was Salman's plan. Whatever it was that someone wanted from that laptop and those tapes, it would remain valuable, but he would make it disappear, at least for now. Go to ground. Make them think it was lost or destroyed. Then, unlike the mad Englishman, discreetly make inquiries. No frontal assaults. No singing to the world. The idiot was probably already dead.

His boy whispered, this way, that way, leading them through a maze of corrugated sheet metal and stinking piles of refuse, up the hill toward the central villa. He paused at a vee-shaped tumble of brick and snow, darting his head out and back before telling Salman it was safe, but urging him to go first. He pointed at an entrance carved into the earth, leading underground.

That had to be the Vivas entrance. A single guard stood nervously by the entrance.

"Lì dentro?" Salman asked his boy. "Is it in there?" The boy nodded, so he straightened up and walked at the uniformed soldier.

"Hey, have you seen Iain? Goddamn it, he was supposed to meet me here."

The soldier's attention alternated from Salman to the whirring in the sky. "Have not seen him, sir."

"Open the door."

"I need your pass, sir."

"Goddamn it, we're under attack."

The door behind the soldier slid open by itself, and four more like him came out at a full run.

Salman strode forward to the still open door.

"Sir, I cannot—"

He grabbed the young man by the throat and pressed his knife into the jugular. "I mean you no harm, I just need my property."

Rita and the boy scrambled across the street and through the door.

His knife still at his throat, Salman guided the soldier through the door and into the curved marble floor that angled downward. Glowing picture frames lined the walls and a door-panel hissed open. He shoved the young man in ahead.

Rita had a length of rope ready, and she tied the guard to a white chair by a brushed metal table in the middle of the room. He didn't resist. The kid was scared, didn't understand what was going on. Boots clattered in the hallway outside. A thundering detonation shook the walls.

"A blond boy, Iain's boy, did he come in here?"

The guard nodded.

"He had a pack with him?"

"He came a minute before you."

"Don't move, you understand?"

Rita brandished her rifle, made sure he understood. He nodded.

Backing out into the hallway, they followed it down. Salman knew they had cameras, that they'd seen him at the entrance, in the room, everywhere here, but it didn't matter. Speed was all that mattered in this confusion. More uniformed soldiers ran past them to the surface. They rounded a corner and found themselves in a huge, brightly lit dome, filled with trees and walkways and flowers.

"*Madonna Merde*," Salman muttered, amazed by the opulence, but there were cracks in the smooth concrete ceiling. Water glistened and leaked from one.

And there, staring at them, was the blond boy.

"Hey!" Salman waved. "Iain told me to come and get the bag."

The boy almost bolted, but froze. In his hand was Salman's prize.

"Stay there, it's okay." He ran to the boy at a jog, not too fast, didn't want to scare him. He grabbed the bag and opened it. There it was. The laptop, the tapes and CDs, the beacon. "Go and hide," he told the boy. "And stay the hell away from Iain, he's a bad man, you understand?"

He didn't wait to see if the boy understood.

Another concussion rocked the ground, bringing down a shower of plaster and debris. Salman took off at a sprint, back the way they came, up the smooth marble hallway that curved around and around. He expected someone to stop them, but in an instant he was back outside and shot straight into the warren of huts across the street. He didn't look back, didn't turn to gawk at the fireballs or the chatter of machine guns, but headed deep into the maze of shacks before stopping.

"*Aspettiamo*," he said to Rita, motioning for them to get low, to be quiet.

Near pitch black, but Salman had good eyes. Now they would wait, move slowly, melt away into the night. By now the Englishman would know, but he was sure Iain had other more pressing issues.

The crack of gunfire faded.

Something whirred past overhead

An uneasy silence descended.

"I believe that is mine," said a voice in the darkness.

A red light clicked on.

Rita raised her rifle, but Salman held the muzzle down to peer at the ragged figure standing in front of them. He'd know that voice anywhere.

Jess knew who it was right away. The curved cleft lip on the man's face was the last thing she saw before she slipped under the ice. "Salman, what's in the bag is mine."

"I thought you were dead," the man replied. "*Morta*. I saw you die."

"I was."

Even in the dim red light of her headlamp, she saw their eyes and mouths open at the sight of her.

251

"*Strega*," Rita whispered.

She crouched beside Salman, the boy between them. Their faces looked like they saw a ghost.

And they did.

A ghost back from the dead.

"And now you live? For what?"

"To stop them."

"Who is *them*?"

"I don't know, not yet."

"And what do you want to stop them from doing?"

"Destroying the world."

Salman couldn't help laughing. "If you haven't noticed—"

"There is still a lot worth saving."

This gave the old Italian a pause. "Run with us," he said, his voice gaining a note of sympathy. "Hide with us. Whatever you want with your father's things, maybe—"

"No more running."

"You want to restore your family honor? Is that it?" It was something Salman would understand, but his tone was sarcastic.

"I want to save them."

"Your parents are dead."

"Giovanni, Hector, they are still alive. Out on the ice."

Rita took her arm. "Raffa. Is he with them?"

Jess nodded, noticed the way her eyes lit up. "I think he's alive."

Rita's father's face softened. "But there is nothing we can—"

"You cannot escape, Salman. Do you want to die here? Do you want *them* to die here?" Jess flicked her chin at Rita and the boy. "Give me the bag, right now."

She'd tracked them using the signet ring. It tapped hard against her index finger—in front, in front—the beacon was in that bag.

Salman had been halfway to bolting, but now stood firm. "How could you save us? If you're not dead anymore, you look more than half dead right now."

She hobbled forward, wincing in pain. "I prefer to think of myself as half alive. Do you think I came here for no reason? Trust me." She held out her hand.

The Italian hesitated, glanced at Rita, but shrugged and handed over the bag. "It is hard to argue with someone who has come back from the dead."

"Then we are together."

He nodded. "Tell me what you need me to do."

She pulled a roll of duct tape from her pocket. "Hold this."

The whirring noises in the dark sky intensified to a deafening rush. A massive dark shape loomed gray overhead. The Englishman's ears rang, his senses still numb from the grenade blast. With a shaking hand, he picked a fragment of shrapnel from his leg and struggled to his feet. Outside the tent, a burst of gunfire, but something else, like fast beating wings.

The gunfire stopped.

A man stepped in through the tent's opening. The guard beside the Englishman opened fire, straight at the man's exposed head, but the bullets bounced off some kind of transparent helmet. The man held up his hand. "Once more, and you die." He turned to the Englishman. "Mr. Radcliff?"

Iain nodded.

"I am Maxim, head of Sanctuary security. Do you have Dr. Rollins laptop and data?"

"It's underground, in Vivas."

The man checked something, a ring on his finger, and nodded. "We will be back." He pointed a finger at Iain. "Stay."

"Let's move." Jess shouldered the backpack.

Rita led the way, her rifle out. Jess gave her one of her spare headlamps. Salman brought up the rear, with Jess and the boy in the middle. They wound their way through the shantytown of rubble and metal, frozen dirt showing through the ice and snow underfoot. Jess did her best to keep up, but her prosthetic had almost torn free in her crash landing, and her other, real foot, exploded in pain on each step.

The chaos Jess had incited with the plane crash had calmed

down. No more yelling voices echoed overhead, no more bursts of gunfire.

"We're going to meet Roger and Massarra at the southern edge of the camp," Jess whispered.

"What about the Englishman?"

"He shouldn't be a problem anymore."

They reached an opening, a flat square between the buildings a hundred feet across, lit by orange sodium lights on posts at each corner.

"They should be a few hundred feet on the opposite side," Jess whispered, crouching low. "We'll go as a group."

Tapping Rita on the shoulder, she hobbled out into the snowy opening as quick as she could. Bits of debris blew away in front of her in sudden breeze.

Except that it wasn't a breeze.

A violent downdraft of rushing air pinned them in place. Shapes dropped from the sky. Men on ropes slid down into the snow and crouched. The cyclone from above evaporated almost as quick as it had started.

"Don't move," Jess whispered without needing to.

A dozen men clad in gleaming black stood, weapons out, but not weapons Jess recognized. Something else. Something different.

"Give us the bag, Miss Rollins." A man stepped between the warriors, his head covered in a translucent dome that reflected the orange sodium lights. In the dim light, she couldn't quite make out the face.

Two more of his men came behind, each of them dragging a body.

It was Roger and Massarra. Jess swore quietly.

"I'll kill them," the man said. "Just give me the bag."

"Shoot them, for all I care."

"Don't test me."

"But what about Giovanni?" said another voice, from the shadows behind them. A voice with a thick German accent. "And what about Hector?"

Jess lowered her rifle.

A pot-belled, older man with a tangle of gray hair and spectacles stepped out from behind the men. "I can help. But you need to give me that bag."

Jess squinted in the dim light. She'd seen this man before, many years ago. At the university with her father, when she was a child. "Dr. Müller?"

33

A BLACK-CLAD SANCTUARY soldier patted Jess down. He slid a hand under her ragged clothing.

"Hey!" she yelped and tried to squirm away, but another held her arms behind her back while a third bound her feet together.

Her arms were covered in taped-on bandages, with more of the tape wrapped around her midsection where she'd attempted a fix for the ribs she cracked in her abortive parachute landing.

"She's clean," the soldier said, forcing her to sit on a wooden bench at the back of the cell.

Back in this stinking jail. That's where she'd ended up. Back where she'd been detained when she first entered Vivas.

The world seemed a more innocent place, back then, when all that had happened was a natural disaster. Now the evil of men had cast its ugly shadow over the events. So much of the death and carnage wasn't a consequence of nature.

Now there were people to blame.

Roger and Massarra were similarly bound and searched in the cell across from her, while Salman, Rita and their boy were in the cell to her right. Through the window bars, the sky wasn't black anymore. The darkest shade of gray colored it.

They were quick-marched here. No time to waste, apparently. The men, the Sanctuary forces, were dressed head-to-foot in gleaming black body armor, even their faces covered.

"Transparent aluminum," said their leader, Maxim, the only one who had introduced himself. He stood at the base of the stairs leading up and watched Jess as she observed his men. "Very tough. Your weapons wouldn't penetrate it. You made the right decision to stand down."

The door behind him opened.

Iain Radcliff entered, now a shadow of his usually well-composed self. Black smudges covered fresh crimson scars on his cheeks. His left eye was swollen, and he limped, a bloody red bandage around his right leg.

"Are you okay?" asked a voice in a thick German accent.

Dr. Müller entered the room behind the Englishman.

"I am fine," Iain insisted. "But these people *attacked* us."

"It was very good work recovering Dr. Rollins data," Müller said. "Would not have been possible without you."

Iain stopped at the base of the stairs. "I only ask that my family and I be granted asylum within Sanctuary."

Müller smiled. "Of course." The smile dissipated as he switched his gaze to looking around the room. "First, we need to deal with this mess. Another terror attack against Vivas. It is too much. It is why I came. We have to stop this madness." He held up a tablet. A video played on it.

Jess leaned forward. It was her. In the airplane earlier. The video tracked her, then followed the spinning aircraft as it exploded into the ground. It was very clear.

"You were following us?"

"When you arrived here, yes, our drones picked you up." He pointed at Massarra. "And this woman, the Queen of Spades, one of the highest terrorists on our watch list. She masterminded the bombing of the Vatican."

"A lie," Massarra spat. "But your kind tell many lies."

"And Roger Hargate, one of our own," continued Müller. "One of Maxim's own men. A traitor." He turned to Salman. "And a convicted *mafioso*. What a motley gathering. The Rollins family never ceases to amaze me." He turned to Jess.

"I don't care what you're doing," she said breathlessly. "Just find Giovanni and Hector, and Lucca and Raffa. They're on a patch of ice, in the sea. Maybe a hundred and fifty kilometers—"

"I'm sorry, but even with the technology at our disposal, and even if I wanted to, that wouldn't be possible. We have no jets, no turbine engines can survive the ash floating everywhere in the skies. The entire Earth is coated in it. No, we have to limit ourselves to internal combustion or electrics—propeller driven aircraft—and even these degrade quickly. It is very expensive to maintain anything that flies, at least for now. And there are very limited resources, you understand."

"But they're only a hundred kilometers—"

"More like two hundred kilometers, straight off Naples, if our radio signal triangulation is correct. We did intercept your latest transmissions."

"So you know where they are." Her voice rose in pitch. "A helicopter. A ship...?"

"A helicopter big enough to make that distance and pick up survivors would require turbine engines, my dear, and ships..." He laughed. "The Mediterranean is an iceberg infested deathtrap, swamped almost daily by massive tsunamis. All the Earth's oceans are, and will be, for some time. There are no ships."

"Please, they'll be dead in a day."

"I'm afraid you must consider them *already* dead." Müller affected a pained smile. "Was this your gamble? As much as I revile you, I am sorry." He turned back to Iain. "And enough of this. Please, escort them to the troop carriers. We will bring them to Sanctuary for interrogation." He turned back to Jess. "Except her. Leave her with me for a moment."

Maxim nodded and the black-clad men grabbed the prisoners.

Müller waited for them to leave, keeping just the Englishman with him. "Such a shame, all of this."

Iain nodded. "I agree."

"But catching a terrible criminal mastermind like Jessica Rollins, you must be proud," Müller said. "Soon the whole world, or at least what is left of it, will find out. You will be famous."

"So what do we do with her?" Iain smiled an greasy grin at Jessica.

"She's going to try and escape."

"She is?"

"And it's such a terrible shame, that you, the hero, will be killed in the struggle."

He turned to Müller. "Wha—"

Müller had a pistol pointed directly at his chest. He pulled the trigger, a muted *thwap* the only noise. It was silenced. The Englishman stared at his chest, a pool of red spreading across it. He crumpled to the floor.

"Do you know, that is the first time I've ever killed anyone?" Müller said, staring at the body.

Jess retreated on her wooden bench and squirmed against the ropes binding her hands and feet. "I doubt that."

"When you put it like that, I see what you mean. I must have killed thousands. Hundreds of thousands. But I take no pleasure in it. Before Nomad hit, we had to…*highlight*…the divisions in our society. Bring them into sharp relief, so people could see more clearly."

"See what more clearly?"

"How we must rebuild. Don't you see? This is a chance for humanity to start with a clean slate, to be rebuilt better and stronger."

"You're nuts."

"Genius is often described as such." He walked into Jess's cell. "You are a remarkable woman, do you know that?"

Jess flinched and pushed her back against the wall. "What do you want? Is it my father's data?"

"You just don't seem to want to die," Müller continued, ignoring her questions. "When Roger was with Nico, at the castle, they assured me you would not survive."

Staring into his eyes, her skin crawled. "So you arranged that? Dragging my family into that castle, into the middle of that mess?"

The German pursed his lips. "Sometimes it is necessary to come up with a myth that people can blame, rather than the cold hand of unfeeling fate."

"So you blamed all this on my father?" As terrified as she was, anger rose up in her. "Blamed him hiding the existence of Nomad, tied him to the terrorists?"

"And you inspire such devotion, Jessica." Müller stood in front of her, his face radiating mock admiration. "Roger, who betrayed your father, even led him to his death, and yet you forgave him. And here he is, working for you. And Salman, uncle to Nico, who terrorized your family—"

"They were all just pawns in your sick game," Jess spat. "Not their fault."

"This is no game." He stopped laughing. "But it does need to end. I'm only sorry that you had to see this. You should have been dead a long time ago. My agents assured me your family was dead after Nomad, and yet you popped up in Vivas and on radio transmissions. We tried to find you, but it was Salman and Iain who reported you dead, again. Yet here you are."

Jess needed more time. "'The Organization' that Roger said he worked for—"

"My organization."

"And the Vatican, that was…"

"You *are* a clever girl. Destroying Rome was a necessary precursor to justifying military control of Sanctuary. They would be dead anyway, at least this way their deaths served a purpose. I am not a monster, but practical, you see?"

She couldn't believe what she was hearing and leaned closer.

"Such a shame that I can't let you live." Müller held his pistol up. "And you know, I get the feeling that even if I put a bullet in your head, somehow you will pop up tomorrow somewhere, taunting me. And I can't have that. So you know what I think I will do?" He leaned close to Jess's face. "I will take your body back to Sanctuary with me, and take you apart, piece by little piece. An autopsy, I'll tell them, to search for microchips, something you might have swallowed. But I will take the bits of you, and scatter them to the four corners of the Earth, just to—"

Jess started to laugh, right in his face. Not just a giggle, but a full blown snickering laugh.

"You find that funny?" Müller's eyes widened, the look on his face incredulous.

"Too little, too late," Jess managed to get out between snorts.

The man waited in anticipation.

"You might have tried searching me better earlier," she laughed.

His look of confused mirth darkened. He grabbed Jess's shirt and ripped it open. Her skeletal frame was crisscrossed with duct tape and bandages, and convulsed violently with each painful sob of laughter. He felt around her body, her hair, and then grabbed her breasts. His jaw fell open, and he ripped her bra off, shredding the fabric apart.

In his hand he held the beacon, Roger's beacon. With Roger's severed thumb duct taped on top of it. The device glowed blue. It was on.

Outside, the loud whirring in the sky had started again, and beams of light stabbed down from the brightening cloud cover.

"It's in broadcast mode," Jess screamed over the rising noise, her face somewhere between a snarl and a grin. "You just told the entire world, all frequencies, everyone back at Sanctuary—even

your men outside—you just explained the monster that you are—
"

The door at the top of the stairs flew open. "Sir, you must come with us." screamed Maxim. "Now!" Debris swirled around him.

Gunfire erupted again outside.

Müller looked at him, back at Jess, then at the pistol in his hand. He raised it.

"…and that you blamed my father," Jess screeched, throwing herself from the bench, using her head as a missile launched straight into the old man's chest.

He fired, but it grazed her left shoulder as she barreled into him, knocking them both hard to the concrete floor. She landed on top of him, knocking his wind out. The pistol clattered across the stone floor. But she was tied at her feet, her hands tied behind her back. He pushed her off and she squirmed to turn around.

"Now! We must leave!" Maxim yelled from the top of the stairs again. He strained to see into the swirl of debris kicked up into the air behind him.

Jess rolled onto her side while Müller got to his feet. He glanced at Max at the top of the stairs, then at the pistol ten feet away inside the cell, and finally at Jess squirming to get upright. A seething frustration boiled in his eyes, his face creased in anger, but there was no time.

He turned to follow Max.

Jess screamed and ripped the stump of her leg free from the duct taped prosthetic. She jammed her stump into the concrete, using it as leverage, and leapt upward with everything she had. Müller flinched away, held out a hand to block her.

And Jess used the only weapon she had left to use.

Her teeth.

She sunk them deep into the side of Müller's hand. He roared in pain and slammed her head with his right fist, but she held on, tasting his blood in her mouth. She bit down, feeling bone and sinew crunch between her teeth.

The man yelped in pain. He punched her face. Blood poured from his hand. She was dragged along the concrete after him, a bloody slug, but Maxim had already disappeared from the top of the stairs.

The last thing Jess saw was more men, rushing through the open door, running down the stairs. Müller roared in frustration and slammed his fist into her head again.

NOVEMBER 15th

Twenty-Two Days A.N.

34

SONGBIRDS WARBLED IN a leafy green canopy. A blue sky burned bright beyond. From the twisted boughs of branches overhead, white orchids spilled down, their sweet scent mixing with the fragrant wet earth. Dappled sunlight danced over the ground, and from somewhere the sound of children laughing echoed. Waves crashed against a shore.

"Where am I?" Jess's vision went in and out of focus, the greens and blues fuzzing together, but not the sounds, not the smells. They almost overpowered her. She exhaled, then inhaled the intoxicating perfume of the flowers.

A fly buzzed past her.

Not a fly. A bird. And no, not even a bird.

The tiny machine darted through the leaves and up into the sky. The sky.

She tried to sit up, but she was restrained. It was all she could do to angle her neck down to look at her body. Encased in a white sheet, on some kind of bed. In the middle of a forest. Or jungle.

And that sky.

Her eyes opened wide to take in the deep, beautiful blue, and the flickering, impossibly bright orb of the sun that she hadn't seen for so long.

Was she dead?

"You're not dead. Not this time."

The platform she was on slowly inclined at her waist, raising her head up. A smiling face greeted her, his skin brown like caramel, his eyes soft, a knitted cap set askew on his slicked black hair and a silver earring dangling from one ear.

"Where...is this..."

"Sanctuary," the smiling face replied.

"And you're..." She closed her eyes. She'd seen him before. "Ufuk Erdogmus."

"At your service."

She tried to move again.

"I'd sit still for now. We're still repairing you. You did quite a

265

bit of damage to your body." He smiled, his teeth perfectly white but gapped in the front.

The other strange thing she couldn't put her finger on. It wasn't something she felt. It was something she didn't feel.

Pain.

For the first time in longer than she could remember, she didn't have any sensation of pain. Her eyes widened and she tried to look at her right foot.

"We saved your toes," Ufuk said, seeing the panic in her eyes. "And you'll have a new leg in a day or two. A robotic one, even better than flesh and blood. It's kind of my specialty."

"What happened to, ah…" Her mind was still groggy.

"Müller? He's in custody. He would have escaped if you hadn't held onto him. I should tell you, there are videos of you, hanging on to his hand like a pitbull…you've got some fans on our intranet. And it would have been a bloody battle, if you hadn't broadcast that message. You saved us. Me. All of us." He held his hands wide. "Müller knew we were coming. He knew we knew. It was a trap that I had to put myself into, and thank God you got us out of it. I pulled my drones from North Africa to attack Müller's men, but he was setting it all up to position me as part of the extremists, cooperating with you. Attacking Vivas."

It was too much for Jess to process. She squeezed her eyes shut as sunlight flashed from above. "Is that the sun?"

"High intensity multi-spectrum LED display over the Dome."

For a moment, a blissful sense of peace eased over Jess. She was safe.

But then like a bolt of lightning: "Giovanni and Hector. Did you…are they…"

Ufuk's brows knitted together. "What Müller said was true. We managed to locate them, or at least, their bodies. My drones mounted a grid search based on the last radio signals and found the tent on the ice floe, but it's too far out to recover."

"God, no…" Her breath caught in a sob. "I wasn't trying to do anything but save them. It was the only way, to get to someone in Sanctuary…"

"You've only been unconscious for six hours." He looked away, seemed to speak into thin air. Another of the tiny flying machines flitted away into the leaves. "We're doing all we can."

Jess did her best to collect herself. "What did he want? What was in my father's data that was so important?"

"It wasn't the data."

"Then what?"

"It was his personal information, his emails, his personal logs. Your dad had kept that laptop for six years; he kept everything on it. Müller was worried that something on there could disprove all the lies he'd been telling about your father. He'd shown information proving your father was connected to the religious extremists, that he leaked info about Nomad, that he hid its existence."

"Why did you try and talk to him in Darmstadt?"

"Because I wanted to tell him the truth, but Müller made sure I couldn't."

"Where's Massarra? Salman?"

He shook his head. "They slipped away. But Roger is here, in the hospital."

"This isn't a hospital."

"No." His warm smile returned. "This is something just for you. We owe you. And your family."

"So the Earth won't hit Saturn?" This was the thing she'd been worrying about ever since she ran the simulation back at the castle. The Earth was a mess, but hitting Saturn, that would be the end of everything.

"We'll come close, maybe even pass through its rings. It will be quite the show in the sky in eighteen months. From what I see, we won't hit any moons or apocalyptic-sized asteroids, but we will have to survive bombardment from Jovian clusters, some weird magnetics, and the sun is unstable. Our solar system has become a hostile place."

"But why…?" Jess whispered. Seeing Ufuk's puzzled face she added: "I mean, why did Müller do it?"

He shrugged. "Right now we can only guess. One of the stated goals of Sanctuary was to retain diversity, to try and recreate the world and culture as it was before. A vault of civilization. Müller didn't see it that way. He complained that the problems of the world stemmed from its diversity. He argued that we should create a homogeneous human population, that we had a chance to build a race of superhumans."

"And why did he try to pile all the blame on to my father?"

Ufuk shrugged again. "He needed a scapegoat, someone for people to focus their anger on. He had videos of your father stealing the car at Darmstadt, escaping into the night. And your father *did* discover Nomad, even if he didn't know it at the time. Even if Müller hid the discovery."

Jess let her head fall back against the pillow. "So what now?" She could hardly imagine taking another breath, she felt so tired. And there was no point anymore. Everyone she cared for was dead.

"I'm pushing to repeal the one-year moratorium. I want to open channels to help anyone left alive out there. We have a world to rebuild. I'm taking an expedition up to the Svalbard seed reposi—"

A tiny whirring drone sped in through the leaves and whispered in Ufuk's ear.

"There was a boy, by the airfield," Jess started to say. "He—"

But Ufuk held his hand up. "I have news." He handed something to Jess that looked like a telephone.

She took it.

The ice tipped back and forth, back and forth, the waves gliding endlessly past and through them. Giovanni did his best to hold his grip on Hector, but the boy was gone. Where was he?

"*Bevi*," whispered Hector. He held a cup to Giovanni's lips.

But he couldn't even take a sip.

He had no energy to lift his head. In front of his eyes, his hands curled into claws, the fingertips blue. In the blue-black light, he saw the mass of Lucca and Raffa, where he knew the faithful teenagers were, or used to be. How long had it been? Everything had been soaked, but now it was frozen solid. What would Hector do when Giovanni was dead? What kind of lonely, painful death would Hector have to endure?

But Giovanni didn't even have tears left to cry.

He closed his eyes and blackness took him.

The boy and his dog crouched in the dark shadows inside the hangar. They huddled together for warmth in the nest of cardboard and old blankets. The dog licked the boy's face. His mother and father died weeks ago, in the flood, before the cold.

"*Mi dispiace, Issa,*" the boy said to the dog.

He had no food, not since the flying woman left two nights ago. And he had to hide.

A loud whirring noise grew in the sky.

At first the boy was scared, but then wondered: was it the woman returning? She reminded him of his mother, and he wished he'd gone with her, found a way to sneak himself and his dog onto the airplane.

But he'd been too scared, too weak.

The buzzing sound grew louder, and now the boy *was* scared. A shape loomed out of the dark sky. It was a flying machine, but not like the one the woman took off in. It had four propellers, one in each corner, and was much smaller than the other machine.

There was a box underneath it.

The machine hovered in front of him, kicking up snow and dirt. It seemed to look at the boy, but he saw no eyes. The box underneath it dropped with a thud onto the snow. The buzzing whirring noise intensified and dust and snow kicked up in a swirl. The machine gained altitude and disappeared into the gloom overhead.

The box popped open.

They would have run away, but the smell.

It drew them toward it.

Edging closer, a light was on inside, and a steaming pot of stew.

Stay there, said a note in Italian, *I am coming to get you*. The boy smiled and looked into the sky.

Blinding white light.

So bright that it hurt to look at.

269

"Hello," echoed a voice.

Dots of brilliant gold floated in space, and a face coalesced from the bright white.

"Can you hear me?" the face said.

Giovanni opened his mouth, but no sound came out. He tried again. "Am I dead?"

The floating white dots swirled in a blizzard.

"Am I in heaven?" he asked, louder this time, hoping, fearful.

"No, mate, I'm Ballie. Ballie Booker. Remember? The Jolly Roger?" The face came into focus. It was a man with a sailor's cap set at an angle, a tattered blue uniform. Behind him, in the sky, Giovanni saw something sweep by. A tiny helicopter.

Ballie held something out to Giovanni. "You're not in heaven, mate." His smile almost went from ear to ear. "But there's an angel on the other end of this phone that wants to talk to you."

From the Author
A sincere *thank you* for reading.
But this story is only half over,
the series continues with the next book
Resistance
Now available from Amazon.

For free advance reading copies and more, join me
www.MatthewMather.com

AND PLEASE…
If you'd like more quality fiction at this low price, I'd really appreciate a review on Amazon. The number of reviews a book accumulates on a daily basis has a direct impact on how it sells, so just leaving a review, no matter how short, helps make it possible for me to continue to do what I do.

OTHER BOOKS BY MATTHEW MATHER

CyberStorm

Award-winning CyberStorm depicts, in realistic and sometimes terrifying detail, what a full scale cyberattack against present-day New York City might look like from the perspective of one family trying to survive it. Search for CyberStorm on Amazon.

Polar Vortex

A routine commercial flight disappears over the North Pole. Vanished into thin air. No distress calls. No wreckage. Weeks later, found on the ice, a chance discovery—the journal from passenger Mitch Matthews reveals the incredible truth... Search for *Polar Vortex* on Amazon.

Darknet

A prophetic and frighteningly realistic novel set in present-day New York, Darknet is the story of one man's odyssey to overcome a global menace pushing the world toward oblivion, and his incredible gamble to risk everything to save his family. Search for Darknet on Amazon.

Atopia Chronicles (Series)

In the near future, to escape the crush and clutter of a packed and polluted Earth, the world's elite flock to Atopia, an enormous corporate-owned artificial island in the Pacific Ocean. It is there that Dr. Patricia Killiam rushes to perfect the ultimate in virtual reality: a program to save the ravaged Earth from mankind's insatiable appetite for natural resources. Search for Atopia on Amazon.

271

NEW RELEASE

The Dreaming Tree is now available! Described by readers as *The Girl with the Dragon Tattoo* meets *Black Mirror*. A new breed of predator hunts on the streets of New York-- chased by Delta Devlin, a detective whose gift and curse are eyes that see things only she can.
Search for *The Dreaming Tree* on Amazon.

SPECIAL THANKS

I'd like to make a special thank you to Allan Tierney, Theresa Munanga and Pamela Deering who did whole edits of the book as beta readers.

AND THANK YOU to all my beta readers (sorry I don't have surnames for all of you) Cliff Shaffer, Ken Zufall, Tomas Classon, Chrissie Pintar, Katrina Archer, Erik Montcalm, Angela Cavanaugh, Amber Triplett, Wendy Matthews, Bryan Scullion, Philipp Francis, Sun Lee Curry, Monte Dunard, David Dai, Ernie Dempsey, Nick Burnette, James McCormick, Fern Burgett, and so many more!

And of course, I'd like to thank my mother and father, Julie and David Mather, and last but most definitely not least my wife, Julie Ruthven, for putting up with all the late nights and missed walks with the dogs.

-- Matthew Mather

About Matthew Mather

Translated into over twenty languages, with 20th Century Fox now developing his second novel, CyberStorm, for a major film release, Matthew Mather is a worldwide name in science fiction. He began his career at the McGill Center for Intelligent Machines before starting high-tech ventures in everything from computational nanotechnology to electronic health records, weather prediction systems to genomics, and even designed an award-winning brain-training video game. He now works as a full-time author of speculative fiction.

AUTHOR CONTACT
Matthew Mather:
author.matthew.mather@gmail.com

Made in the USA
Columbia, SC
04 March 2020